For twenty years, I have earned my livelihood here on Detectives' Row. I have tried to uncover the truth of every circumstance, unravel the most tangled of plots, and bring even the most dangerous criminals to justice. More often than not, I have been fortunate enough to succeed in these aims. Even the greatest detectives must make way for a new generation of talented investigators, however, and I am no different. It is time for me to pass on my good fortune to one of my neighbors: in other words, to one of you!

On the first weekend in May, I will be hosting a friendly competition at Coleford Manor. Food will be served, games will be played—and a crime will be committed. Who will the guilty party be? That is for you to deduce. You must work quickly, though, for whoever is first to solve the crime will win ten thousand dollars, my personal recommendation, and the title of World's Greatest Detective.

I hope you will join me in this contest of wits, and I look forward to seeing you soon.

Yours,
Hugh Abernathy

THE WORLD'S GREATEST DETECTIVE

Caroline Carlson

HARPER

An Imprint of HarperCollinsPublishers

The World's Greatest Detective
Copyright © 2017 by Caroline Carlson
All rights reserved. Printed in the United States of America.
No part of this book may be used or reproduced in any manner whatsoever without written permission except in the case of brief quotations embodied in critical
articles and reviews. For information address HarperCollins Children's Books, a
division of HarperCollins Publishers, 195 Broadway, New York, NY 10007.
www.harpercollinschildrens.com

Library of Congress Control Number: 2016957943
ISBN 978-0-06-236828-7

Typography by Andrea Vandergrift
19 20 21 22 23   PC/BRR   10 9 8 7 6 5 4 3 2 1
❖
First paperback edition, 2019

For Nora

CONTENTS

PART I: DETECTIVES' ROW

PART II: A CONTEST OF WITS

PART III: SUSPECTS AND SECRETS

DETECTIVES' ROW

CHAPTER 1

THE LAST RELATIVE

Most people who made their way to Detectives' Row were in trouble, one way or another, and Toby Montrose was in a heap of it. He had been living with his uncle Gabriel for only two months, but trouble had always been good at finding Toby. This time it had tracked him down more quickly than ever.

Currently, the trouble's name was Mrs. Arthur-Abbot. She sat across from Toby in the one good chair Uncle Gabriel reserved for clients. "I'm sorry, ma'am," he said to Mrs. Arthur-Abbot. "I don't understand what you're asking me to do."

Mrs. Arthur-Abbot picked up the cup of tea Toby had brought her. She frowned at it. Then she frowned at the damp ring it had left on the dusty tabletop. "I want you," Mrs. Arthur-Abbot repeated, "to tell me why I have paid you this visit."

Her words didn't make any more sense to Toby the second time he heard them. Somewhere in the walls, behind the peeling flowered paper and the pictures yellowing in their frames, a mouse scampered past. Toby hoped Mrs. Arthur-Abbot wouldn't notice the noise. "I don't mean to be rude," he said, "but wouldn't it be easier for *you* to explain to *me* why you're here?"

Mrs. Arthur-Abbot set down her cup without drinking from it. Her gold bracelets clacked together on her wrist. "You are a detective, are you not?"

"Yes, ma'am." Strictly speaking, Toby was only a detective's assistant, but he didn't think Mrs. Arthur-Abbot would like the sound of that.

"Then detect! Deduce! Study my person—the splatter of mud on my shoe, perhaps, or the faint scar above my left ear—and tell me what troubles have caused me to seek a detective's assistance." Mrs. Arthur-Abbot leaned forward, and Toby leaned away; the legs of his ancient chair creaked dangerously under him. "I've read my fair share of stories in the *Sphinx Monthly Reader*, young man, and I know how these things work. Hugh Abernathy is always able to determine his clients' problems a good five minutes before they open their mouths. I'm sure any halfway decent investigator can do the same." Her eyes narrowed. "Or aren't you half-way decent?"

"I've read the *Sphinx*, too, ma'am," Toby said quickly. He hated to admit it under Uncle Gabriel's roof, but at least Uncle Gabriel himself wasn't home to hear the confession. He'd asked Toby to watch the office for him while he went into town, and he'd given Toby the usual jumble of old case records to organize, but he hadn't said a word about what to do if a new client came to visit. The thought probably hadn't occurred to him. Mrs. Arthur-Abbot was the first new client Toby had seen since he'd moved to Detectives' Row, and he'd been so surprised when she knocked on the door of Montrose Investigations that by the time he realized he didn't have any idea what to do with her, she was already sitting in Uncle Gabriel's parlor and asking for tea.

"I can see you're not willing to help me," she said now, rising from her chair. "In that case, I'll take my business to another agency. I'm told Mr. Abernathy can identify criminals by doing nothing more than glancing at their fingernails."

"Wait!" said Toby. "Please don't go!"

He wished he didn't sound so small and panicked, but he had to fix this trouble before Uncle Gabriel came home. In the motorcar on the way from Grandfather Montrose's, with his small suitcase bouncing on his knees, Toby had made himself three promises: he would be polite, he would not forget to use soap anymore, and he wouldn't disappoint Uncle Gabriel. The third promise was the most important. He couldn't lose a potential client, her mystery, or her undoubtedly hefty fortune to another detective—and he especially couldn't lose them to Hugh Abernathy. Just the sound of Mr. Abernathy's name sent Uncle Gabriel into a fury whenever he heard it. "If you'll only sit back down," Toby told Mrs. Arthur-Abbot, trying to sound a little less panicked, "I'll deduce why you're here."

With a smile more fierce than friendly, Mrs. Arthur-Abbot slipped back into her seat. "That's more like it," she said. "Whenever you're ready, Mr. Montrose."

Toby wasn't sure he'd be ready anytime soon. Two months of organizing case records hadn't taught him all that much about the art of detection. He couldn't afford to visit any of the famous crime scenes tourists were always flocking to, and Uncle Gabriel never took him along on business. Still, he'd read enough detective stories to know the sort of thing Mrs. Arthur-Abbot was expecting. He stared dutifully at her peach-colored silk dress, her tightly laced boots, and her untidy hair, searching for clues. He'd already learned a few things about her—she was rich, for example, and very unpleasant—but he was smart enough to avoid saying any of this aloud. Instead, he tried to imagine that he was Hugh Abernathy himself, pacing back and forth in his parlor in an issue of the *Sphinx*. What conclusions would the world's greatest detective have drawn from Mrs. Arthur-Abbot's appearance? He might have been able to tell by the number of bangles on her wrists if she'd been robbed by a jewel thief, or by the soles of her boots if she'd run away from a band of kidnappers. But nothing about Mrs. Arthur-Abbot looked all that unusual to Toby. He could feel his skin prickling with sweat, and he wondered if Mrs. Arthur-Abbot had deduced how nervous he was. Even the worst detective on the Row would have been able to manage *that*.

There was a twitch of movement over Mrs. Arthur-Abbot's head, and Toby let his gaze slide upward. Dangling from the edge of one bedraggled window curtain was a small brown mouse. It must have gotten tired of running through the walls, but Toby didn't think its new situation was much of an improvement: it clung desperately to the curtain fringe, hanging just above Mrs. Arthur-Abbot's tangle of curls and looking for all the world like a fashionable lady's hairpiece. Toby knew he should be horrified, but he couldn't help grinning at it.

"Is my predicament amusing to you?" Mrs. Arthur-Abbot asked. "Or haven't you guessed it yet?" She raised a hand to tuck a lock of hair back into place, almost brushing the mouse's tail as she did so.

Toby swallowed his grin. "I'm sorry, ma'am," he said again. There *was* something unusual about Mrs. Arthur-Abbot's hair, now that he thought about it. She seemed like a very neat person—the sort of person who wouldn't be happy to find a mouse hanging over her head, if you wanted to be specific about it. Her dress was neat and her bootlaces were neat and all the buttons on her dress were fastened into the correct buttonholes. If Toby's aunt Janet had been there, however, she would have taken a comb to Mrs. Arthur-Abbot's hair with a vengeance. Had she been wearing something over her head? Toby stole a glance at the coatrack in the hall, where a wide-brimmed black hat hung from a peg, half-shrouded by a black veil. On the peg below that, Mrs. Arthur-Abbot had hung a long black coat.

Of course! Toby could have kicked himself. He'd been so shocked by the new client's arrival that he'd barely noticed her clothes, but now that he saw them again, he felt sure he could guess why she needed his help. "You've just come from a funeral," he told Mrs. Arthur-Abbot. For the first time in his life, he felt like the hero in a detective story, and the sensation was thrilling. "That's why you were wearing a black coat and veil; you've been in mourning. Now, people at funerals don't usually need to hire detectives, but something about the death seemed suspicious to you. You don't think the person died normally." Mrs. Arthur-Abbot was staring at Toby now, with her mouth slightly open; was that the sort of reaction people usually had to famous detectives? Toby hoped so. "There's been a murder," he announced, "and you want Uncle Gabriel to find the killer."

Mrs. Arthur-Abbot sat back in her chair. She didn't stop staring at Toby. Then, horribly, she began to laugh.

"A murder?" she said. "These are my motoring clothes! Haven't you seen a lady's driving veil before?"

Toby hadn't. He'd only ridden in a car twice himself, and most of the women he knew weren't rich enough to need driving veils. The thrill he'd been feeling melted away, and trouble wound itself around him like an awful, itchy scarf. "But you didn't come here in a motorcar," he said. "There's not one parked in the street."

"That's because it was stolen!" Mrs. Arthur-Abbot crowed. "*That* should be obvious to any decent detective. A thief puttered away in my car while I was visiting my sister, and I walked here to find someone who could help me get it back. I can see that you, Mr. Montrose, are not that person. I only hope the line won't be too long at Hugh Abernathy's."

"Won't you wait for my uncle to come home?" There was that small, panicked voice again, sneaking out of Toby before he could fix it. "I'm sure he'll be able to help you. He's one of the best detectives on the Row, and—"

The mouse chose this moment to fall on Mrs. Arthur-Abbot's head.

With a shriek, Mrs. Arthur-Abbot jumped to her feet. Tables overturned and knickknacks crashed to the floor as she tore through the parlor, swatting at her hair. One wild swipe of her hand knocked over the stack of case files that Toby had spent all morning putting in order. The mouse, which seemed to sense that it was in danger of becoming a murder victim, darted down her neck and slipped inside one of her capacious sleeves.

Toby jumped up, too. "I'm sorry!" he said for the third time. He batted at the part of Mrs. Arthur-Abbot's sleeve where he thought the mouse might be, but this only made her shriek more loudly. Toby was surprised half of Detectives' Row didn't come running in hopes of finding a convenient crime in progress.

Eventually, Mrs. Arthur-Abbot's shrieks turned into words. "This," she sputtered, "is a sorry excuse for a detective agency!" She flung her arms wide. The mouse sailed out of her sleeve and across the room, where it took refuge behind one of Uncle Gabriel's file cabinets; Toby wished he could do the same. "And *you*, boy, are a sorry excuse for a detective!" Mrs. Arthur-Abbot pulled on her long black coat and squashed her hat down on her head. "I don't know why your uncle bothers to employ you, but rest assured he'll be receiving a lengthy complaint from me, along with a bill for a new gown. I can't imagine wearing this one again after it's been so thoroughly *moused*."

The trouble had really outdone itself this time. How many more crimes would Uncle Gabriel have to solve before he'd made enough money to pay for Mrs. Arthur-Abbot's new dress? Hundreds, probably. "Thank you for visiting Montrose Investigations," Toby said miserably, wishing he hadn't promised to be polite. Mrs. Arthur-Abbot, who must not have made a similar promise, scowled at him and slammed the front door behind her, leaving Toby alone to start cleaning up the mess.

Until the year he turned eight, nothing very terrible had ever happened to Toby. He'd grown up in a stout white farmhouse where sunlight poured through the curtains his mother had sewn, and the old floorboards creaked with his parents' comfortable footsteps. On his eighth birthday, the whole family, all three of them, had walked to the riverbank for a picnic. Nothing went the way they'd planned: Toby's mother dropped the cake in the grass, and his father tripped and fell into the river, and a rainstorm swooped in from the west, washing away the lumpy frosting and making them all as damp as Toby's father. It should have been a disaster. But Toby's mother draped the picnic blanket over a branch to make a sort of tent, Toby's father sliced the sodden cake, and they all sat in the grass, licking crumbs from their fingers and almost bursting with laughter.

Then Toby's parents had left for a trip to the seashore,

and Toby himself had been sent to stay for a week with his aunt Janet. Aunt Janet had six children of her own, whom she mothered with military precision; she administered a kiss to Toby's cheek each morning after checking his fingernails for dirt. Toby had never heard her laugh. She had, however, cried exactly once, when the police officer from the seashore came to the door to tell her there had been an accident.

Toby hardly remembered the funeral. There had been eye-dabbing ladies in drab gowns and nose-blowing gentlemen in suits, he knew, but they'd floated around him in a thick black cloud, murmuring sad words he couldn't make out. Since the rowboat his parents had disappeared in had never been found, there hadn't even been any caskets at the front of the church. The only thing that had seemed real to Toby was the trouble. It wrapped itself around him for the very first time, filling his ears like cotton wool so he could hardly hear Aunt Janet saying she would take care of him from now on.

The trouble, however, had other plans in mind. After a few months of daily fingernail inspections, Aunt Janet determined that she couldn't afford to care for a seventh child, particularly one who tracked mud across her carpets and often forgot to scrub behind his ears. "It's fortunate your parents had so many relations," she told Toby as she handed him off to his uncle Francis, who managed a fancy hotel. "Otherwise, poor dear, you'd have to be sent to an orphanage."

The thought of being crammed into a cold, smelly bunk room with dozens of other miserable little boys turned Toby's insides to jelly. A small piece of him still hoped that disappearing in a rowboat was just another kind of disaster his parents could fix, and that they'd turn up one day to collect him and bring him home. When this didn't happen, however, he decided to be so well behaved and useful that Uncle Francis would have no choice but to keep him.

It didn't work. Toby tried to help in the hotel restaurant, but when he spilled an entire bottle of expensive wine all over a loud and short-tempered duke, Uncle Francis hurried Toby along to Aunt Ingrid, who owned a bakery. When he fell asleep at the oven and burned the morning's bread loaves, Aunt Ingrid sent him to Cousin Celeste at the hospital, and when Cousin Celeste couldn't find the money to pay for the clothes Toby was constantly growing out of, she sent him to Uncle Howard at the stables. In this way, Toby was passed around the family like a bowl of cold mashed potatoes at dinner until the day three years later, when ancient Grandfather Montrose unfolded his newspaper, took one last wheezing breath, and passed away right in the middle of the society pages. The housemaid shrieked and sent for Aunt Janet.

"It's a shame," Aunt Janet had said as she packed Toby's

few belongings into his suitcase, "but we can't avoid it any longer. You'll have to go to your uncle Gabriel."

"The detective?" Toby had asked. He was as fond of detective stories as everyone else in the city of Colebridge, and the outside pocket of his suitcase was stuffed with his parents' old copies of the *Sphinx Monthly Reader*. Living on Detectives' Row sounded a hundred times more interesting than pouring Grandfather Montrose's medicines, and Toby said so to Aunt Janet.

Aunt Janet had wrinkled her nose as if she'd smelled something stale. "Gabriel," she'd said, "is not a good influence. He spends his time rummaging through morgues and lurking in alleys, and as for his reputation—well, the less said about that, the better. He's not fit to take care of a young boy, and I doubt he can afford to keep you on for more than a few months, but neither can the rest of us." She'd snapped the suitcase shut and placed it in Toby's hands. "Be good for your uncle, Toby," she'd told him. "And for heaven's sake, don't give him any reason to turn you away. He's your Last Relative, you know."

That was why Toby had to be clean and polite, and why he couldn't possibly disappoint Uncle Gabriel, no matter what kind of influence he was. Toby had learned enough about his family to know by now that if Uncle Gabriel couldn't afford to keep him—or worse, if Uncle Gabriel didn't *want* to keep him—he'd be sent to the orphanage, and that would be that.

Toby was still sweeping pieces of knickknack into the dustpan when Uncle Gabriel returned. "Good news, Tobias!" he said as he stomped inside. His enormous voice was slightly muffled, for once, by the pile of brown paper–wrapped parcels in his arms. "The butcher had a handsome stewing hen he needed to part with, so I took it off his hands. I'll place it straight into Mrs. Satterthwaite's stew pot, and we'll all feast like kings for the rest of the week. Except for Mrs. Satterthwaite, that is; I expect she'll feast like a queen."

As his uncle teetered into the kitchen with his stack of parcels, Toby hid the dustpan behind his back. He was pretty sure most actual kings and queens would turn up their royal noses at Uncle Gabriel's cook's chicken soup, but he wasn't about to do the same. He didn't even mind the rubbery carrots. They probably didn't have any carrots at all at the orphanage.

"So, Tobias," said Uncle Gabriel, coming back into the hall, "did you solve any crimes while I was away?" He said this every time he left Toby in charge of the agency, and then he would let out a boom of laughter, and Toby would laugh, too.

This time, though, Toby couldn't even manage a chuckle.

He had to tell Uncle Gabriel about Mrs. Arthur-Abbot, her silk dress, and all the rest of it, but the truth was bound to make Uncle Gabriel upset, and Toby didn't know where to begin. "I tried to solve the crime, sir," he said; "I swear I did, but I don't know much about motorcars, and I couldn't figure out how to get the mouse out of the dress."

This stopped Uncle Gabriel's laughter in a hurry. He looked around the parlor at the crooked drapes Toby had tried to tug into place and at the files he'd hurriedly stacked. He peered at the dustpan behind Toby's back. Then he frowned and ran his fingers over the bristles of his beard. "I can see that something unusual has taken place in this room," he said, "but, as a professional investigator, I find it hard to believe that a well-dressed rodent could have caused quite so much destruction. As much as I'd enjoy deducing the true course of events, it would probably consume most of the evening, and Mrs. Satterthwaite sinks into a gloom when I pay more attention to my work than I do to her dinner. You'd better tell me exactly what happened." He lowered himself into a chair, which creaked even more under his weight than it had under Toby's, and pulled out the small blank book he carried with him to crime scenes. "The mouse was driving a motorcar, you say?"

"Not the mouse, sir," said Toby. "Mrs. Arthur-Abbot. Only she *wasn't* driving a motorcar; that was exactly the problem."

14

In a rush, Toby told his uncle as much as he could bear to confess. Uncle Gabriel scratched away in his notebook, interrupting Toby every so often to ask a question about the soles of Mrs. Arthur-Abbot's shoes or the precise species of the mouse. By the time Toby had finished speaking, his mouth was dry. Uncle Gabriel set his notes aside, and Toby tried to read them upside down to see if any of them said *orphanage*.

"There's one more thing I'd like to know, Tobias." Uncle Gabriel folded his hands together, looking grave. "When Mrs. Arthur-Abbot stormed out of our home, where did she go?"

Toby wished he hadn't asked. "To Mr. Abernathy's," he said as quietly as he could. "I'm sorry to say the name, sir; I know you don't like hearing it."

"Mr. Abernathy!" said Uncle Gabriel. "That puffed-up, self-serving old ostrich! There'll be no chance of getting the woman's business back now, and I don't suppose she'll be recommending Montrose Investigations to any of her wealthy friends." He slumped down in his chair and shrugged. "Truthfully, she sounds like an awful nuisance. I would have liked to get acquainted with her money, but I don't envy Hugh Abernathy for having to tolerate her company."

Toby thought there were plenty of reasons to envy Hugh Abernathy, but the idea of seeing Mrs. Arthur-Abbot again, even for a moment, made him feel queasy. "She wants us to pay for the dress that got ruined," he admitted. "She said she'd be sending you a letter about it."

"The peach silk." Uncle Gabriel sighed. "I suppose it cost a fortune? Of course it did; the woman's got her own motorcar." He squinted at Toby. "You don't happen to have any cash reserves hidden under your mattress, do you? Any gemstones scattered in the back lawn?"

Toby squirmed. "I was hoping *you* did."

"I," said Uncle Gabriel, "haven't had a new case in weeks. I'm not the only one, either. Miss Price next door says business is as bad as she's ever seen it. There are too many detectives in this town, Tobias, and there's not enough crime to put food on all of our tables—or silk dresses on all of our backs, for that matter. If something doesn't change soon, we'll all be boarding up our windows by the end of the year, and Mr. Abernathy will have the whole Row to himself." He pressed his fingers to his brow as though he felt a headache coming on. "Maybe I can persuade Mrs. Satterthwaite to make us a loan. Do you think she might secretly be a duchess?"

"Probably not," Toby said glumly. He didn't think secret duchesses usually found work as part-time cooks, and he was sure Mrs. Satterthwaite couldn't afford even one sleeve of a silk gown on the meager paycheck they gave her every month. "This is all my fault, sir. If I could only do something to fix it—"

He hadn't even finished his sentence before Uncle Gabriel started shaking his head. "My business troubles have nothing to do with you, Tobias, and I shouldn't have brought them up. Forget I said a word. Eleven-year-old boys shouldn't be worrying about money—and while we're at it, they certainly shouldn't be calling me *sir*. Do you understand?"

Toby nodded. He wondered what eleven-year-old boys *should* be worrying about, but this didn't seem like the right moment to ask. He didn't want Uncle Gabriel to call him an ostrich.

The clock on the mantel struck five, accompanied by a symphony of sharp knocks at the door—Mrs. Satterthwaite, prompt as usual. Uncle Gabriel stood up to let her in. Halfway across the hall, however, he paused. "There is one thing you can do," he said, turning back to Toby. "The next time any clients show up when you're here alone, why don't you ask them to have a seat and wait until I return? That's all a detective's assistant really needs to do."

So much for not disappointing Uncle Gabriel. "Yes, sir," said Toby. "I mean—well—yes."

"Excellent," said Uncle Gabriel. The symphony of knocks had progressed into its next movement, much more energetic than the first. "Now, Tobias, let's banish all thoughts of detection from our minds and think only of the mystery of tonight's dinner."

CHAPTER 2

INSPECTOR WEBSTER'S DETECTION CORRESPONDENCE COURSE

From the window of his bedroom at the top of the house, Toby could see the entire length of Detectives' Row. To the east, it bumped up against the busy High Street, lined with mansions and shops; to the west, it sputtered out in a weedy little garden that Toby had never seen anyone tend. The detectives who lived at the western end of the Row were talentless newcomers—or at least that was what Uncle Gabriel said—and the nicer, eastern end of the Row was where the more successful investigators kept their offices. They had been there since the early days of detection, long before the famous Colebridge Cutthroat murders had captivated the city and turned half its residents into armchair sleuths.

Even now, the people of Colebridge loved a good crime.

The Cutthroat had been locked up in Chokevine Prison years earlier, but following crime reports in the newspapers, swapping theories about unsolved cases at dinner parties, and visiting famous murder sites on the weekends were still the city's most fashionable hobbies. No one would dream of missing the serialized detective stories that ran in the *Sphinx Monthly Reader*, and every neighborhood park was full of children playing at sleuths and robbers. Even Toby's parents had promised him that one day, when Toby was old enough, they would scrape together the funds to pay for a grand tour of Entwhistle House. That was where the Colebridge Cutthroat had planned to commit one last, terrible murder—and been caught in the act by a heroic young detective named Hugh Abernathy.

Hugh Abernathy wasn't young any longer, but he was more heroic than ever, and he lived with his assistant, Mr. Peartree, in a tall white house at the easternmost end of the Row. Times were lean for the detectives of Colebridge: the surge of interest in crime solving had sent a number of criminals to jail and encouraged the rest to reconsider their careers. Still, crowds of visitors gathered outside Mr. Abernathy's door each weekday morning, waiting for a chance to hire the detective or just to catch a glimpse of his famous silhouette. Toby would have liked to catch a glimpse of his own, but he didn't dare join the crowds outside the door; he knew perfectly well what Uncle Gabriel thought of Hugh Abernathy. On the day he'd brought Toby to Detectives' Row, Uncle Gabriel had spotted the stack of *Sphinx*es in Toby's suitcase and wrinkled his nose as though he'd smelled something rotten. "Keep that nonsense out of my sight, Tobias," he'd ordered. "Better yet, burn it. That miserable man may have charmed the whole city, but he hasn't charmed me." Toby had been shocked (didn't everyone like Hugh Abernathy?), but he supposed it wasn't easy for his uncle to live only a few houses away from the world's greatest detective. After all, the *Sphinx* never published any stories about Gabriel Montrose.

Uncle Gabriel's house, number one-fifteen, sat squarely in the middle of Detectives' Row, although he was quick to tell anyone who asked that its walls tilted ever so slightly to the east. Toby's third-story window gave him an excellent view of all the carriages and motorcars that squeaked down the street toward Montrose Investigations, though lately there hadn't been many of either. More importantly, on the morning three weeks after Mrs. Arthur-Abbot's disastrous visit, it allowed him to keep a careful eye on the mailbox that stood in front of the house.

Everything looked just as it usually did at seven o'clock on a Tuesday. A line of anxious clients was already starting to form outside Hugh Abernathy's door. Miss March and Miss Price, the detectives who lived in the house next to Uncle Gabriel's, were taking their morning constitutional down to the High Street, their elbows linked together and their heads bent low in conversation. Across the street, a girl stood on the curb looking bored as her small brown dog investigated a patch of weeds. (This was a little surprising, since Toby had never seen the girl or the dog before, and he especially hadn't seen them at seven o'clock on a Tuesday. Then again, he'd been watching the mailbox for only twelve days.) And at two minutes past seven, just as Toby had hoped he would, the mailman strode down Detectives' Row, reached Uncle Gabriel's house, and stopped to remove a bundle of letters from his sack.

Toby catapulted himself away from the window, out of his bedroom, and down two flights of narrow, brown-carpeted staircase. "Getting the mail!" he called as he slid across the front hall in his socks. Uncle Gabriel looked up from his desk in the parlor, but Toby was into his shoes and out the door before his uncle could ask any questions. It had been this way for the past eleven mornings.

Toby could already tell, though, that *this* morning was different. To start with, the girl across the street was still walking her dog. She wore a wool coat that looked too big for her and a pair of square-framed wire spectacles that kept sliding down the bridge of her nose, and she was staring intently at Toby. Toby stared back at her. The girl frowned. Finally, after what seemed to Toby like ages, she dropped her gaze and tugged her dog away toward the garden at the end of the Row, leaving Toby alone to sort through the contents of the mailbox.

There was the usual bundle of envelopes—bills for Uncle Gabriel, mostly, and letters from his few remaining clients. At least there wasn't anything new from Mrs. Arthur-Abbot. Her promised nasty note had arrived last week, and although Uncle Gabriel hadn't told Toby how much the peach silk would cost them, he'd sworn under his breath as he'd read the letter. In addition to the bills and notes, there was a catalog from a detection supply company, its illustrated pages full of advertisements for fingerprint powders and little pistols with ivory handles. There was also a square envelope addressed to Uncle Gabriel in elegant green calligraphy; it looked like it might be a party invitation. Uncle Gabriel would like that, Toby thought. He didn't get invited to many parties.

At last, Toby reached the bottom of the mail stack. There, underneath the letters and bills, was a lumpy brown parcel stuck shut with an abundance of tape. To anyone who wasn't a detective's assistant, it would have looked very much like a plain, unremarkable package. Toby, however, knew better: unlike all the other pieces of mail that had landed in the box over the past eleven days, this package was addressed to him.

Toby grinned and did a little hop there on the sidewalk. He wanted to tear the brown paper open right away, but the dog down at the end of the Row was starting to bark, and the girl was frowning at him more intently than ever, so he stuffed the parcel into the back waistband of his pants instead and pulled his sweater over it as well as he could. It made a sort of crunching noise as he walked up the stairs and into the house. Toby hoped he didn't look too suspicious.

"You're up early again," Uncle Gabriel said as Toby handed him the rest of the mail. "What have we got today? Oh dear." He flipped through the envelopes, sighing a little every time his fingers brushed against an unpaid bill. His desk was covered with stacks of similar envelopes; most of them were stamped *PAST DUE* in bright red ink, and one or two said *FINAL WARNING*. In front of them, the Montrose Investigations money ledger lay open to the page Uncle Gabriel had been studying. Toby wasn't allowed to touch the ledger—it was another of the things eleven-year-old boys weren't supposed to worry about—but he couldn't help sneaking a look at it over Uncle Gabriel's shoulder. All he could see were long, gloomy columns of zeroes.

"Uncle Gabriel," said Toby, "do we have any money left at all?"

Uncle Gabriel looked startled. He pushed the stacks of bills to the back of his desk and snapped the money ledger shut. "You're an observant child, Tobias," he said. "It's a useful quality for a detective to have, but it's far less useful in a nephew."

What Uncle Gabriel meant, as far as Toby could tell, was that he wasn't going to answer the question. Toby wished he'd never asked it. His cheeks prickled with embarrassment, and he could feel the brown paper parcel sliding farther into the seat of his pants. It was going to be hard to move without crunching. "I'm sorry," he said. "I'll go back up to my room now."

"Well, there's no need for that!" Uncle Gabriel stood up from his desk. "I'm famished, Tobias, and I suspect you are, too. Why don't we see if we can scrounge up some food?"

"Oh! I can't." The parcel was heading down Toby's pant leg now. "Not yet, at least. I've got to, um, get ready."

Uncle Gabriel frowned. "You look ready enough to me."

"My hair!" said Toby in a hurry. "I haven't combed it! Aunt Janet always says you can't eat a meal with messy hair."

"That does sound like Janet," Uncle Gabriel admitted. "I'm sure she means well, but I'd never dream of bringing that sister of mine along to a crime scene; she'd tidy up all the evidence." He ran a hand through his own thicket of hair. "All right, then, Tobias. You make sure you're suitably coiffed, and I'll make breakfast. I think we've got just enough flour left for pancakes."

Back in the safety of his bedroom, Toby shut the door, rolled up his pant leg, and let the parcel drop onto the carpet. His fingernails (freshly trimmed and very clean) were useless against the bulwark of tape, but this room had been Uncle Gabriel's storage space before Toby had moved in, and all sorts of useful objects from previous cases were still stashed in boxes and stacked along the walls. In one of these boxes, Toby found a silver-handled dagger. Its blade was edged with something red that he hoped was rust. In any case, it was sharp enough to slice the parcel open.

Inside the brown paper wrapping were a small black notebook, a round fabric badge, and a thick sheaf of paper that had been folded over twice. The badge read JUNIOR DETECTIVE in wobbly embroidery, and the top piece of paper in the sheaf said INSPECTOR WEBSTER'S DETECTION CORRESPONDENCE COURSE, LEVEL ONE.

Toby flopped happily onto his bed and flipped through the pages of instructions and exercises. Inspector Webster had written out lessons on dozens of subjects, from deciphering codes to assembling disguises. It would take days for Toby to read through it all, but the advertisement in the back of the *Sphinx Monthly Reader* had promised that Inspector Webster's correspondence course could turn even the most untalented beginner into a first-class detective in only three months, and a first-class detective was exactly what Toby needed to become. The sight of Uncle Gabriel's money ledger had made him more certain than ever: if

Montrose Investigations didn't bring in more clients, the business would close, Uncle Gabriel would board up his windows, and he'd have no more use for a troublesome nephew who needed to be clothed and fed. Toby couldn't risk that. He needed to make himself useful, and being useful meant making money. With two detectives on its staff, wouldn't Montrose Investigations be able to solve twice as many crimes? Instead of pouring tea for new clients, couldn't Toby impress them with his talents? Uncle Gabriel had already said he was observant, and now that he was a Junior Detective (Level One), he was sure he'd be able to learn enough to solve a few smaller cases here and there. He could make back the money he owed to Mrs. Arthur-Abbot, and he might even convince some of the people waiting outside Hugh Abernathy's house to come down the street to Montrose Investigations instead. Uncle Gabriel would swell with pride.

For now, though, Toby would have to pretend that nothing had changed. He'd paid for the correspondence course with the last of the pocket money Grandfather Montrose had given him before he died, and if Uncle Gabriel learned that Toby had sent almost ten dollars to an utter stranger with only a stack of lessons to show for it, he'd probably send Toby to the orphanage on the spot. Even holding the papers from Inspector Webster felt dangerous in the daylight, so Toby rolled off his bed and stuffed them into his suitcase alongside his collection of *Sphinx*es. In spite of what Uncle Gabriel had said, Toby hadn't burned the magazines; some nights he couldn't sleep without reading a few more pages of a Hugh Abernathy story. The pages were smudged with soot and fingerprints, and the words were all familiar, but Toby didn't mind. His parents had read those stories aloud by the fireplace after dinner—"The Adventure of the Clockwork Spider," "The Case of the Fourteen Lemons," and dozens of other tales that Toby knew practically by heart. As he tucked his new lessons away, it occurred to him in one wild and thrilling moment that someday, if he studied hard, the *Sphinx Monthly Reader* might even write stories about *him*.

Two floors below, there was a huge and echoing crash. "THAT PUFFED-UP, SELF-SERVING OLD OSTRICH!" shouted Uncle Gabriel.

Toby took the stairs three at a time. Even a junior detective could tell that something awful had happened.

CHAPTER 3

A CURIOUS INVITATION

Toby found Uncle Gabriel in the kitchen. He was standing in front of a bowl of pancake batter and wearing one of the cook's frilly flowered aprons, with a spatula in one hand and a steaming frying pan at his feet. Something thick and brown was leaking out of the frying pan onto the floor. The square envelope that had arrived in that morning's mail lay on the counter, covered in a fine layer of flour. There was a fine layer of flour all over Uncle Gabriel, too. But he didn't seem to notice the mess or the steaming pan; he didn't even seem to notice Toby. He just kept glaring at the envelope.

"What is it, sir?" Toby asked, remembering too late that he wasn't supposed to say *sir* anymore.

Uncle Gabriel looked up at him as though he'd been pulled away from a dream. "Hugh Abernathy," he muttered, poking at the envelope with the blade of his spatula as though the letter inside might bite him. "Hugh Abernathy has ruined my pancakes."

Toby couldn't believe this accusation was entirely fair. "I heard you call him an ostrich again," Toby said, picking up the hot frying pan and putting it back on the stove before it had a chance to burn him. "Why did you do that?"

Uncle Gabriel glowered. "Because I hate ostriches." He lifted the flour-covered envelope onto his spatula and held it out to Toby. "Just look at what that insufferable man dared to send me!"

Gingerly, Toby took the envelope. It had been ripped open without much care, and the green-inked letter inside was splotched with pancake batter. "You can read the dratted thing if you'd like," said Uncle Gabriel, "but it might put you off your breakfast."

Dear Esteemed Friend and Colleague,
For twenty years, I have earned my livelihood here on Detectives' Row. I have tried to uncover the truth of every circumstance, unravel the most tangled of plots, and bring even the most dangerous criminals to justice. More often than not, I have been fortunate enough to succeed in

these aims. Even the greatest detectives must make way for a new generation of talented investigators, however, and I am no different. It is time for me to pass on my good fortune to one of my neighbors: in other words, to one of you!

On the first weekend in May, I will be hosting a friendly competition at Coleford Manor. Food will be served, games will be played—and a crime will be committed. Who will the guilty party be? That is for you to deduce. You must work quickly, though, for whoever is first to solve the crime will win ten thousand dollars, my personal recommendation, and the title of World's Greatest Detective.

I hope you will join me in this contest of wits, and I look forward to seeing you soon.

Yours,
Hugh Abernathy

"Disgraceful, isn't it?" Uncle Gabriel spooned more circles of batter into the frying pan. "'Esteemed Friend and Colleague?' We're barely colleagues, and we're certainly not friends."

Toby didn't hear much of this. He wasn't sure he'd taken a breath since he'd started reading the letter, and he worried he might faint into the bowl of pancake batter.

"Ten thousand dollars!" he shouted. "We could buy Mrs. Arthur-Abbot a whole new motorcar with that!" It was more money than he'd seen in his life, maybe even more than his parents had ever seen. It was enough to keep Uncle Gabriel from worrying about clients and heating bills and groceries and nephews; it was enough to shove all thoughts of Inspector Webster's correspondence course out of Toby's mind. Ten thousand dollars could change his life.

Then he saw the look on Uncle Gabriel's face.

"You *are* going to enter the competition," Toby said, "aren't you?"

Uncle Gabriel set down his spatula and put both his large hands on Toby's shoulders. "We may not know each other very well yet," he said, "but I promise you I have more self-respect than that. I've been doing this work for decades, I've done it well, and I don't see why Hugh Abernathy's opinion of my talent should matter in the least." He snorted. "Can you imagine it? Wasting a perfectly good weekend sipping champagne in the countryside, solving a made-up crime when I could be working on a real case instead? The idea is ridiculous!"

Toby thought of all those bills stacked on Uncle Gabriel's desk, and all the ones that hadn't arrived yet. "But the money—"

"Yes, Tobias, it's true we don't have any." Uncle Gabriel looked Toby straight in the eye. Behind him, the pancakes were starting to smoke. "Our roof leaks whenever it rains, our pipes freeze whenever it snows, our floorboards creak, and our walls are overrun with mice. I can't deny that ten thousand dollars would be enough to solve our troubles, but I've got too much dignity to beg for it from Hugh Abernathy. We don't need his charity, and we certainly don't need him to tell us who is the world's greatest detective." He frowned. "Oh dear. Have I upset you?"

"It's the pancakes," Toby said nervously. "They're . . . well . . . they're on fire."

Uncle Gabriel wheeled around. "I need tea towels!" he boomed. "The damper the better. This is all Hugh Abernathy's fault!" Toby scrambled through the kitchen, gathering the towels that had been tossed into drawers and flung over chairs, while Uncle Gabriel doused them in water and did his best to smother the flames. "Take that letter away from me, Tobias," he called across the smoky kitchen. "Put it out with the trash. And don't bother to send a reply. It would only flatter Abernathy's ego, and I can't think of anything worse than that."

Toby couldn't bring himself to throw the letter away. In the washroom, he smoothed out the corners of the paper that Uncle Gabriel had crumpled. Then he folded it so its edges and corners were perfectly lined up, and he tucked it into his pocket. There it sat all through breakfast, poking into Toby's leg and refusing to leave his thoughts as he spread the last of the week's butter on his blackened pancakes. "Uncle Gabriel," he said, "may I ask you something?"

"Anything," said Uncle Gabriel, "and always."

"Why do you dislike Mr. Abernathy so much?"

Burned bits of pancake crunched between Uncle Gabriel's teeth. "I didn't always dislike him. We were friends once, if you can believe it. Then we quarreled. It was the sort of quarrel a friendship can't recover from. In fact," said Uncle Gabriel, "I broke his nose."

"You didn't!" Toby was horrified.

"I certainly did. It was up to me to either forgive the man or punch him, and since I couldn't bear to forgive him, I chose the punch instead. It wasn't my proudest moment." Uncle Gabriel smiled. "Still, I can't say I regret it."

"What did you quarrel about?"

"If it's all the same to you, Tobias," said Uncle Gabriel, "I'd rather not discuss it."

Toby considered this as he chewed. Mr. Abernathy's nose had probably healed ages ago, but it was obvious that Uncle Gabriel still felt sore about their argument. "If he did something unforgivable to you," he suggested, "and you took his money, it might not be charity. It might be revenge."

This made Uncle Gabriel laugh. "I like your view of things," he said, "and I can't deny that I'm curious about that contest. I wonder what Hugh Abernathy thinks he's up to. Whatever it is, though, I won't be in town to find out about it. I've already made traveling plans for the first weekend in May: there's a long-term case of mine that's on the verge of cracking open, and I'll need to go abroad for a few days."

"Really?" Toby had never traveled before, not far enough to count. The promise of a trip abroad was almost as exciting as a weekend with Mr. Abernathy. "Will you need a detective's assistant to help you with the case?"

Uncle Gabriel fidgeted with his fork. "Actually," he said, "I won't. I've booked only one ticket on the overnight ferry to Gallis. I'll ask Mrs. Satterthwaite to stay here with you, though, so you won't be entirely alone."

"Oh," said Toby. "Right. Of course." He couldn't believe he'd let himself get his hopes up. After all, he wasn't a real detective yet, and the overnight ferry probably wasn't cheap.

"I'm sorry, Tobias," Uncle Gabriel said. He sounded like he really *was* sorry, too, which made it even worse. "I'd like nothing more than to take you with me, but it just isn't possible."

"Don't worry, sir," said Toby. "It's all right. I understand." Then he pushed his chair away from the table, gathered up the plates even though they were still halfway full, and ran back to the kitchen before Uncle Gabriel could get any kinder. The kinder he was, the worse it would be when Toby had to leave him.

Late that night, Toby lay on the floor of his bedroom. He pressed his ear to the floorboards and tried not to make a sound until he was sure he could hear Uncle Gabriel snoring in the room below. Then he lit the candle next to his bed, pulled out his suitcase, and settled into his blankets with Inspector Webster's Detection Correspondence Course, level one.

The first lesson was all about interviewing suspects, and the second was about tracking a criminal's movements. Toby couldn't practice these techniques very well by himself in the middle of the night, but he hoped Inspector Webster would understand. By the time he was starting to yawn, he'd read through two more lessons, drawn a map of a crime scene in his new notebook, and learned to identify the three most popular poisons. Still, he knew it wasn't enough. He'd have to do much more than that if he wanted to make enough money for Uncle Gabriel to keep him. At breakfast, Uncle Gabriel had said that ten thousand dollars would solve their troubles. How long did it take to make ten thousand dollars? Toby had a feeling he'd be conducting interviews and drawing crime scene maps until he was ninety.

The candlelight in Toby's room reflected off the glass boxes that held mementoes of Uncle Gabriel's past cases, flickering over old ransom notes and bullet casings. Uncle Gabriel may not have been a wealthy detective, but it didn't look to Toby like he was a bad one, either. Why did he have to hold a grudge against Hugh Abernathy? Why couldn't he just cancel his trip abroad and enter that contest? If Toby'd had the chance to win ten thousand dollars, he never would have let it pass him by. He'd march up to Coleford Manor, solve the crime before the other contestants had time to realize they'd been bested, accept that prize money from the most famous detective in the city, and hand it all over to Uncle Gabriel. He'd never have to worry again that the trouble would sneak up behind him, sink in its teeth, and drag him away. If he won Mr. Abernathy's contest, he could afford to be fearless.

Toby sat straight up in bed, sending the pages of the correspondence course flying. What was he thinking? The first weekend in May was only a few months away. He wouldn't be more than halfway through Inspector Webster's lessons by the time the competition began; he could never win that contest himself. It was a terrible idea, even worse than the time he let Uncle Howard's horses run free and half of them never came back. Toby knew he didn't stand a chance of winning that money.

Then again, what if he did?

The trouble creaked in the eaves.

"Go ahead," Toby told it, suddenly feeling bold. "Creak as much as you like. No matter what you do, I'm going to find a way to stay here."

CHAPTER 4

A VISIT TO MR. ABERNATHY

Making an excuse to leave the house the next day turned out to be easier than Toby had expected. Uncle Gabriel was so absorbed in his long-term case that he hardly even raised his eyes from his work when Toby told him he was going for a walk.

"All right," Uncle Gabriel said, "but be careful, Tobias. Miss March came by this morning to say that another convict's escaped from Chokevine Prison, and the city coppers haven't found him yet. If they left these matters to private detectives, we'd have the man back in cuffs by now." He shook his head, just as everyone on Detectives' Row always did when the subject of the local police came up. Convicts were as common as fruit flies in Colebridge, but they had a worrying habit of escaping. "In any case, if you're not back in an hour, I reserve the right to start worrying about you."

"I won't be long," Toby promised. "I'm just going down to the High Street." He paused with his hand on the doorknob. "Are you sure there's no chance you'll enter Mr. Abernathy's competition?"

"Let me put it this way," said Uncle Gabriel. "There's more of a chance that you and I will both grow wings this very evening and fly over the rooftops of Colebridge, squawking at each other like ravens. Do you take my point?"

"I do," said Toby. "I'll let you know if I feel any feathers poking through."

Uncle Gabriel boomed with laughter, and Toby slipped out the door before the sound of it could make him change his mind. He hoped his uncle wouldn't choose that afternoon to take his own stroll down Detectives' Row. If he did, he'd almost certainly spot Toby waiting to speak to Hugh Abernathy.

Toby had spent all night thinking about exactly what to say to Mr. Abernathy and exactly how to say it. He rehearsed his lines quietly to himself as he walked down the street. "Thank you for agreeing to see me, sir," he whispered. "I've been reading about your adventures for years. I'm a huge fan, actually, even though my uncle broke your nose, and—oh! Hello there, boy!"

This wasn't part of what Toby had planned to say to Mr. Abernathy. A small brown dog with wiry fur and bushy eyebrows had run up to him and placed its forepaws on Toby's knee. Now it was waving its tail like a flag and doing its best to lick whichever parts of Toby it could reach. Toby knelt down to scratch its ears. He liked dogs. There had been a pack of foxhounds at Uncle Howard's stables, and Aunt Janet had once owned a friendly white dog named Eglantine. Eglantine was just about the only thing Toby missed about living with Aunt Janet.

"What are you doing here all alone?" Toby asked as the dog set to work licking his nose. "Are you lost?" He had a sudden, terrible thought. "You don't belong to an escaped convict, do you?"

"Percival! Come back here!" A girl ran up to them, holding a bright red collar and leash in one hand. "He's always running off," she said, sounding a little out of breath. "You shouldn't let him jump up on you like that; it'll only encourage him."

"I really don't mind," said Toby. He got to his feet and watched the girl as she fastened Percival's collar. Even the worst detective on the Row would have noticed her: she wore a long, sea-green evening gown, white gloves that stretched almost to her shoulders, and a grimy fedora, which she'd pulled low over her black hair. Toby was pretty sure she wasn't a convict after all, but she did look familiar. "You were here yesterday morning, too, weren't you?" he asked. "You watched me from across the street when I went to get the mail."

"You're wrong." The girl glared up at him so fiercely that Toby took a few steps backward. "That absolutely, definitely wasn't me."

"Yes, it was! You were wearing spectacles, and you didn't have that awful hat on, but your dog was with you, and he still looks exactly the same."

The girl sighed. "Well, maybe it *was* me, but I wasn't watching you. I was just taking Percival for a walk." She stood up and dusted herself off. "And I like this hat. I hope you're done making fun of it, because I have to get home."

Toby felt a little guilty about forgetting to be polite—the hat wasn't *that* awful—but the girl didn't seem interested in waiting for an apology. She picked up the train of her evening gown, tugged at Percival's leash, and started down the street toward Uncle Gabriel's. "Do you live on the Row?" he called after her. "I haven't seen you here before."

The girl turned back to Toby. "I'm visiting my grandmother. She lives on the next street over."

"On Slaughter's Lane?" Toby was surprised. Uncle Gabriel wouldn't allow Toby to set even one foot in Slaughter's Lane. The city's most notorious pickpockets, kidnappers, and con men were rumored to gather in its grimy gaming parlors and shadow-filled alleys—that is, when they

40

gathered at all. Only the shiftiest criminals still roamed free in Colebridge, and they knew better than to spend too much time near Detectives' Row. "Is your grandmother a criminal?" Toby asked.

The girl hesitated. "Yes," she said, "that's right. She's a murderess, in fact. And she's training me to be one, too, so you'd better not interrogate me again."

"I wasn't—" Toby started to protest, but the girl was already hurrying away, with Percival trotting along behind her.

Toby had lived with Uncle Gabriel long enough to know that unlike the rest of Detectives' Row, where clients turned up at unpredictable hours if they bothered to turn up at all, Mr. Abernathy's office operated according to a strict routine. The detective saw clients every weekday from ten until three. Each morning, at ten o'clock exactly, the shiny black front door of his house would swing open and a man dressed from head to toe in green would bow to the crowd of people gathered on the sidewalk. Then he would lead one lucky client into the house. Several long, boring minutes would pass while the people in the crowd checked their watches, tried to peer through the windows, and speculated about the great feats of detection Mr. Abernathy might be performing at that very moment. Eventually, the door would swing open again, the client would be ushered out (sometimes looking hopeful, other times in tears), and the man in green would begin the process all over again.

Toby knew this was how it always went at Mr. Abernathy's, but now that he was here, he realized he couldn't waste time standing on his tiptoes at the back of the crowd. He'd already spent too long talking to the strange girl in the evening gown, and he had less than an hour before Uncle Gabriel came looking for him. Apologizing in his head to Aunt Janet, who strongly believed that everyone should wait their turn, he began to weave his way through the cluster of ladies and gentlemen in front of him.

Mr. Abernathy's admirers smelled like sweat and smoke and fancy perfume. Out of habit more than anything else, Toby scanned their faces as he squeezed past: some were anxious and others were excited, but none were familiar. This wasn't a surprise: after three whole years, Toby had almost stopped believing that he might spot his parents' faces in a crowd someday—his father's eyes sparkling above his whiskers, his mother's smile shining out from under a flowered bonnet or a big straw hat. Still, he couldn't bring himself to stop looking.

Some of Mr. Abernathy's clients were looking back at him now, and a lot of them were scowling. There was still a thick wall of people standing between him and the detective's house; he couldn't see how he'd ever get to the front of the crowd. "Please let me through!" Toby said, turning

42

sideways to fit himself into the space between a man's buttoned-up stomach and a woman's velvet elbow. "I'm not a client, I swear! I've got something important to tell Mr. Abernathy."

"So do the rest of us!" said the man with the buttons. He was twice Toby's size, and he wasn't budging.

"That's right," said the woman in velvet. She glared down her nose at Toby. "I've been waiting here for hours, and you can very well do the same."

"Excuse me!" someone called, and the crowd went silent.

The man in green had opened the door again. He stood at the top of the steps, and he, too, was looking straight at Toby. "Make way for that boy, please," he said.

Toby thought he'd heard the man wrong. "For me?"

"Indeed." The man clapped his hands together. "Move aside, move aside. Mr. Abernathy's orders."

Reluctantly, the crowd parted. Their eyes lingered on Toby as he passed, and he wondered if this was how criminals felt when they were marched into the city courthouse for their trials. Finally, he reached the man in green. "Thank you, sir," he said.

The man in green bowed stiffly. "As I said, you may thank Mr. Abernathy. He noticed you from his office window when you arrived, and he has asked to see you next. You *are* Gabriel Montrose's nephew, correct?"

Toby had no idea what to do with himself. He had never

been bowed to before. Were you supposed to bow back, or were you just supposed to stand there? Then he realized he hadn't answered the man's question, and he decided he'd better do that first. "Yes," he said, "I'm Toby Montrose."

"Mr. Abernathy thought so," said the man in green. He stepped to one side and held the door open for Toby. "Please come in."

This made the crowd on the sidewalk unhappier than ever. The man with the buttons grumbled, and the woman in velvet groaned, but as Toby stepped through the doorway, he hardly noticed the noise. Hugh Abernathy had asked for him! He didn't understand quite how it had happened, and he almost couldn't believe it, but he was about to meet the world's greatest detective.

Mr. Abernathy's front hall was as wide as the entire ground floor of Uncle Gabriel's house, with high ceilings and floors that were tiled in black-and-white stone. Standing on a gleaming white square, Toby felt a little like a playing piece in an enormous game of chess. He tried to smooth out the wrinkles in his shirt as the man in green closed the door and walked to Toby's side.

"It's a pleasure to meet you, Mr. Montrose," the man in green said. Everything about him was neat and precise, from the cut of his emerald wool vest to the click of his moss-colored shoes on the tiles. "I am Mr. Peartree, Hugh Abernathy's assistant."

"Oh!" said Toby. "I thought you were a butler!"

Toby knew all about Mr. Peartree, of course, even though he hadn't expected the detective's assistant to be quite so *green*. In the *Sphinx Monthly Reader*, Mr. Peartree usually took care of the more routine parts of an investigation—studying train timetables, for instance, or compiling lists of everyone in the city who wore a certain shoe size—while Mr. Abernathy got to do exciting things like dressing up in elaborate disguises and exchanging gunfire with fugitives. During the Case of the Left-Handed Banker, which Toby had read about the previous evening, Mr. Abernathy had chased a band of robbers through the streets of Colebridge while Mr. Peartree, perched on a rooftop and serving as lookout, had dozed off and missed the whole affair. It was no wonder Toby had always thought of Mr. Peartree as a boring sort of person.

The real Mr. Peartree, however, with his mint-green leather gloves and his perfectly waxed brown mustache, seemed much more interesting. "I've read all your stories, sir," Toby added, scrambling to make up for what he'd said about being a butler. "I think they're wonderful. Working for Mr. Abernathy must be an exciting job."

"Thank you," Mr. Peartree said crisply. "The work is constantly surprising, I'll grant you that." His mouth twitched under the curve of his mustache. "If you'll come with me, I'll take you to see Mr. Abernathy now."

Toby followed Mr. Peartree across the hall and up a wrought-iron spiral staircase. At the top of the staircase was another wide, high-ceilinged space, with doors leading in all different directions. As they passed by one doorway, Toby caught a glimpse of glass vials and test tubes laid out on a long table. Another door was latched with a padlock; a third door boasted a label that said *SKULLS*.

Mr. Peartree must have noticed Toby's eyes getting wider as they walked. "Mr. Abernathy likes to have every supply he might need for an investigation close at hand," he said. "I imagine your uncle has a similar collection."

"Sort of," said Toby. Uncle Gabriel's collection of supplies was limited to the odds and ends in Toby's bedroom and a few unsorted boxes he'd stashed under his desk in the parlor, but Toby didn't want Mr. Peartree to think that Montrose Investigations was small or shabby. Truthfully, he was relieved that none of the doors in Uncle Gabriel's house said *SKULLS*. "How did Mr. Abernathy guess who I was?" he asked.

"I can promise you," said Mr. Peartree, "it wasn't a guess." He stopped in front of a tall set of double doors and pushed the knobs inward. "As for his methods, however, you're welcome to ask him yourself."

Toby walked forward into a room lined from floor to ceiling with bookshelves. He knew he shouldn't stare, but he couldn't help himself; even the city library didn't store so many books in one place. There were medical journals and city directories, at least three full sets of encyclopedias, several volumes with titles written in languages Toby didn't understand, and what looked like a lifetime subscription to the *Sphinx Monthly Reader* squashed into its own tall bookcase. The only wall free of books was the one directly across from Toby, where a man sat in a swiveling leather chair, looking out the window to the street below.

"Mr. Montrose!" Hugh Abernathy turned around and unfolded himself from the chair. He looked just the way Mr. Peartree always described him in the *Sphinx*: golden-haired and clean-shaven, with a smile warm enough to put a murderer at ease. He was no taller than his assistant, and equally slim, but while Mr. Peartree faded away into the corner of the room, Mr. Abernathy seemed to fill every inch of it. "Toby, is it? I did my best to read your lips when you introduced yourself to Mr. Peartree, but I don't always get these things exactly right. It's a pleasure to meet you."

Toby tried to remember what he'd planned to say to Mr. Abernathy, but it had all fallen out of his mind somewhere on the staircase or along the hall. That didn't seem to matter, though, because Mr. Abernathy just kept talking. "Let me take a look at you," he said, studying Toby at arm's length. "Ten—no, eleven years old. Smart, I think, and responsible." Mr. Abernathy narrowed his eyes. "*Too* responsible. You've been taking care of yourself for a while now, haven't you, Toby? I'm very sorry about that. I wonder—have you spent much time with a strict aunt, perhaps? In any case, you've lived with Gabriel for the past three months, and you're here to respond to the invitation I sent him. You were delayed by a terrier on the way here, but I won't keep you long; I can see you need to get home quickly." He stepped back and crossed his arms. "Tell me: how'd I do?"

Toby felt almost breathless. He knew Hugh Abernathy was brilliant—everyone knew that—but Toby had never imagined that anyone in the world could know so much about *him*. Even Uncle Gabriel had never made such an accurate deduction. "That was just like in the stories!" he said. "You've got to tell me how you did it, sir. How did you know about my aunt Janet?"

"So it was an aunt after all?" Mr. Abernathy looked relieved. "I have to admit that was a hunch on my part. When a child has cheeks and fingernails as neatly scrubbed as yours, there's always a fastidious relative in the background who's given him the habit. Aunts are most common, in my experience. Sometimes it's mothers"—Mr. Abernathy paused—"but I don't think that's true in your case."

"No, sir," said Toby. "My mother is gone. Anyway, she never minded getting dirty." During the planting season, she'd always been covered with smudges of soil, and Toby's father had once threatened to sow carrot seeds behind her ears.

Mr. Abernathy nodded. "You had me fooled for a moment with your size," he continued, "but boys of ten are really nothing like boys of eleven, and I expect you'll sprout up soon. Then there's the matter of the fourth button on your shirt." He took a pen from behind his ear and used the end of it to tap the button in question. "It fell off in the past, and it's been fixed by someone with a pinch of improvisation and a bucketful of good intentions. If you're mending your own clothes—and cutting your own hair, for that matter—you must be used to looking after yourself."

He didn't say it unkindly, but Toby felt his cheeks flame up. He'd been really proud of that button. It had come off while he was chasing after Uncle Howard's horses, and he'd spent hours working out how to knot it back in place. Unlike the lost horses, it had been one piece of trouble he'd actually managed to fix. "I hoped no one would be able to tell," he said.

"Most people won't." Mr. Abernathy slipped the pen back behind his ear. "But most people aren't detectives. It's my job to notice the small things of the world, the things that are usually overlooked. The animal hairs at your wrists and ankles, for instance."

Toby looked to where Mr. Abernathy was pointing. A few strands of Percival's fur clung to the sleeves of his coat and the cuffs of his pants. "That's how you knew about the terrier."

"As it happens, I've collected a number of fur, feather, and scale samples from animals around the world. It took me a decade to gather them and another six months to memorize them all."

In the corner of the room, Mr. Peartree raised his green-gloved hand. Toby had almost forgotten he was standing there. "I wonder," he said, "how you knew the dog wasn't the boy's pet?"

"Ah!" Mr. Abernathy beamed. "I'm glad you asked, Peartree. A less experienced detective easily could have leapt to that conclusion. But take another look at our friend Toby here." He put his hands on Toby's shoulders and spun him around slowly, as though Toby were modeling a new fashion. "If he owned a dog, its fur would be everywhere, not only on his sleeves and cuffs. Since it's not, I knew his meeting with the wretched creature must have been brief. Recent, too, or he would have dusted himself off by now." Mr. Abernathy let Toby go. "He's a very tidy person."

"Thank you, sir," said Toby, hoping it was a compliment.

"And his relationship to Gabriel Montrose?" Mr. Peartree asked.

Toby had been thinking about this. "Actually," he said, "I've got that one figured out already." He pointed to the pocket of his coat, where he'd tucked Mr. Abernathy's invitation earlier that afternoon. It was sticking halfway out of his pocket now, with most of Uncle Gabriel's name and address clearly visible.

Mr. Abernathy laughed. While Uncle Gabriel's laughter was booming and thunderous, Mr. Abernathy's sounded more like a spring drizzle. "Well done, Toby," he said. "I see I was right about your smarts, too. The letter certainly helped. To be honest, though, news travels quickly on the Row. I'd heard that Gabriel's nephew had come to live with him. You look very much like he did when he was younger, and I recognized you right away when I saw you in the crowd." Mr. Abernathy rubbed the bridge of his nose, where there was an almost imperceptible bump. Toby wondered if that was the spot where Uncle Gabriel had broken it.

"Now that I've satisfied your curiosity," Mr. Abernathy said, "I hope you'll satisfy mine. What message has your uncle asked you to bring me?"

Toby sucked in his breath. The detective may have praised his smarts, but Toby wasn't sure a really smart person would lie to Hugh Abernathy's face. He hadn't done it yet; he could still turn around and go back to Montrose Investigations, where Uncle Gabriel would mutter about the bills and stare at his meager case files while Toby sat in the hallway, waiting to open the door for clients who never came. Toby could swear he heard the trouble rustling through the pages of Mr. Abernathy's encyclopedias.

He needed those ten thousand dollars.

"It's about the contest," Toby said, "to choose the world's greatest detective. Uncle Gabriel says—well, he says he'd like to enter."

"Really!" Mr. Abernathy frowned. "I'm pleased to hear it, naturally, but I'm frankly surprised. I thought Gabriel's arm would need more twisting than that."

"He does have some requirements, though," Toby said quickly, "and he says he won't come unless you meet them."

"That sounds more like Gabriel." Mr. Abernathy sat down in his chair. "You'd better go ahead and tell me what they are."

"Well," said Toby, "he's got to be allowed to stay alone in his bedroom all weekend to think about the case. He can't have any distractions. He doesn't even want to go downstairs for dinner. It's all part of a new investigative strategy he's trying."

"It doesn't sound likely to work," Mr. Peartree observed from the corner. "Won't he want to interview suspects? Search for clues?"

"That's why he needs me!" said Toby. His throat felt dry and his feet felt damp, but he couldn't ask for a glass of water or kick off his shoes; he couldn't risk looking suspicious. This part of the lie was the most important of all. "Uncle Gabriel wants me to come to the competition with him. I'll do the legwork, collecting clues and things, and I'll bring it all back to Uncle Gabriel so he can think about it."

For the first time that afternoon, Mr. Abernathy looked baffled. "Let me make sure I've heard you correctly. Gabriel Montrose actually believes he can solve a crime—a crime of my creation!—by sitting in his room all weekend and *thinking*?"

"Thinking very *hard*," Toby amended.

Mr. Abernathy cast his eyes to the ceiling and shook his head. "Fine!" he said. "Peartree, make a note of Detective Montrose's requirements, as bizarre as they may be. I want him at this competition." Then he looked at Toby. "I hope joining us at the manor won't be too boring for you."

"I can't wait for it," said Toby. It felt wonderful to tell the truth again. "How could one of your mysteries possibly be boring?"

There was another spring drizzle of laughter. "I don't like to compliment myself too often," Mr. Abernathy said, "but it *is* an awfully good case."

In the corner of the room, Mr. Peartree coughed.

"Excuse me, sir," he said. "If Mr. Montrose has finished delivering his message, we should bring in the next client." He stepped out of his corner, pulled a pocket watch from his emerald-green vest, and held it out to Mr. Abernathy. "We're running well behind schedule."

Mr. Abernathy considered the watch. Then he pinched it between two fingers, lifted it from Mr. Peartree's palm, and tossed it over his shoulder.

Pieces of glass and clockwork flew everywhere as the pocket watch cracked against the floorboards. Toby put his arms up to protect his face from the wreckage. He expected Mr. Peartree to swear or shout, but the detective's assistant didn't seem all that surprised by the destruction of his watch. He only sighed, as though he were used to this sort of thing, and brushed a shard of glass from his lapel.

Mr. Abernathy kicked up his feet. "There's another problem solved," he said over the sound of skittering cogs and popping springs. "As you can see, Peartree, time is no longer an issue. It's a good thing, too, because our business with Mr. Montrose isn't entirely finished. There's still one more thing we need to discuss."

Toby had no idea what Mr. Abernathy was talking about, but he didn't think it was anything good. Did the detective know he'd been lying? Was he going to pick Toby up and toss him over his shoulder, just like he'd done with the pocket watch? Toby imagined his own insides bursting out and bouncing across the carpet; it wasn't a nice thought.

"Come here, Toby," Mr. Abernathy said. He tapped the arm of his chair. "Tell me about your parents."

Toby didn't move. "My parents, sir?"

"You said earlier that your mother is gone, and I assume

your father is, too; that's why you're living with Gabriel." He studied Toby's face. "I have to admit I'm curious. What happened?"

"They went to the seashore for a holiday." Toby didn't like talking about it, and he couldn't imagine why Mr. Abernathy wanted to hear about it, either, but adults were always asking Toby questions like this, and he'd learned by now that it was easier not to argue. "They took a rowboat out into the cove one afternoon," he said, "and a storm came up out of nowhere. My parents disappeared. The police think they drowned."

"But you're not so sure, are you?"

"What?" Toby stared at Mr. Abernathy. No adult had ever asked him *that* before.

"I can tell from the way you speak about them. You say they're gone, you say they've disappeared, but you never say they died. Was the rowboat ever found?"

"No," said Toby, "but—"

"And your parents' bodies? Were they recovered?"

Toby shook his head. "We couldn't even have a burial."

"Just as I thought." Mr. Abernathy leaned forward in his chair. "I know hope when I see it, Toby, and you've got a speck of it in your eyes right now. You're a practical child, but there's a part of you that hopes your parents might walk through that doorway at any moment." He pointed to the tall double doors behind Toby. "Isn't there?"

Toby couldn't help looking over his shoulder. The doors, of course, stayed closed. "It's been three years, sir," he told Mr. Abernathy. "Even if my parents did survive, I don't think anyone would be able to find out what happened to them."

At this, Mr. Abernathy looked wounded. "My boy!" he said. "You're standing in front of the world's greatest detective! It's perfectly obvious to me that you want to know the truth of your parents' disappearance, and when it comes to solving mysteries, I happen to be something of an expert." He smiled at Toby. "Why don't you let me look into it? If your parents are anywhere to be found, I'm sure I can find them."

It was tempting to imagine it: just like he did in all those stories in the *Sphinx*, Hugh Abernathy would comb the beach sand for clues and plumb the truth from the ocean's depths. Maybe he'd even let Toby come with him. But real life wasn't a detective story, Toby reminded himself, and the police officer from the seashore had seemed awfully confident when he'd knocked on Aunt Janet's door. "Do you really think there's a chance my parents are alive?"

"If there's one thing I've learned in my line of work," Mr. Abernathy said, "it's that nothing is likely, but everything is possible. I can't make any promises, but I'd like to take your case."

"Are you sure?" Not even Uncle Gabriel had ever offered

to do anything of the sort. "You must have more important work to do," Toby said, "finding lost jewels and kidnapped millionaires and things."

Mr. Abernathy waved a hand, as if jewels and millionaires meant nothing to him. "To be honest, Toby Montrose, you interest me."

"But I can't pay you!"

"Then consider it a favor." Mr. Abernathy stood up. The springs and gears from Mr. Peartree's shattered pocket watch crunched under his shoes as he walked Toby to the door. "We'll see each other at Coleford Manor, won't we? I'm sure you'll have a chance to repay me then."

PART II

A CONTEST OF WITS

CHAPTER 5

IN SLAUGHTER'S LANE

"Where in the world is Mrs. Satterthwaite?" Uncle Gabriel pushed the parlor curtains aside and squinted through the glass. "She should have been here ten minutes ago. If I don't leave by eight, I'll miss my train, and the ferry after that." He picked up the suitcase at his feet, shifted it from hand to hand, and set it down again; Toby could tell he was a mess of nerves. "Do you think she could have forgotten she'd agreed to stay with you this weekend?"

"I'm sure she didn't," said Toby. He was a mess of nerves, too, but for an entirely different reason: while Uncle Gabriel was hoping Mrs. Satterthwaite would appear on the front step, Toby was hoping she wouldn't. The letter he'd sent her the evening before had been perfectly clear, even if it had taken him three whole nights to copy out in his best approximation of Uncle Gabriel's handwriting:

Dear Mrs. Satterthwaite,

I am writing to inform you that my nephew, Tobias, has been invited to stay with his dear aunt Janet while I am traveling in Gallis. Since she will be taking care of Tobias this weekend, I no longer need you to come to Detectives' Row tomorrow morning to look after him. Please stay at home instead.

Sincerely yours,
Gabriel Montrose

Toby had been proud of that letter, but he hadn't been at all certain that it would work. What if it didn't arrive in time? What if Mrs. Satterthwaite spotted his forgery, and what if she showed it to Uncle Gabriel? He half expected the cook to come charging down the Row, waving his letter in her fist and dooming his plan to enter Mr. Abernathy's contest before he'd even left the house. But the seconds ticked by on the mantelpiece clock, its chime struck the hour, and there was still no sign of her.

"Eight o'clock. I can't stay any longer." Uncle Gabriel stepped back from the window and picked up his suitcase, more confidently this time. "I'm sorry, Tobias. Will you be all right on your own until Mrs. Satterthwaite gets here? I hate to leave you in the lurch, but this trip is too important to miss, and this case is too important to lose." He'd been working on nothing else for the past few weeks, going out at odd hours and staying awake late into the night, poring over Gallian newspaper clippings Toby couldn't understand. More than once, Toby had come downstairs in the morning to find Uncle Gabriel asleep at his desk. He refused to discuss the case with Toby—Toby guessed it was another of the things he wasn't supposed to worry about—but whatever it was, it had darkened the circles under Uncle Gabriel's eyes and deepened the furrows in his brow.

"I'll be fine," Toby promised him. "I hope you solve your case."

"I hope so, too." Uncle Gabriel strode to the door. "If all goes well, you'll hear my shouts of joy all the way from Gallis. If it doesn't—well, let's not waste time thinking about that." He swung the door open and tipped his hat to Toby. "Either way, Tobias, I'll see you soon. Be good for Mrs. Satterthwaite, and don't let her tidy up too much."

The windowpane in the parlor was cold and grimy, but

Toby pressed his nose to it and watched as Uncle Gabriel ran down the Row toward the train station, his tweed coat billowing out behind him and his shoes kicking up clouds of spring dirt. Soon he was as small as Toby's thumbnail. A few moments after that, he turned the corner into the High Street, and Toby couldn't see him anymore.

Six dollars and fifty-three cents wasn't a lot of money, but it was the amount Toby had managed to collect off the city sidewalks over the past few months, and he hoped it was enough to get him to Coleford Manor. He slipped it into the pocket of his pants, dragged his own suitcase down the stairs from his bedroom, and locked the front door of Montrose Investigations behind him with the key Uncle Gabriel had given him for emergencies. Under the door, he'd tucked another letter, this time in his own handwriting, though he hoped he'd be safely back at home before anyone else had a chance to read it:

> To the person who finds this note:
> I have gone to become the world's greatest detective. Please do not worry about me. I'm sorry to sneak away, but I had to find a way to stop the trouble, and I think ten thousand dollars should be enough to do it.
>
> Your friend,
> Toby Montrose

Detectives' Row was quiet for half past eight on a Friday morning, but Toby walked quickly and tried to keep his head down. Once he reached the High Street, with its busy bakeries and newspaper stands, he felt safer: he could blend into the crowd without worrying that one of Uncle Gabriel's eagle-eyed neighbors might spot him and ask what he was doing. Horse-drawn carriages rolled up and down the High Street, carrying Colebridge's moneylenders and lawyers and merchants to work at the banks and courts and market stalls in the city center. The train station was only a few blocks north, but no trains ran near Coleford Manor, and anyway, Toby didn't want to risk running into Uncle Gabriel.

But hailing a carriage on the High Street was impossible. At first, Toby tried to copy the well-dressed men and women all around him, whistling and waving his hat hopefully whenever a driver approached. Although they stopped more often than not for the well-dressed men and women, none of the drivers seemed particularly interested in stopping for *him*, no matter how loudly he whistled or how hopefully he waved. People on the sidewalk jostled Toby from his left and his right, brushing past him as if they didn't even realize he was there. A man in a pin-striped suit kicked over his suitcase, and a woman carrying loaves of bread shoved Toby so powerfully that he fell into the street. As he picked himself up, brushing the dirt from his knees, all the well-dressed people gathered around him and shook their heads. Toby could feel the trouble there, too, squeezing him in. "Be careful, child!" someone shouted. "And for goodness' sake, get out of the way!"

For once, Toby didn't pause to search for his parents' faces in the crowd: he grabbed his suitcase, pulled his hat low over his eyes, and made his way out of the High Street as fast as he could.

The street he'd turned into was narrow and empty. Dead-limbed trees crowded out the sunlight, and no flowers bloomed here, but at least it was quiet. Toby was so flustered that he walked almost a whole block, past rows of tall gray buildings and darkened storefronts, before he realized it: this was Slaughter's Lane. No wonder all the well-dressed people from the High Street had disappeared; only the most eager tourists and the most desperate detectives were brave or foolish enough to come this way.

Now that Toby knew where he was, he couldn't help looking around. This was, after all, the street where the Colebridge Cutthroat's career had begun, and the street Uncle Gabriel had warned him to avoid. Over his head, a curtain in a window flicked open and closed again. A yellowing piece of newsprint blew down the sidewalk, past a billiard parlor and a deserted pub, before settling in the shadows. Something in the alley beyond him made a noise that might have been a laugh or a scream; he wasn't sure he wanted to know which. Even though the weather was warm for May, Toby could feel goose bumps racing up his arms. If his suitcase hadn't been so heavy, he would have turned around and run.

The noise came from the alley again. It was louder this time: not a laugh or a scream, after all, but a bleating sort of sound, like a horse asking for hay. Toby remembered that sound from the few weeks he'd spent working for his uncle Howard. *Was* it a horse? Toby inched forward toward the corner where the alley met the street. In Inspector Webster's correspondence course (lesson thirty-six), he'd learned about using mirrors to look around corners; he didn't have a mirror with him, but in the pub's plate-glass window, he could see the dim reflection of two thin animals harnessed to a carriage.

"Who's there?" The voice came from the alley. Too late, Toby realized he hadn't been the only one using the pub's window to watch the business of Slaughter's Lane: a tall, sturdy man in a suit that had seen better days stepped around the corner and straight into Toby's path. He looked Toby up and down, but his eyes lingered on the suitcase. "You're a new one," he said. His voice crackled like dead leaves. "What brings you here? Looking for work? You're small enough to make a decent pickpocket."

"No, sir." Toby wasn't sure whether you were supposed to be polite to men who were most likely on their way into prison or out of it, but he figured it couldn't hurt.

The man shrugged. "Then you're going somewhere. That case of yours looks heavy."

"It's not," said Toby, although it was.

"You'll never catch a cab on the High Street at this time of day—but it looks like you've found that out already." He smiled, more at the suitcase than at Toby. "Lucky for you, and lucky for me, I've got a carriage around the corner and no fares to pick up for the rest of the morning. Where can I take you?"

Toby looked back over his shoulder toward the bustling High Street. The man with the carriage obviously couldn't be trusted, but he was right: Toby had no hope of hailing a ride, and no other way of leaving the city. If he wanted to enter Mr. Abernathy's contest, he didn't have much of a choice. "I'm going to Coleford Manor," he said, "a few miles over the river. And I've only got six dollars."

"Six dollars?" The man raised his eyebrows. "That's exactly my price."

"I'm a detective, you know," Toby said. "So is my uncle. He'll be very upset if anything happens to me."

The man laughed, showing all of his teeth. "Don't worry about that, my boy. Climb aboard, and I'll have you safe at the manor as quick as my mares can take us."

As the carriage shuddered and squealed through the city streets, Toby pulled out his packet of lessons from Inspector

Webster and studied it again to be sure he hadn't forgotten anything. He hadn't quite reached level three of the correspondence course yet, but over the past few months, he'd learned how to follow strangers in the street, how to encipher a secret message, and how to set a trap for thieves using only a tablecloth and a few pieces of wire. He'd tested this trap a few weeks earlier in the downstairs hallway, and Mrs. Satterthwaite had walked straight into it when she came to cook dinner. She hadn't seemed particularly impressed with Toby's investigative skills when he'd helped her out from under the tablecloth, but at least she hadn't mentioned the whole incident to Uncle Gabriel. Toby wasn't sure he was entirely qualified to be the world's greatest detective yet, but knowing he had Inspector Webster's lessons to help him through the weekend made him feel as though he might have a chance of winning the prize money after all.

The carriage groaned to a halt, and Toby looked up. The horses had stopped on one of the small bridges that led over the river and into the countryside. "Where are we?" he asked the driver.

"City limits," said the man, scratching his ear. He'd taken his jacket off in the morning heat, and his arm was scarred and hairy, tattooed with a thick black line that curled around it from his wrist all the way to his elbow. "That's as far as your fare will take you."

"But I have to get to Coleford Manor!" said Toby. "It's

miles down the road still. You said six dollars was enough to get me there."

"Did I say that?" The man turned in his seat and winked, not kindly. "I must have meant it'd be six to the city limits, and six more to the manor." He held out an empty palm. "Pay up, my boy, and we'll be on our way."

Toby wriggled away from the man's hand. He should have known better than to expect the truth from a driver he'd met in Slaughter's Lane. "I don't have any more money," he said, "so don't bother trying to frighten me out of it."

The driver shook his head. "It's a shame," he said, "leaving a boy as small as you out here all alone, so far from his home. I hate to do it." His eyes went again to Toby's suitcase. "Of course, I don't need to be paid in money. Why don't you hand that case over to me instead?"

Toby pulled the suitcase to his chest. "It's just luggage, sir," he said. "Clothes and things. You wouldn't want any of it."

"I don't know about that. Those papers look worth a read." The driver pointed to Inspector Webster's lessons. "And aren't those old Hugh Abernathy stories in the front pocket? Folks will pay more than a few pennies for those."

"I don't care," said Toby. He could see the trouble now, swirling in the murky water below them. No matter where he went, it always caught up sooner or later—usually sooner. "You can't have them."

"Then you won't be getting to the manor." The driver turned back to his horses. "Do you think your uncle is a good enough detective to find you wandering along the riverbank a few days from now?"

The trouble began to curl its way out of the water and onto the bridge. Toby looked down at his suitcase. He'd packed his very best clothes—the only ones that still came close to fitting, and the ones Aunt Janet had ordered him not to lose. He couldn't afford to lose the correspondence course, either; he didn't know what he'd do at Coleford Manor without Inspector Webster's instructions to guide him. Worst of all was the thought of putting his parents' old *Sphinx* issues into the driver's grimy hands. But he couldn't see any way out of it. He might have been gullible enough to trust a third-rate criminal, but he wasn't going to let this man ruin his chances to become the world's greatest detective. At least he still had fifty-three cents in his pocket and his junior detective badge pinned under his coat. That would have to be enough.

"Fine," he said, shoving the suitcase into the driver's seat. His eyes stung at the corners, but he couldn't let the man see him cry. "You've got what you wanted. Now take me to the manor."

The man gave Toby's suitcase a pat and flicked his horses' reins. "Right away, Detective."

CHAPTER 6

CREEPING IVY

The road outside Coleford Manor was still puddled with the last evening's rain, and the carriage splashed muddy water all over Toby as it rolled away. In front of him, two gateposts marked a curving drive that led through perfectly tended flower beds and fishponds, past a summerhouse and a hedge maze, and up the hill to the most impressive house Toby had ever seen.

The closer he got to it, the more enormous it looked. It might have been half the size of Colebridge's government hall, with pointed towers rising from its corners, carved stone griffins perched along the roofline, and fluted columns sprouting from the walls, as though the builders had been so excited about constructing the manor that they'd forgotten to stop. It was the sort of house, Toby thought, where you lived if you didn't mind losing track of everyone else in your family. All of his own aunts and uncles and cousins could have lived there for years without ever bumping into one another in the hallways. Toby wondered what sort of people *did* live at Coleford Manor, and whether they liked each other very much.

Over the manor's front entrance, two dark-suited footmen on wobbly ladders were attempting to hang a banner that read *WELCOME, DETECTIVES!* in hand-painted letters that looked awfully wobbly themselves. Just beyond the ladders, a small crowd of people had gathered. Toby recognized most of them from Detectives' Row: at the front of the group, handing his luggage to a waiting servant, was Mr. Rackham, Uncle Gabriel's across-the-street neighbor. Miss Price was exclaiming happily over a flowering lilac bush, while Miss March had fallen into conversation with a young woman Toby sometimes saw riding her bicycle down the Row. Julia Hartshorn, he thought she was called. She was tall and serious-looking, and she lived in the house next door to Hugh Abernathy's. On busy days, the line of clients waiting to see Mr. Abernathy stretched all the way to her doorstep. The only person Toby didn't recognize at all was a young man wearing a white linen suit and a straw hat that shaded his face. He stood apart from the others, looking up at the manor's stone griffins as though they might swoop down from their parapets and bite him. The young man didn't look much like a detective, Toby thought—but then, neither did Toby. As he joined the others, he did his best to brush the mud from his clothes and wished for the tenth time in as many minutes that he still had his suitcase.

Only the young man in white seemed to notice him. "Hello," he said to Toby. "Are you here for the contest?"

Toby nodded. "I'm here as my uncle's assistant," he explained. "I'm Toby Montrose."

"Then your uncle must be Gabriel Montrose!" The young man looked awfully proud of himself for deducing this. "I've heard of him, of course, though I'm afraid we've never met. I'm Philip Elwood." He held out a hand, and Toby shook it. "I hope you'll introduce me to your uncle as soon as you can."

"I hope so, too," said Toby. He didn't know quite where Uncle Gabriel was at the moment, of course—he might be on a ferry halfway across the sea, or squashed in a Gallian train compartment—but he wasn't going to tell Philip Elwood that.

Before Philip could ask any uncomfortable questions about Uncle Gabriel's whereabouts, the manor door opened and Mr. Peartree stepped outside. To Toby's disappointment, Mr. Abernathy wasn't with him. He wore a coat the color of a spring meadow and a verdant felt hat, and he crossed off names on a list with a green fountain pen as he greeted each of the guests. First, Mr. Rackham passed into the manor, then Miss March and Miss Price, then Julia Hartshorn. Philip Elwood fiddled with his straw hat the whole time; he hurried off toward the *WELCOME, DETECTIVES!* banner before Mr. Peartree had even finished crossing off his name.

Then Mr. Peartree blinked down at Toby. "Welcome to Coleford Manor, Mr. Montrose," he said. He raised his fountain pen over the list of guests and let it hover over Uncle Gabriel's name. "It's a delight to see you again, but I hope you aren't the *only* Mr. Montrose who has joined us this weekend. Is your uncle here?"

Luckily, Toby had planned for this moment. *When you must be deceitful*, Inspector Webster had written in lesson thirty-four of his correspondence course, *deceive with confidence! A confident liar is much more difficult to spot than one who is wishy-washy.* Hoping the inspector knew what he was talking about, Toby lifted his chin and met Mr. Peartree's gaze. "He's gone around to the back entrance," he said. A house as huge as Coleford Manor was sure to have at least one back entrance, wasn't it? "Uncle Gabriel's brought some top secret detection devices with him this weekend, and he doesn't want any of the other investigators to see them. He asked me to let you know he's arrived."

Had Toby been confident enough? Mr. Peartree gave

him a curious look. Then, slowly, he put his pen to paper and drew a bold green slash through the name *Gabriel Montrose*. "You and your uncle will be in the Marigold Room on the second floor," Mr. Peartree said. "One of the servants will show you the way. Does your uncle need any help carrying his—ah, his devices?"

Toby let himself breathe. "I don't think so," he said. And then, because he couldn't help himself, "Is Mr. Abernathy here? Do you know if he's found out anything about what happened to my parents?"

"I'm afraid Mr. Abernathy hasn't kept me up-to-date on that particular case," Mr. Peartree said briskly, "but you'll be seeing him soon. He's asked all the guests to gather in the parlor at eleven o'clock."

According to the shiny new watch Mr. Peartree flipped open, it was already a few minutes past ten. "All the guests but Uncle Gabriel, you mean," Toby said. "He's got to stay in his room and think."

"Of course; I'd forgotten." Mr. Peartree looked down at Toby and scratched the side of his nose. Then he lowered his voice to a murmur. "Are you sure you don't need my assistance, Mr. Montrose?"

If Toby hadn't had a knack for observation, he might not have noticed the slight suspicious edge to Mr. Peartree's voice. He *did* notice it, though, and he was suddenly horribly certain: Mr. Peartree knew everything. He knew Uncle

Gabriel wasn't really dragging mysterious devices up the servants' stairs, and he knew Toby was there all alone, where he didn't belong, trying to fib his way past Hugh Abernathy's assistant and doing a spectacularly bad job of it. A brown blur dashed past Toby's feet: it was the trouble and it had caught up with him, just the way it always did.

Then someone shouted, the ground shook, and something fell from the sky onto Mr. Peartree's head.

It was the *WELCOME, DETECTIVES!* banner—though now that it had draped itself over Mr. Peartree, it was much harder to read. One of the wobbly ladders had come crashing down, bringing one of the dark-suited footmen with it. Now he lay on the ground next to Toby, clutching his ankle. "That damned dog!" he shouted. "Get him away from me, or I'll wring his neck!"

The dog—small, brown, and enthusiastically exploring the insides of the footman's ears—didn't seem to take the threat seriously, but Toby did. He scooped the dog up and hurried into the manor, passing Mr. Peartree, who was still stumbling around under the billowing cloth like a ghost in a children's play. "There's a man outside who's hurt his leg," he told the worried-looking maid who'd come running to see what had happened, "and I think Mr. Peartree needs to be rescued from that banner."

The maid ran out the door. The dog licked Toby's nose and put his muddy paws on Toby's chest. He seemed to think they'd known each other all their lives.

Actually, Toby realized, there *was* something familiar about him. "Percival?" he asked, setting the dog down on the carpet. "That's your name, isn't it?"

The dog stared at Toby as though it were obvious.

"We met on Detectives' Row," Toby explained. "Do you remember?" Of course he did; dogs were good with memories. "I was going to visit Mr. Abernathy, and you were with that strange girl. . . ."

Toby trailed off. The strange girl stood in the doorway in front of him, looking just as shocked as he was.

"It's you!" they both said at the same time. And then, "What are you doing here?"

"I *live* here." The girl set down the bags she was holding—a whole armful from the nicest shops in Colebridge, stuffed with colorful tissue. She wasn't wearing a fedora today, or spectacles, either; she was dressed as though she were the sort of girl who always got lots of presents on her birthday and never had to do chores. "Come here, Percival," she said.

Percival looked up at the girl. Then he looked at Toby. He sighed through his nose.

"I think you're making him uncomfortable," said Toby. "And anyway, how can you live here? Aren't you a murderess?"

The girl frowned. "A murderess-in-*training*," she said.

"That's different. And it's beside the point, Toby Montrose. You still haven't told me why you're standing in our front hall."

"I'm here for the contest," Toby explained, "the detectives' competition, and—how did you know my name?"

"Ivy!" A dark-haired woman hurried through the front door, followed by a younger woman with her own armload of shopping bags. They both looked like taller, more glamorous versions of the girl in front of Toby. "Ivy, you know we all love Percival, but you've *got* to keep him on his lead when he's outdoors," the woman said. Her voice was stern, but not angry—the sort of voice that usually belonged to mothers. "Norton says he's broken his ankle, and from the color of it, I think he might be right; I've never seen anything quite so purple. The driver's gone to fetch Doctor Piper, but you should apologize to Norton before she gets here. And for heaven's sake, keep Percival away from him! I think he'd like to roast that dog on a spit."

The girl—Ivy—wasn't staring at Toby any longer, thank goodness. And he'd learned her name, too! Now they were even. "I'm sorry, Mother," Ivy said. "I don't know what got into Percival. He never runs away like that, except . . ." Her eyes darted back to Toby. "Never mind. Should I pick some flowers for Norton?" Toby thought she sounded awfully reluctant about the idea.

"That would be thoughtful," the woman said, guiding

79

Ivy out the door. "Not the roses, please!"

Toby didn't know what to do. He wanted to go to his room before Mr. Peartree came inside and started questioning him again, but he couldn't remember which room was supposed to be his. The Magnolia Room? The Marmalade Room? Whichever it was, if he didn't get there quickly, he'd be stuck here in the middle of the rug with mud flaking off him while Ivy's mother studied him as a scientist might examine her latest specimen.

"You look lost," she told him. "Don't feel bad about that; it's the house's fault. We've lived here for years, but I still feel I ought to have a compass to navigate the place." She raised her eyebrows at Percival, who had settled himself on Toby's feet. "I see Percy has already introduced himself to you, so I'll do the same. I'm Amina Webster, and this is my older daughter, Lillie."

The younger woman, who was putting away her hat and gloves, nodded to Toby. "Are you a friend of Ivy's?" she asked.

Whatever Ivy thought of him, Toby didn't think it was friendly. "I'm here with my uncle, actually," he said. "He's a detective. His name is Gabriel Montrose."

"Which must make you Toby!" Mrs. Webster exclaimed. "Of course. Mr. Peartree told us Detective Montrose's assistant would be joining him, but I assumed he'd be much more grown-up and dull. What a relief he's not." She thought for a moment. "You and your uncle are in the Marigold Room, aren't you? Would you like me to show you the way?"

Marigold—that was it. "Yes, please," said Toby. He was having a hard time believing that a girl as strange as Ivy could have a mother as stubbornly normal as Mrs. Webster. She took Toby's hat and coat herself—she didn't even ask a servant to do it—and carried them across the hall and up the staircase. Toby followed at Mrs. Webster's heels, and Percival followed at Toby's.

On the second-floor landing, Mrs. Webster turned left and led the way down a narrow hallway lined with doors. Each door had a different sort of flower carved into its wood, but Toby didn't know any of their names. He'd always been more interested in the plants you could eat than in the ones you couldn't. Besides, something much more important than flowers was tugging at the corner of his mind. "Excuse me," he said, hurrying to keep up with Mrs. Webster's long strides, "but have you ever heard of an *Inspector* Webster? Is he your husband?"

"My husband," Mrs. Webster said over her shoulder, "would have a difficult time finding eggs under a hen, let alone solving a crime." She laughed. "Robert is a historian—he studies antiquities—and I'm an archaeol-gist. We're very good at digging up ancient pots and things like that, but our family is almost useless when it comes to detection."

"Lots of people are," said Toby, thinking of some of Uncle Gabriel's neighbors on the western end of the Row. "But that's all right. At least you're not all criminals."

Mrs. Webster gave him an odd look. "Why in the world would all of us be criminals?"

"Because of Ivy's grandmother," Toby explained. "Since she's teaching Ivy to be a murderess, I thought that maybe she'd taught the rest of you, and—"

Mrs. Webster looked so confused by now that Toby stopped talking. Of course: Ivy had been lying to him. Why had he ever bothered to believe her? They'd met before he'd become a junior detective, but still, he should have known better. "Never mind," he said to Mrs. Webster. "I was just thinking of a story Ivy told me once."

"A story about murder?" Mrs. Webster shook her head and sighed. "Yes, that sounds like Ivy."

At the end of the hallway, Mrs. Webster stopped in front of a door carved with a round-looking blossom that might have been a marigold. "Since there will be two of you," she said, "I've given you the largest room in the wing. I hope you like orange."

When she opened the door, Toby saw what she meant. The Marigold Room was as big as Uncle Gabriel's parlor on Detectives' Row, and almost everything in it, from the curtains at the windows to the piles of cushions on the two beds, was the color of a brightly blooming marigold. He had to squint to take it all in. There was a pitcher full of water on a nightstand, a shelf of interesting-looking old books, and a tree just outside that looked close enough to climb down if Toby needed to escape in a hurry. "It's wonderful," he said, hoping Mrs. Webster would leave soon so he could stop being polite and dive into the piles of cushions.

She hung his coat and hat in a closet and looked around the room. "Your uncle hasn't made his way here yet," she said. "Would you like me to send out a search party?"

"That's all right," Toby told her. "I think I can find him myself."

"Then I'll look forward to meeting him later." Mrs. Webster smiled at Toby. "Now, if you'll excuse me, I've got to speak to the doctor, apologize to poor Norton, and pour a cup of coffee for Mr. Abernathy."

The cushions were even softer than they'd looked. Toby let out a huge sigh as he collapsed into them: he'd actually done it! He was finally at Coleford Manor, in the fanciest bedroom he'd ever seen. Somewhere in the house, Hugh Abernathy himself was having coffee, and in only a few days, Mr. Abernathy might be putting ten thousand dollars in Toby's hands. Still, there were other detectives to outwit, and he'd already lost Inspector Webster's lessons. He had to make sure that nothing else could possibly go wrong. To start with, if he wanted to last more than five minutes at the manor, he had to build himself an uncle.

Toby stood up, gathered a few of the cushions in his arms, and arranged them in the marigold-colored armchair in the corner, fluffing and poking them until, when he glimpsed them out of the corner of his eye, they looked a little like a well-upholstered detective deep in contemplation. If he'd still had his suitcase, he could have dressed the cushions up a little more convincingly, but he did what he could, draping his coat around the figure's shoulders, placing his hat on its squarish head, and balancing a book in its lap. Then he turned the armchair to face one of the windows and pulled the curtains closed. Anyone who looked closely would be able to tell that the pile of pillows was nothing more than that, but if the other detectives saw the figure from the hallway or spied its silhouette behind the curtains, they might believe they'd actually caught a glimpse of the real Gabriel Montrose. "Think hard, Uncle Gabriel," Toby said, patting the cushion person's head.

Percival, who had followed Toby into the Marigold Room, didn't seem all that impressed by the fake Uncle Gabriel. He put his forepaws up on the bed, leaving mud prints on the coverlet. Toby would have scolded him about it, but he'd tracked in an awful lot of grime himself. "Don't you think you ought to go back outside?" he asked instead. "I'm not sure you're allowed to be in here."

Percival gave him a long and meaningful look.

"Oh, all right. I guess that servant won't be able to

84

wring your neck as long as you're with me." Toby lifted Percival up and watched as he made himself comfortable on the orange blanket. "Thanks for distracting Mr. Peartree, by the way. I might have gotten in a lot of trouble if you hadn't." Percival yawned to show Toby that this didn't surprise him at all.

With water from the pitcher, Toby cleaned up the mud he and Percival had tracked inside. Then he wiped off Percival's paws and scrubbed his own fingernails to a shine that even Aunt Janet would have approved of. He didn't look exactly like the world's greatest detective yet, he thought as he studied himself in the mirror: his shirt was rumpled from the journey, and his junior detective badge was a little bent, but at least he was clean and ready to solve a mystery. That would have to do for now.

Through the open window of the Marigold Room, Toby could see Ivy stomping through the manor's flower beds, pulling up plants by their roots and shoving away the hair that kept falling in her face. Even from a distance, she didn't look happy. Toby felt a little guilty about spying on her until he remembered that she'd probably been watching *him* for months. "Why has she been following me?" Toby asked Percival. "How did she know my name?"

Percival twitched his eyebrows. He might have known the answers, but he wasn't talking.

CHAPTER 7

LET THE GAMES BEGIN!

At eleven o'clock, Mr. Peartree rang the gong, and six detectives gathered in the parlor. Five of them were among the finest investigators in Colebridge, which was, in turn, the finest investigative city in the world.

The sixth was Toby. He had waited in the hallway for almost ten minutes, hoping for a chance to speak to Hugh Abernathy. He hadn't heard a word from Mr. Abernathy since the day he'd snuck out to visit him, and he was anxious to find out if the detective had made any progress on his parents' case. As soon as he was allowed inside the parlor, however, he could see he'd wasted his time: Mr. Abernathy wasn't anywhere in sight. He was probably still having coffee in some distant wing of the manor. There wasn't any time to go looking for him, though, so Toby sat down in a high-backed chair close to the doorway, where Mr. Abernathy would be sure to notice him when he finally arrived.

"Hello, dear." Miss Price slid into the chair next to Toby and patted his hand. "What a nice surprise! We didn't expect to see you here, did we, Anthea?"

"We certainly didn't," said Miss March. She was as sharp as Miss Price was round, and half a foot taller than her partner, but no less cheerful. "I could hardly believe it when I saw Gabriel's name on Mr. Peartree's guest list. After all that's happened between him and Hugh Abernathy, I expected he'd want to stay as far away as possible. Leave the country, even!" She and Miss Price both chuckled at the thought.

Toby didn't join them. He liked Miss March and Miss Price, but they were dangerous. No morsel of information stayed a secret for long once they got hold of it, and their talent for spreading gossip up and down Detectives' Row was second only to their knack for uncovering the truth of every situation. If Toby didn't stop them, they'd have the truth about *him* uncovered in minutes. "Uncle Gabriel didn't want to come," he explained, "but I convinced him to enter the contest. To be honest, we could use the money."

"So could we all," said Miss March. "Flossie and I haven't seen business so slow in years."

Miss Price shook her head. "It's no surprise half the detectives on the Row turned up here this weekend."

"Philip Elwood doesn't live on the Row, does he?" Toby pointed across the room to the man in the white linen suit. "I've never seen him before today."

Miss Price practically glowed with delight at the chance to talk about her fellow guests. "That," she said, "is because he's *international*."

"He's got an office in the city, but he's almost always abroad," Miss March explained. "He's got a good reputation on the Continent. They don't have so many detectives over there, of course."

"They don't even read mystery novels!" Miss Price said in grave tones. "Not nearly as many as we do, at least. And they haven't got any famous murder sites to visit. I can't imagine what they do for fun on the weekends."

"Philip Elwood rounded up a whole gang of thieves near Gyptos last spring," said Miss March. "Awfully impressive, but I hear it was more luck than logic. Now, a girl like Julia Hartshorn—*she* doesn't need luck."

"Why not?" Toby looked over at Julia Hartshorn, who sat with her shoulders squared and her jaw clenched, staring straight ahead. He'd never seen someone who didn't need luck before. She looked brave, as though she'd grab luck by its forelegs and hoist it over her shoulders if she ever did need it after all.

"Julia Hartshorn," said Miss Price, "has got *science*. She's a whiz with calculations and devices, and she's got all sorts of horrible chemicals in jars. I've heard she can work out how a poor soul was killed just by examining a bit of hair or a slice of stomach."

Toby's own stomach churned at the thought of it. Miss Hartshorn *was* brave. "And what about Mr. Rackham?" he asked. The elderly detective was studying his wristwatch, sighing loudly through his nose, looking up at the parlor door, and shaking his head before turning back to his wristwatch and repeating the whole performance. "How does he solve crimes?"

Miss Price and Miss March exchanged a look. "The same way he does everything else, dear," Miss Price said. "The old-fashioned way. Rackham was quite the thing forty years ago, and he hasn't changed a bit—except in the usual places." She patted her own stomach. "Do you know, I've never seen him out of his formal coat, even when he goes out to collect the eggs from his henhouse. Our Mr. Rackham likes to keep up appearances."

"He's not the only one." Miss March looked around at the other detectives and laughed a little. "After all, there are plenty of people in this house who aren't quite what they seem."

Mr. Peartree chose this moment to open the parlor door. Even Miss March stopped talking as a small parade of people filed into the room, led by Mrs. Webster and a responsible-looking man in a suit. Toby guessed this must be Mr. Webster. Behind them were Lillie, who smiled prettily at the detectives, and Ivy, who didn't. If Toby's aunt Janet had been there, she would have gone after Ivy with a scrubbing brush. Her tights had a new ladder in them— Toby wondered if she'd gotten stuck in a rosebush—and she'd tracked in more than a few clumps of garden dirt, which Mr. Peartree quickly swept up into his palm. Ivy was obviously trying to walk as elegantly as her sister, with her chin up and her shoulders back, but it only made her look uncomfortable. At least, Toby thought, there was someone in the room who felt even more out of place than he did.

When the Webster family had taken their seats, Mr. Peartree cleared his throat. "Ladies and gentlemen, boys and girls," he said, "and dog"—he looked pointedly at Percival—"I am delighted to introduce the man who is my employer and the host of this weekend's festivities. Please welcome the world's greatest detective, Hugh Abernathy."

Toby clapped so hard his hands hurt. Mr. Abernathy strode through the doorway with a wave for the crowd and—although Toby might have imagined it—a hint of a smile just for him. "Welcome!" he said, sweeping to the front of the room as if it were the only reasonable place for him to stand. "My dear friends and neighbors, I can't tell you how pleased I am that you've joined me this weekend.

But first, I must thank the Webster family for allowing us to overrun their lovely home. I hope you'll agree with me that it is the perfect location for a crime." He bowed to the Websters, who didn't seem particularly flattered by the compliment. "Now, I've promised you a game, and a game you shall have. By the end of our time together, someone in this house will be rich. Someone will be the world's greatest detective. And someone"—Mr. Abernathy paused, looking reluctant—"well, someone might be dead."

"Dead!"

Julia Hartshorn was the one who said it. She stood up from her chair and looked Mr. Abernathy in the eye. "What in the world are you talking about, Hugh?"

"I'd like to know the same," said Mr. Rackham. "I didn't come all the way out here just to get myself murdered."

"I doubt any of us did," Miss Price murmured to Toby.

"Never fear!" Mr. Abernathy said hastily. "The death will be merely temporary. In the next few hours, one member of the Webster household will *pretend* to die."

"Thank goodness," said Julia, sitting down. "You should have said so from the start."

Toby agreed with her. He could still feel his heartbeat thudding in his ears. The last thing he needed was for Uncle Gabriel to return from Gallis and find him dead; he'd have been in more trouble than ever.

"As for the identity of the murderer," Mr. Abernathy

continued, "that will be up to the six detectives to discover. Miss Hartshorn, Miss March, Miss Price, Mr. Rackham, Mr. Elwood—and, of course, Mr. Montrose." He raised an eyebrow at Toby. "You will each have the weekend to interview suspects, examine the evidence, and determine how and why the crime was committed. All I ask is that you do not leave the manor grounds. If you are first to uncover the solution to my mystery before we all depart on Sunday afternoon, you shall win the title of world's greatest detective, along with my eternal good regard."

"And your money," said Julia.

Mr. Abernathy nodded. "Ten thousand dollars, Miss Hartshorn, straight from my pocket to the winner's."

"And if no one wins?" Philip Elwood stretched out his legs. "What happens then?"

"Then I suppose I'll have to suffer the blows of fame and fortune myself for a few years longer. But I sincerely believe there is a winner among you. There's more crime-solving potential in this room than there is in the rest of the country put together." Mr. Abernathy looked at each detective in turn. "Of course," he said, meeting Toby's gaze, "there's also an alarming amount of deception, duplicity, cunning, and fraud. Most of you have secrets, and all of you have faults. If you can't overcome them, you'll almost certainly leave this house empty-handed."

"Faults?" Mr. Rackham rapped his walking stick on

the floor. "Nonsense! Haven't had any of those for fifteen years!"

Toby wished he could say the same. He knew from his trip to the end of Detectives' Row that if anyone could read people's secrets right off their faces, it was Hugh Abernathy. Did Mr. Abernathy already know about Uncle Gabriel's trip abroad, the letter Toby had forged, or the detective-shaped pile of pillows upstairs in the Marigold Room? And what did the others have to hide? As much as Toby didn't want anyone knowing his secrets, he had to admit he was curious about everyone else's.

"About this crime," Miss March said, raising her hand. "Will we be allowed to work together to solve it?"

"You may work with anyone you choose," Mr. Abernathy said. "I'll remind you, though, that the Webster family and their servants will all be murder suspects, and even your fellow detectives might not have your best interests at heart." His smile grew even broader. "To be frank, Anthea, I wouldn't trust a soul."

"Don't worry," said Miss March with a smile of her own. "I never do."

When Mr. Abernathy had finished speaking, two maids rolled a silver dining cart into the parlor and began to set out sandwiches and lemonade on the tables. While they worked, Toby sized up his competition. Philip Elwood was still scribbling away in his notebook; was he collecting clues already? Mr. Rackham looked like he was about to doze off, but maybe that was part of his crime-solving strategy. Toby was especially worried about Miss March and Miss Price, who probably knew so much about everyone in the house that they'd have the case cracked by dinnertime. As for Julia Hartshorn, when Toby turned to study her, he realized that *she* had been studying *him*. Mr. Abernathy had been right: he couldn't trust a soul. Even Percival was starting to look a little shifty.

Toby helped himself to three sandwiches and wrapped two more in a napkin. "For Uncle Gabriel," he said loudly, just in case someone was watching—and since the room was full of detectives, someone probably was. Then, with his mouth still full of watercress and salmon paste, he made a beeline for Hugh Abernathy.

Mr. Abernathy stood by the fireplace, sipping lemonade through a long paper straw and chatting with one of the Websters' footmen. "When you caught the Colebridge Cutthroat," the footman asked, "was it really as thrilling as Mr. Peartree made it sound in his story?"

"It was even more thrilling than that," said Mr. Abernathy. He caught sight of Toby and gave him a wink. "Quite a few prominent members of government had already been attacked, as you'll recall, and Lord Entwhistle believed he'd be the Cutthroat's next victim. That's when he hired me to keep an eye on Entwhistle House. I watched every man coming and going from the house, but it never occurred to either of us that the Cutthroat might be a woman! If I hadn't noticed the knife hidden in the young lady's hair, she might have succeeded in her aim. She came dangerously close to ending Lord Entwhistle's life, and as I wrestled the blade away from her, I thought she might end mine as well. I asked Mr. Peartree to spare his readers the bloodiest details." Mr. Abernathy gave a little bow to the footman, who was staring at him now in full-fledged awe. Then he turned to Toby. "I hope my story hasn't alarmed you, Mr. Montrose."

"No, sir. I've read it at least five times." Toby hoped the tattooed carriage driver was taking good care of the *Sphinx* issue that contained "The Adventure of the Colebridge Cutthroat"—it was one of Toby's favorites. "May I ask you a question, sir?"

"You may ask anything you'd like." Mr. Abernathy took a sip of lemonade. "I only hope I can answer you."

"It's about my case, sir." Toby clutched his packet of sandwiches more tightly. "About my parents. I was just wondering if you've learned anything new."

Mr. Abernathy slurped the rest of his lemonade and handed the glass to Mr. Peartree, who was passing by. "I apologize," he said. "I should have come to find you earlier. Of course you've been wondering. As a matter of fact, I've uncovered some information that I think you'll be excited to hear."

Toby nearly dropped his sandwiches. "Are you sure?"

"Entirely." Mr. Abernathy hesitated. "We shouldn't discuss the matter here, though. I've brought the case file with me, and I'd be happy to share it with you this evening. Can you come to see me tonight before dinner?"

"Of course!" said Toby. He felt a little unsteady, as though he'd just wandered into the pages of the *Sphinx*. Had Mr. Abernathy actually managed to find his parents? No ordinary person would have been capable of it—but Hugh Abernathy wasn't an ordinary person, not by a long shot.

"Excellent. I'll see you then." Mr. Abernathy's eyes flicked to the right, past Toby's shoulder. "I'd suggest leaving your spy behind when you come to see me, though. She's been watching you for the past five minutes."

Toby spun around. Just behind him was a large potted palm, and behind *that*, peeking over the rim of the ceramic pot, was the top of Ivy's head. "You don't look much like a palm frond," he told her. "You're not even green. Next time you should borrow Mr. Peartree's hat."

Ivy got to her feet and gave Toby a steely look. "You wouldn't have seen me if it weren't for *him*," she said, jabbing a finger in Mr. Abernathy's direction. "After all, you're only a junior detective." Then she turned on her heel and ran out of the parlor, leaving Toby staring after her.

"How interesting," Mr. Abernathy said mildly. "It looks to me, Mr. Montrose, like you've got more than one mystery to solve this weekend."

CHAPTER 8

THE INVESTIGATORIUM

Toby was quick, but Ivy was quicker, and she knew the tangled hallways of Coleford Manor much better than he did. In the time it took him to say good-bye to Mr. Abernathy and squirm loose from the crowd of detectives, she'd escaped out the parlor door and up the front stairs, giving Toby nothing but a glimpse of her scuffed patent-leather heel disappearing around a corner.

He thought of leaving her alone, but the thought didn't last more than a second. Ivy was definitely up to something, and if he didn't even try to find out what it was, he might as well cut up his junior detective badge and send himself home. Besides, all the adults were still chatting in that dull, droning way they had, and anything was better than that.

He started up the stairs himself, hoping he could figure out which way Ivy had gone.

Two hallways branched out from the second-floor landing: a left-hand one, with the Marigold Room at the end of it, and a right-hand one, lined with glass-knobbed closed doors. Neither of the hallways contained Ivy. Toby stood on the landing as quietly as he could, holding his breath and listening for the creak of floorboards in the distance, or the patter of footsteps, but he couldn't hear anything like that. If it hadn't been for the hum of conversation floating up from the parlor, he would have thought he had the whole vast manor to himself.

Toby tried to remember what else he'd learned from the correspondence course about tracking suspects. He couldn't exactly follow footprints indoors, but Ivy had tracked all that mud into the parlor; maybe she'd left a trail behind her as she ran away. As soon as Toby knelt down to look more closely at the floorboards, though, he could tell they wouldn't be much help: crumbs of dirt were scattered along both hallways and up the stairs to the third floor, too. Those could have come from anyone's shoes. If there was a way to tell the difference between flower-garden dirt and the regular kind, Toby had no idea what it was.

Then, somewhere above Toby's head, a door slammed so loudly that he almost laughed. He took the stairs to the third floor two at a time and turned left, where the noise had come from. The corridor was dim and shadowy, with only a small window at one end to let the sunlight in, but Toby was almost sure he could hear someone moving behind the farthest-away door—the one right above his own room. He took off his shoes and slid down the hall in his socks, staying close to the wall to keep the floorboards from creaking.

If it hadn't been nearly so dim, or quite so shadowy, Toby might have seen the wire before it caught his ankles. But he didn't, and half a second later he was sprawled on his stomach, trapped under a heavy tablecloth that had dropped on him from the ceiling. It smelled of mothballs and disaster.

A door opened nearby, and Toby poked his head out from underneath the tablecloth to see Ivy's feet coming toward him. It was enough to make him pull his head right back in again. Being caught in a trap would have been bad enough under any circumstances, but being caught in *this* trap was completely humiliating. Toby had even set it himself once, when he'd accidentally trapped Mrs. Satterthwaite. He wondered how Ivy had figured out how to build it—and then, horribly and all at once, he knew.

"You did a good job sneaking silently," Ivy told him, pulling the tablecloth off of him. "For a minute, I thought you weren't following me after all. But you should probably read the lesson about trap detection again. I'm going to put 'needs improvement' in my notes."

Toby sat up too quickly, which made him dizzy. "You're Inspector Webster," he said. He wasn't sure whether to be horrified or amazed. "But you're supposed to be a man!"

"And you," said Ivy, folding the tablecloth crisply, "are supposed to be smarter than that. Get up and come inside before someone overhears us. If Mother finds out what we're up to, she'll scold us both, and at least one of us doesn't deserve it." It was pretty obvious which one she meant.

"I didn't do anything wrong!" said Toby as he scrambled to his feet. "You're the one who set the trap, and spied on me, and pretended to be a detective. I sent you ten whole dollars!"

"I wasn't *pretending* to be anything." Ivy grabbed Toby by the wrists and tugged him into the room at the end of the hall. She was stronger than she looked. "If you don't believe a girl can be a detective," she said, shutting the door behind her, "then you're just as hopeless as that old bore Hugh Abernathy."

"Mr. Abernathy isn't a bore! And of course I know girls can be detectives. But you're not any older than I am, and . . ." Blinking in the sunlight, Toby looked around the room where Ivy had dragged him. He promptly forgot what he'd been going to say. The space was bright and cramped, and every inch of it was crammed with investigators' tools. A microscope stood on a desk; a pair of binoculars waited by the window. On a rack that ran the length of one wall, dozens of disguises hung from pegs: there were hats and wigs, shawls and gowns, even a pair of motoring goggles. Long coils of rope and wire were stacked in a corner behind a life-sized and perfectly complete human skeleton that Toby desperately hoped was just a model. A set of encyclopedias filled one bookshelf, a row of thick notebooks filled a second, and a third was stuffed with volumes about every subject Toby could think of and several more he couldn't, from swordplay to snake venom. The only normal piece of furniture in the room was an old, worn-out velvet couch, but even this was covered in back issues of the *Sphinx Monthly Reader*. Toby spotted at least three he hadn't read before.

He tried to cross the room to get a better look at them, but Ivy held him back. "You don't want to go that way," she said. "More traps. Percival got stuck in that one last week, and it took forever to get him out of it. He's awfully squirmy."

Toby stopped and stared up at the ceiling, where a perilous-looking contraption made out of silver netting looked ready to fall on him. "What kind of place is this?"

For the first time since Toby had met her, Ivy came very

close to smiling. "I call it the Investigatorium," she said. "What do you think?"

"It's amazing," said Toby. He hated to admit it, but it was the truth. "Where did you get all of this?"

"In the city, mostly. Doyle's Detection Goods, Secondhand Sleuthery, those sorts of places. Some of the old gowns are Mother's, and Doctor Piper gave me Egbert as a loan."

"Egbert?" Toby looked around to see if there was another detective lurking in a corner somewhere.

"Egbert's the skeleton," Ivy explained. "I told Doctor Piper I wanted to study anatomy, and she said I could borrow him. It was awful smuggling him up the servants' stairs, though. Percival kept trying to chew on his femurs."

Cautiously, Toby walked along the edge of the room, keeping his eyes peeled for traps. The sunlight glinted off a wicked-looking knife on the bookshelf; not even Uncle Gabriel owned anything quite that dangerous. He took a step back from it. "Do your parents know you have this?"

Toby hadn't meant to make a joke, but Ivy laughed anyway. "Of course not," she said. "They don't even know the Investigatorium exists. Hardly anyone ever comes up to the third floor, and Mother believes children should have their privacy. She thinks I borrowed those gowns to play dress-up." Ivy shook her head. "Mother is a very nice person, but she'd make a horrible detective. Father's just the same, and so is Lillie. One of the maids tried to clean this room once, though. That's why I had to set traps."

"They definitely work." Toby rubbed his ankle where the wire had caught him. He couldn't even imagine what it was like to live in a house so big that whole chunks of it went unexplored for years at a time. And he couldn't understand why Ivy seemed so angry. If Toby had a whole Investigatorium to himself, he'd be in heaven. "I wish you hadn't trapped me by accident," he said.

"Oh, it wasn't an accident." Ivy sat down on the couch, in the middle of the pile of magazines. "I had three good reasons for trapping you. Would you like to hear them?"

Toby nodded. He was a detective, after all, and detectives were curious by nature.

"Good," said Ivy. "Reason one: you were following me. I don't like being followed."

"You follow *me* all the time," Toby pointed out.

Ivy ignored him. "Reason two: I wanted to test your detective skills. You're all right for a beginner, I suppose, but you've still got a lot to learn."

This didn't seem entirely fair to Toby. "You only sent me a lesson on how to build traps, not how to avoid them."

"Oh." Ivy frowned. "Well, here's your lesson: if you see a trap, don't step in it."

Inspector Webster wasn't turning out to be anything like

Toby had expected. "Thanks, I guess," he said. "What's reason three?"

"Reason three," said Ivy, "is that I want to find out what you're doing here. It doesn't make any sense. When I asked Mr. Abernathy if I could enter his silly old contest, he laughed at me and said it wasn't for children. Now I'm stuck here all weekend, watching other detectives solve a murder while I have to be quiet and fetch coffee and pick flowers for everyone Percival crashes into. But Mr. Abernathy let you into the contest, and you're my student! You haven't even gotten to level three of the correspondence course!" She leaned forward to give Toby an extra-powerful stare, making the couch springs squeak under her. "If you can be the world's greatest detective, why can't I?"

"So *that's* why you're so angry all the time!" Toby said. "I wondered." He didn't think Ivy really needed the prize money, but still, he couldn't blame her for being upset. He hated feeling left out.

"I'm not angry all the time," Ivy grumbled. "I'm angry right *now*." She sighed and flopped onto the couch, letting a *Sphinx Monthly Reader* slide onto her face. "Usually, I'm delightful."

"Well, I don't think you have to be angry anymore—unless you'd like to be, of course." Toby made his way over piles of paper and cartons stamped with mysterious

WARNING labels. "I'm only here as my uncle's assistant. I'm sure Mr. Abernathy never would have let me enter the contest by myself."

"Your uncle?" Ivy lifted the magazine from her face. "Gabriel Montrose? But he's gone abroad!"

Toby felt as if another one of Ivy's traps had come crashing down on him. "He hasn't!" he said frantically. "He's downstairs! In the Marigold Room! He's, ah, sitting in a chair! Thinking important thoughts!"

Ivy was sitting up again now, and this time, she was beaming. "At least you're deceiving with confidence," she said. "Good job, Toby. I'm not surprised the others believed you."

"I don't think Mr. Peartree did," Toby admitted. "Percival had to rescue me. But how did you know about Uncle Gabriel?"

"Look around you!" said Ivy. "I'm an investigator! It's my job to know absolutely everything." She looked a little uncomfortable. "Also," she said, "when your uncle left your house this morning with his suitcase, I might have been hiding behind a lamppost."

"You were spying on me again?" Toby had caught Ivy twice in Detectives' Row, which meant she'd been there at least three times—and, knowing Ivy, it had probably been a lot more than that. He wished he'd been paying better attention. "Do you spy on all your students?"

"It's not spying; it's investigating. And of course I don't investigate all my students. They live all over the world!" Ivy stood up and pulled one of the thick notebooks from her bookshelf. Toby's own name was printed on the front of it. "When I got an application from someone who already lived on Detectives' Row, though, I had to find out who that someone was. I'd never heard of any detective named Toby Montrose before. When I saw you picking up the mail, I deduced that Toby Montrose had to be you."

"But you kept coming back," said Toby. "Why?"

Ivy shrugged and flipped through the notebook with Toby's name on it. "I was curious about my student," she said, "and Percival likes you. Besides, you're sort of interesting to watch. You clean your fingernails a lot. Why is that?"

Toby could feel his cheeks growing warm. "Does it say that in your notes?"

He reached for the notebook, but Ivy pulled it away. "I'm sorry," she said. "That's confidential."

"I don't see how taking notes about people's fingernails makes you a good detective," Toby said. Since Ivy was still holding the notebook out of his reach, he pulled a different one from the shelf and started to flip through it, hoping that another of Inspector Webster's students liked to waltz with his cat or sing in the shower.

"Put that down!" said Ivy. She'd given up being delightful and gone back to being angry. "Those notes are private!"

But Toby had already closed the notebook. All of its pages were blank. So were the pages in the next book, and the next after that.

"Ivy," he said carefully, "am I your only student?"

Ivy rolled her shoulders back and clenched her jaw in the way that adults sometimes did when they were starting to find Toby tiresome. "No," she said. "That's ridiculous."

But her voice was a little higher than it had been, and a little faster, too. Toby looked at her hard. "Are you deceiving me with confidence?"

Ivy's jaw clenched tighter. Then, grudgingly, she put her observations of Toby back on the shelf with the rows of empty notebooks. "All right," she said. "I suppose there's no point in lying to a fellow detective. I put that advertisement in the *Sphinx* almost a year ago, but you're the only person who's ever signed up for my course. If you think about it, though, you're not really my *only* student; you're my *first* student!"

She said this as though it were an honor, but it didn't really feel that way to Toby. "Your advertisement said you've taught hundreds of successful sleuths!" he said. "You said results were guaranteed!"

"Oh, Toby, *everybody* says those things in ads. And you've already had results, haven't you? You knew I wasn't being truthful just now. That's a result!"

"In your lessons, you talked about all the cases you've

worked on with your assistant." Toby looked around the Investigatorium. It had impressed him at first with all its dazzling tools and devices, but now he thought it looked more like a child's playroom than an inspector's office. He glared at the skeleton in the corner. "Is Egbert your assistant?"

"Of course he's not," Ivy snapped. Then, in a very small voice, she said, "Percival is my assistant."

This was too much for Toby. All this time, he'd been imagining two bold inspectors chasing down clues, cracking codes, and matching wits with the criminal element of Colebridge—not a girl and her dog spying on him from across the street. He'd been counting on Inspector Webster to make him the world's greatest detective, but Inspector Webster was nothing but a fraud. She'd probably already spent his ten dollars on one of her awful disguises. "No real detective has a dog as an assistant!" he shouted. "Have you ever even solved an actual mystery?"

"Well," said Ivy, "not exactly—"

"Here. You can have this. I don't want it anymore." Toby pulled off his junior detective badge and shoved it into Ivy's hand. "And I want my ten dollars back." All he *really* wanted, truthfully, was to get as far away from Ivy as possible before he started to cry. He didn't have long; his nose was already getting sniffly. He turned his back on Ivy, who was staring down at the badge as though she'd lost her best friend, and ran across the Investigatorium, heading toward the door.

"Don't go that way!" Ivy shouted, but it was already too late. With a mechanical whirr, the silver trap had released itself from its moorings and swung down from the ceiling, heading straight for Toby. He froze—which was, of course, exactly the wrong thing to do.

Then Ivy barreled toward him. She moved so quickly that her shiny shoes screeched on the floorboards and the grass stains on her tights blurred together into one enormous smudge. With both arms outstretched, she tackled Toby. They crashed to the ground, and the trap crashed next to them, barely half a foot away.

Toby could hardly breathe. This was partly because he'd had the wind knocked out of him when he fell, and partly because Ivy's elbow was digging into his chest. "I'm sorry," she said, moving it. "About the traps and the lies and the spying and everything. What I was going to say before is that I might not have solved a real mystery yet, but I've read a lot and practiced even more, and I know I'm a good detective. I *promise* I am. If you stop being my student, I'll feel just awful about it. I won't have anything to do except torture Lillie all day, and I'm sure Percival will be completely miserable. Won't you please forgive me?"

Toby sat up. "The trouble's going to find me again," he said, "and it's all your fault. I'm not a real detective after all, not even a junior one. I'm not going to win the competition, I'm not going to get ten thousand dollars, Uncle Gabriel is going to lose his job, he'll send me to the orphanage, and I'll have to eat gruel for the rest of my life." He wasn't entirely sure what gruel was, but he knew it was the kind of food they served in orphanages, and it didn't sound good.

Now Ivy was the one with the sniffling nose. "I don't entirely understand what you're talking about," she said, "but I do think you're a real detective—or you *can* be one, if you want to be." She wiped her nose with a grubby hand-kerchief. "What if I helped you with the competition? We could work together. You could use the Investigatorium, too—the magnifying glasses and Egbert and everything!"

Toby shook his head. "Forget it," he said. "I'm not interested."

He couldn't look at Ivy as he left the Investigatorium. He didn't even glance back over his shoulder as he ran down-stairs to the Marigold Room, slammed the door behind him, and lay down on the soft orange carpet. The plump, pillowy face of the fake Uncle Gabriel gazed down at him. The real Uncle Gabriel would have raised his voice to a cheerful boom and asked what in the world was so terrible that Toby was forced to squelch across the floor like a snail, but the real Uncle Gabriel was miles away, and nothing had gone right since Toby had left Detectives' Row. Most of the things he owned were being sold from the back of a carriage in Slaughter's Lane. He was a long way from home, he had no idea how he was going to solve Mr. Abernathy's mystery by himself, and he wished he hadn't given his junior detective badge back to Ivy. Maybe she wasn't exactly who she'd pretended to be, but Toby had felt a lot better with that badge on his shirt. Now all he had left was fifty-three cents—and the trouble, of course. It must have let itself into the manor, because Toby was sure no one had invited it. He could see it skulking under his bed, just beyond the orange dust ruffle.

There was a knocking noise outside his room; just a few quick raps. As Toby scrambled to his feet, someone slid two small, flat items underneath the door. The first was his junior detective badge, a little crumpled but otherwise as good as ever. And the second was a shabby but very real ten-dollar note.

When Toby opened the door, he found Ivy and Percival standing on the other side of it, waiting. They looked very professional.

"Please?" said Ivy.

Toby sighed. "Okay."

CHAPTER 9

DETECTIVES IN AND OUT

With his badge pinned back on his shirt and a borrowed notebook under his arm, Toby ran down the hall after Ivy. He hadn't known her very long, but he was learning quickly that Ivy liked to be in charge, and she didn't like to be kept waiting. "Why are we hurrying?" he called to her. "The competition hasn't started yet. We've got nothing to do!"

Ivy turned to face him, but she didn't stop walking. "If we're going to solve Mr. Abernathy's case," she said, "we've got to be at least two steps ahead of all the other detectives, and we might as well start now. Do you know how to make observations?"

Toby nodded. "I'm pretty good at it, actually."

"I thought you might be," Ivy said. "Mother says I don't notice much because I'm usually too busy talking, but you obviously don't have that problem."

"We'll make a good team, then," said Toby. He'd finally caught up with Ivy, but he wasn't sure she'd heard him.

"Anyway," she said, "the things we observe *before* the murder takes place might help us figure out what's happened *afterward*. We need to know who's arguing, who's acting suspicious, who's wandering through the hedge maze with a particularly sharp knife. If we're lucky, we could catch the murderer in the act!"

Toby didn't think Mr. Abernathy's mystery was going to be quite that easy to solve. "If the crime hasn't happened yet," he said, "how do we know who our suspects are?"

"Everyone in the household is a suspect," Ivy said grimly. "That's what Mr. Abernathy said. Mother, Father, the servants—even silly old Lillie, though I don't think she'd ever do something as interesting as murdering someone."

Toby was surprised. "Don't you like your sister?"

"I love her," said Ivy, "but she's awfully *good*."

"Is that a bad thing?"

"The worst," said Ivy. "She never tears her stockings, she writes little notes thanking Mother and Father for her birthday gifts, she takes music lessons once a week in the city, and I'm beginning to suspect that she actually enjoys them. Do you know what it's like to live with someone like that?" Ivy sighed. "No one can be perfect all the time, though. She's been well behaved for eighteen years straight, so one of these days, she's bound to do something completely awful." The thought of it seemed to cheer her up as they wound down a steep back staircase into the servants' quarters. "Now, we're not really allowed to be back here, so we'll have to be careful. Do you remember how to observe suspects without getting caught?"

Toby thought back to his earliest correspondence course lessons. "Don't get too close," he recited. "Don't draw attention to yourself. If anyone notices you, act like you're supposed to be there."

Ivy nodded. "And stay out of Cook's way, or she'll boil your bones for soup stock."

The kitchen was a churning, rumbling machine at the back of the house, at least ten degrees warmer and ten times louder than the Websters' living quarters. It reminded Toby of his uncle Francis's hotel, with people coming and going, shouting for things and hurrying to retrieve them. The preparations for dinner had started hours ago, from the smell of it. "Mrs. Webster wants that lamb roasted, not stewed!" Cook called across the room. "And mind you don't put any cream in the soup tonight. That poor Mr. Peartree can't tolerate it."

Toby looked sideways at Ivy, who was already buried in her own notebook. There was a lot to observe, but he

115

didn't think most of it had anything to do with a murder. Still, he wrote down as much as he could. *Cook has a lot of sharp knives*, he scribbled. *A kitchen maid is pouring a bottle of something into the soup. Wine? Poison?* Two footmen passed by, gossiping about a nearby farmer who swore he'd spotted an escaped convict from Chokevine in the pole beans, and Toby wrote this down, too.

In most ways, however, the kitchen was perfectly ordinary, and Toby had almost run out of suspicious things to notice by the time Norton the footman hobbled past. His ankle was wrapped in a bandage, and his expression was stormy. When he spotted Percival, who had given up making observations and gone to beg for a soup bone, it became even stormier. Then he saw Toby and Ivy. *Norton looks angry*, Toby wrote frantically as the three of them ran out of the servants' quarters and through a narrow hallway. *He's not very fast with his ankle wrapped up, but he's excellent at shouting.*

Toby was so busy making observations, in fact, that by the time he noticed Philip Elwood stepping out into the hallway in front of him, it was too late to stop running. His notebook collided with Philip's stomach, and his pen went flying. "I'm sorry, sir!" he said, trying to ignore the sound of Ivy sighing behind him. "I didn't see you there. Are you all right?"

"Oh, I've been in worse collisions than that." Philip

said it kindly enough, but his eyes darted from one end of the hall to the other, as though he'd rather look at anything other than Toby. "Where are you off to in such a hurry?"

"Getting away from Norton," Toby said.

Ivy picked up Toby's pen from the floor and handed it to him. "What my colleague means," she said, "is that we're conducting a covert investigation, and we're not at liberty to divulge our methodology."

Toby was impressed. He didn't know half the words Ivy had just said, but they seemed to mean something to Philip. "That's right," he said. "I meant to say that, about divulging the methodology." If he and Ivy sounded official enough, maybe it would make up for the fact that their investigative partner was trying to eat Philip's left shoelace.

Philip nodded seriously. "I understand. And don't worry; I won't be poking my nose into your investigation. I prefer to work alone." He bent down and removed his soggy shoelace from Percival's mouth. "Has anyone been murdered back there, by chance?"

"In the kitchen?" Toby was about to tell Philip that everyone except the lamb was alive and well, but Ivy looked sharply at him, and he swallowed his words. This *was* a competition, after all, and a famous international investigator like Philip Elwood didn't need any help from Toby. "I guess you'll have to find out for yourself," he said instead. "Like you did with those thieves in Gyptos!"

117

Philip smiled at this, as though he was pleased to be reminded of what a good detective he was. "Fair enough," he said, putting his hand on the brim of his hat. "Best of luck to you both."

Philip passed through the swinging door into the servants' quarters, and Ivy frowned after him. "That was odd," she said. "Did you notice anything unusual about Mr. Elwood, Detective?"

Toby hadn't, to be honest, but he wasn't going to admit that to Ivy after telling her how observant he was. He closed his eyes and tried to picture how Philip had looked. "He was wearing a hat inside," he said at last, doubtfully. "My aunt Janet used to say that wasn't polite, but maybe it's how people do things abroad?"

"It's not, actually," said Ivy. "Mother is from Gyptos, and she and Father have traveled all around the world, but they always take their hats off as soon as they step inside. Good work, Toby; I hadn't thought of that."

Toby couldn't help feeling proud as he wrote this latest observation in his notebook: *Philip Elwood wears a hat indoors. I wonder what's under it.* "You must have noticed something else, then," he said to Ivy. "What was it?"

Ivy walked over to a plain-looking door in the wall and turned the knob. "The reason you crashed into Mr. Elwood," she said, "is that when he stepped right in front of you, he was coming out of this room."

Toby peered into the darkness. "A broom cupboard?" he asked. "What would Mr. Elwood be doing in there?"

"That," said Ivy, "is exactly what I'd like to know."

In the stories Mr. Peartree wrote, Hugh Abernathy was always breaking into creepy old buildings, sneaking into seedy crime dens, and stumbling across murder scenes. If they'd been in a Hugh Abernathy story, Toby thought, they would have stepped into the broom cupboard to find a murderer looming over them. But the only things that actually loomed in the cupboard were tall, rickety ladders and thin, lifeless mops. A wall of shelves held sheets and towels and other mysterious fabrics, all neatly folded and stacked, and bottles full of oils and polishes. When Toby brushed against one of the bottles, it left his hand covered in something as dark and wet as blood. "Ugh," he said, trying to wipe away whatever it was on a towel.

"I wish Mr. Elwood had been more careless." Ivy was on her hands and knees next to Percival, peering under the shelves. "He didn't leave any clues behind—not even anything boring like a dusty footprint. What do you think he came in here for?"

"He might have been looking for a washroom," Toby suggested. "Or maybe he needed a mop."

"Maybe," said Ivy. "But I think we should keep an eye on him. I don't trust that man." She looked at Toby upside down. "It's my detective's instinct."

Toby followed Ivy and her instincts all over the house, winding through skinny back corridors and wandering through huge open rooms decorated with artifacts the Websters had collected on their travels. These fascinated Toby. He was used to houses full of practical things, like shovels and jam jars and potbellied stoves; even the investigative oddities in his bedroom at Uncle Gabriel's all served a purpose. But he couldn't imagine what purpose the round, earth-colored urn in the corner of the conservatory might serve, except for being interesting. A carved hunter with a bow and arrow chased a carved deer around and around the crackled surface.

"The urn is from Mother's hometown," Ivy said proudly. "It was one of her first discoveries. It's at least two thousand years old."

"That's amazing," said Toby. He felt sorry for the hunter. Two thousand years was a long time to spend chasing anything. "What's inside this one?" he asked, pointing at a wooden box painted with faded, colorful symbols. "Can I open it?"

Ivy made a face. "I wouldn't," she said, "unless you like mummified cats."

Toby didn't. He moved away quickly. "Do your parents have a lot of—um—*dead* things?"

"Only the usual," said Ivy. "Butterflies and beetles,

mostly. Their really gruesome discoveries are all in the Colebridge City Museum. Father wants to take the cat there, too, but Mother won't let him. That's one of the things they argue about—along with money, of course."

Toby was surprised to hear this. "But they have so much of it!"

"That just means there's more to argue about. You know how parents can be." Ivy hesitated. "Or maybe you don't. I overheard you speaking with Mr. Abernathy earlier." Her voice had slipped into that soft, worried tone people had always used around Toby in the days after the funeral. He'd forgotten how badly it made his stomach hurt. "Are your parents still alive?"

Toby had answered this particular question hundreds of times before, but this was the first time he hadn't known quite what to say. "I didn't think they were," he said, "but Mr. Abernathy has been looking into their accident, and he says he's got news for me."

Ivy's eyes went wide. "Good news?"

"I think so. I mean, I hope so. I'm supposed to meet Mr. Abernathy this evening to find out."

"This *evening*?" Ivy groaned. "For heaven's sake, Toby, how can you possibly stand to wait? Your parents might be somewhere out there looking for you!"

Toby sat down on a velvet chair. "I guess they could be," he said. "I haven't been letting myself think about it.

What if they're not alive after all?"

"What if they are?" said Ivy. "If Mr. Abernathy's found them, I swear I'll apologize for every mean thought I've ever had about him." She gave Toby a guilty smile. "It may take an awful lot of breath, though."

Behind them, the conservatory door swung open. "I can't put up with it much longer, Amina," Ivy's father was saying in a low voice. "We're being taken advantage of. We can't afford to go on like this."

"What else can we do?" Mrs. Webster didn't bother to keep her voice low. "We haven't got a choice. He made that perfectly clear."

"I'll tell you what I'd *like* to do to the fellow," Mr. Webster said. "First of all, I'd—"

Mrs. Webster put a hand on her husband's shoulder. "Look, Robert," she said, "it's the children."

"Oh!" Mr. Webster coughed. "Hello there, Ivy. Hello, um . . ."

"Toby," said Toby helpfully.

Mrs. Webster smiled at them. "You two shouldn't be indoors when the weather is so pleasant," she said. "Why don't you take Percival for a walk in the yard?"

Toby and Ivy exchanged a look. This was the sort of thing adults said when they wanted you to go away. Toby would have liked to stay and hear what the Websters were arguing about, but it was clear they weren't going to say another word until he and Ivy were safely outside. *Ivy's parents are angry at someone*, he wrote in his notebook as they trudged out of the room. Then he drew a long row of question marks on the page and tucked the book away in his pocket. Even the best detectives had to know when to admit defeat.

On the front lawn of Coleford Manor, the visiting detectives had fallen into a game of badminton. Hugh Abernathy and Julia Hartshorn faced off against Miss March and Mr. Rackham, while Miss Price watched from under a shady oak tree, clapping politely each time a detective scored a point. "Has anyone died yet, dears?" she asked Toby and Ivy as they sat down next to her. "I must admit I'm wild to find out who the victim will be! I've heard the Websters' cook trod the boards on the Colebridge stage back in her day; perhaps she's been enticed to play the role of the corpse."

After what Toby had seen of the cook, he thought she'd make a better murderer than victim. "I don't think the competition's started yet," he told Miss Price.

"Not that we'd know if it had," said Ivy. "Mother kicked us out of the house." She looked as though she might like to murder someone herself.

"Well, you're welcome to wait here with me." Miss Price leaned back in her lawn chair and let out a sigh of contentment. "I do hope the crime scene will be good and bloody."

"Heads up, Flossie!" called Miss March from the badminton court. A gust of wind had caught the birdie she'd hit over the net, and it flew toward Miss Price and Toby with surprising speed.

"I've got it!" said Julia Hartshorn, who was closest. She stepped back to return the lob, but just as she reached out with her racquet, Mr. Abernathy dove in front of her and thwacked the birdie away. It sailed back over the net and landed meekly at Mr. Rackham's feet. Toby and Miss Price burst into applause.

"Another point for us!" Mr. Abernathy called. "Give that racquet a swing next time, Rackham; you just might hit something."

Julia was looking thunderously at Mr. Abernathy. "I told you I'd get that shot, Hugh," she said. "You might let me score a point for once."

"But we're winning, my dear! We make an excellent team, don't you think?" In the stories Toby had read, Hugh Abernathy was always smiling charmingly at luckless young ladies, grieving mothers, and injured kittens; he delivered this same smile to Julia now.

But Julia was nothing like an injured kitten. Toby thought for a moment that she would punch Mr. Abernathy in the nose, just as Uncle Gabriel had done years ago. Instead of making a fist, though, she drew in her breath, tightened her grip on her badminton racquet, and turned back to the net without bothering to answer Mr. Abernathy's question.

I don't think Julia Hartshorn likes Mr. Abernathy, Toby wrote in his detective's notebook, turning away from Miss Price in case she tried to sneak a glimpse over his shoulder. *His charming smile doesn't work on her. Find out why.*

It was warm for early May, and even in the shade, Toby could feel the back of his neck prickling with sunburn as the game continued. This made it much more difficult to focus on the work of detection. Even Ivy had stopped making observations and started to play fetch with Percival instead. Toby was considering joining them when Miss Price nudged his arm.

"Here comes dear Mr. Peartree," she said, looking back toward the house. "If we're lucky, he might have some gruesome news to report."

Toby squinted across the lawn in the direction Miss Price was pointing. From a distance, it wasn't easy to see Mr. Peartree in his green finery against the backdrop of boxwood hedges. He was holding his watch—the new one Mr. Abernathy hadn't broken yet—and he flipped it open as he hurried toward the badminton court. When he'd passed the oak tree where Toby was sitting, he slowed his pace, walked up behind Mr. Abernathy, reached out a hand, and tapped the detective on the shoulder.

Mr. Abernathy must have jumped a foot. Toby hadn't imagined that the world's greatest detective would be so easy to startle, but apparently even Hugh Abernathy himself could be taken by surprise. "Peartree!" he said, composing himself in a hurry. "You're very soft-footed this afternoon. What is it?"

"It's almost three o'clock, sir," said Mr. Peartree. Even in the heat, he hadn't taken off his coat or loosened his necktie. "If we don't start preparing for the evening's events, we'll fall off schedule."

"So we will. Thank you, Peartree." Mr. Abernathy pulled a green handkerchief out of Mr. Peartree's coat pocket and wiped the sweat from his forehead. "I'm sorry, everyone, but I've got other tasks to take care of this afternoon. When the competition calls me, I must answer. Step in for me, Flossie?"

"Gladly," said Miss Price. She got up from her lawn chair. "I used to be badminton captain at school," she whispered to Toby. "Rackham's looking smug at the moment, but I've got a backhand that will make his head spin."

Mr. Abernathy handed Miss Price his racquet and followed Mr. Peartree back toward the house. As they passed Toby, Mr. Abernathy paused. "This evening, Mr. Montrose, before dinner. I'm in the Orchid Room. You won't forget our meeting?"

"No, sir!" said Toby. "I'll be there."

Mr. Abernathy tucked the green handkerchief into his own pocket and smiled. "I'm extremely pleased to hear it."

The evening couldn't come fast enough for Toby. At six o'clock, an echoing boom rang out through the manor, and Ivy explained that this was the dressing gong. "That means dinner's in an hour," she said, "and we have to get dressed."

"But I *am* dressed!" said Toby.

"Dressed for *dinner*," Ivy said, as though she expected this to help. "I have to let Mother try to throw some clean clothes over my head, but I'll see you later in the dining room. And you've got to promise you'll tell me what Mr. Abernathy's found out about your parents. I want to hear everything."

Toby promised. Back in the Marigold Room, he scrubbed at the brown stain he'd gotten on his hand from whatever he'd brushed against in the broom cupboard. It didn't come off easily, even with soap. At least it hadn't gotten all over his clothes. Since the outfit he was wearing was the only one he had left, he couldn't exactly change for dinner. Instead, he smoothed his hair, took a few exploratory sniffs to make sure he didn't smell too awful, and went out to find Mr. Abernathy.

The Orchid Room was at the other end of the second-floor hallway, closest to the main staircase. Toby recognized the elegant petals carved into its door; Grandfather Montrose had grown orchids, and he'd occasionally let Toby look at them, though no one in the house had been allowed to touch them. They had been anxious, delicate flowers. Feeling a little anxious himself, Toby raised his hand to the door and knocked.

No one answered.

"Hello?" Toby called. "Mr. Abernathy? Are you there?"

The door across the hall opened, and Mr. Peartree poked his head out. "I couldn't help overhearing you, Mr. Montrose," he said. "Can I be of any assistance?"

"I'm supposed to meet Mr. Abernathy before dinner," Toby explained. "He told me to come to the Orchid Room, but I'm not sure he's inside."

"That's peculiar," said Mr. Peartree. He stepped out of his room. It had a fern carved into its door, and from what Toby could see of it, the room was just as green as Mr. Peartree was. In one corner, a record spun on a gramophone, filling the hallway with the scratchy sound of a lady warbling a song in a language Toby didn't recognize.

"I spoke to Mr. Abernathy about an hour ago," Mr. Peartree said over the warbling, "and I don't believe he's left his room since." He walked across the hall and turned the Orchid Room's doorknob. "Sir? Toby Montrose is here to see you."

The door swung open.

At first, all Toby could see was that everything was purple. Purple curtains cloaked the windows, letting in only a sliver of late afternoon light. On the woven purple carpet, plump folders stuffed with papers were stacked untidily; the purple bedsheets on the slim four-poster bed were rumpled. A half-empty bottle with a paper label rested on a purple tray. The tray lay on a table, the table stood next to an armchair, and in the armchair sat Hugh Abernathy, the world's greatest detective.

He was definitely dead.

CHAPTER 10

DEAD!

It wasn't a performance; Toby knew that right away. He would have known even if Mr. Abernathy's face weren't as purple as an orchid blossom, even if Mr. Peartree hadn't choked back a cry and rushed to the detective's side. The trouble that had followed Toby for years had slithered out from all its hidden corners, and now it writhed in the heavy folds of the curtains, in the shadows under the bed, and in the gasping, frozen expression on Mr. Abernathy's face. He had never looked that way when he was alive.

"Oh no," Toby whispered. "Oh no, oh no."

"He's not breathing." Mr. Peartree stepped away from the body. "This wasn't supposed to happen! This wasn't part of the plan!" He pulled out his notepad and started flipping through the pages, as though somewhere in his papers were instructions about how to proceed if your employer suddenly turned up dead.

"What do we *do*?" Toby cried. This was nothing like the famous murder sites he'd walked past in the city, where peddlers sold commemorative ribbons to tourists and all the actual bodies had been long since carted away. Mr. Peartree had been to crime scenes before, though; Mr. Peartree was an expert.

"*Do?*" Mr. Peartree threw his pages of notes to the floor. "I have no idea what to do! I'm not a detective! I just write the stories. It's not the same thing at all."

"Then I'll go get help." Toby wasn't sure which was more terrifying: the corpse in the armchair or the sight of Mr. Peartree, panicked and disheveled, rubbing his forehead with his green-gloved hands. All Toby knew was that he had to get out of the Orchid Room, and fast. He backed out of the room, almost tripping over the untidy stacks of papers, and slammed the door shut behind him. Maybe, he thought, that would make the whole purple nightmare disappear for good.

Then he ran.

There were plenty of people in Coleford Manor, but Toby couldn't imagine how any of them could help him. The other detectives wouldn't be able to bring Mr. Abernathy back to life; neither would the Websters or their servants.

Even Uncle Gabriel wouldn't have been able to fix this mess. Toby skidded across the second-floor landing and into the opposite hallway; these were the Websters' rooms. "Help!" he shouted, knocking on each door as he passed it. "Come quick! Something awful has happened!"

One of the glass-knobbed doors flew open, and Ivy ran out. She was a mess. Only the left side of her hair had been brushed and braided, her shoes were missing, and she was hopping up and down on one foot. Percival stood behind her, looking significantly more dignified.

"I stubbed my toe on the wardrobe when you started shouting," she said, "so this had better be worth it. What's the matter?" She stopped hopping and balanced on one leg, looking sort of like a flamingo in a party dress. "Has the murder happened?"

"Yes," said Toby, "only it's not a fake murder; it's a real one. It's Mr. Abernathy. He's very, very dead."

Ivy's leg wobbled beneath her. "I don't believe it. It's just not possible. Mr. Abernathy can't die! He's famous!"

"Oh, he can die," said Toby. "I promise he can. He's *purple*."

Slowly, Ivy put her foot down. "You're not pretending, are you?"

"I went to see Mr. Abernathy in the Orchid Room before dinner," Toby said, "and when no one answered the door, Mr. Peartree let me in. We went inside, and—well—we

132

found him. His body, I mean." Toby felt sick at the thought of it. "That's when Mr. Peartree sent me to get help."

Ivy looked a little shaken, but she didn't fly into a panic. Toby was impressed; his heart was still racing as fast as the engine in Grandfather Montrose's motorcar. "All right," Ivy said, pulling on her shoes. "Percival and I will get Mother and Father, and you'd better alert the other detectives. We'll all meet back at the scene of the crime." She glanced up at Toby. "You don't look so good, Detective Montrose. Are you the fainting type?"

Toby hoped he wasn't. "Of course not!" he said. He was willing to bet that if Ivy had been the one who'd just found a dead body, she wouldn't have looked so good, either. "I'm not going to faint. I'll get the others and meet you in the Orchid Room."

"Good," said Ivy. "And hurry."

Running as quickly as he could, Toby gathered Mr. Rackham from the Rose Room, Julia Hartshorn from the Sunflower Room, Miss March and Miss Price from the Daisy Room, and Philip Elwood from the Delphinium Room. The detectives scurried down the hall after him, shedding half-arranged hairpins and unfastened cuff links as they went. "What an inconvenient time for a murder," Miss Price said to no one in particular as Toby fumbled with the Orchid Room's doorknob. "I just stepped out of the bath!"

Toby pushed the door open, and the whole crowd stumbled inside. "I've brought the other detectives," he told Mr. Peartree, who was sitting on the purple bedsheets and paging desperately through his notes. "I'm sure it'll only be a few minutes until they figure out what's happened."

But the other detectives had gone silent. They all stood over the body.

"My goodness!" said Miss Price at last. "He's really quite dead, isn't he?"

"Perhaps it's one of his performances," Philip Elwood said uncertainly. "Mr. Abernathy has always had a flair for drama."

Miss March shook her head. "I've seen plenty of dead bodies in my day, and I can tell you this isn't a performance. Step back, Flossie; you're dripping on the corpse."

"I don't like it," Mr. Rackham said. "Detectives aren't supposed to be murdered. It makes the rest of us look careless."

Julia Hartshorn had knelt down to examine Mr. Abernathy's body. "He's been dead for an hour, maybe more. I'll have to perform some tests, but I'm almost sure he's been poisoned." She turned to Toby. "And you were the one who found him?"

"Mr. Peartree and I did." Toby felt all the detectives' sharp, steady gazes land on him. In the Hugh Abernathy stories, he realized, the people who found dead bodies were almost always highly suspicious. "I didn't kill him, though!" Toby said quickly. "I wouldn't even know how!"

There was a storm of footsteps in the hall, and all four Websters appeared in the doorway. Ivy, in the front, was flushed and breathless. "See?" she said. "I wasn't telling tales. He's really dead!"

"My heavens," Mrs. Webster said softly. "So he is." She put an arm around Lillie, who was already blinking back tears.

"What's the meaning of this, Peartree?" Mr. Webster pushed his way through the crowd of detectives. "I never agreed to a real murder in this house!"

"I doubt Mr. Abernathy agreed, either," Julia murmured, "but look what's happened to him."

Mr. Peartree finally raised his head from his notepad. "I don't know what went wrong," he said. His voice was hoarse and low, and the whites of his eyes had turned pink. "Mr. Abernathy had the contest all planned out. One of the serving maids was assigned to play the role of victim, and the false murder was supposed to happen tonight at dinner. She was scheduled to drop dead during the soup course!" He blew his nose into a jade-colored handkerchief. "But I suppose there's no point in continuing the contest now."

"It'll have to be canceled at once," Mr. Webster agreed.

"Has anyone sent for a doctor? Must we call the police?"

Everyone gasped. Mr. Webster might as well have suggested that the house should be attacked by ravening wolves.

"Not the police!" Julia said firmly. "They'll only muck things up as usual. But I suppose a doctor would be all right."

Mrs. Webster rushed downstairs to contact Doctor Piper, though Toby couldn't see what good it would do. He'd thought that the other detectives would take charge of the investigation, plucking up clues and setting off to uncover the truth of the matter, but most of them were only wringing their hands, talking in low, worried whispers, or pacing the length of the Orchid Room. This never happened in the sorts of stories Toby loved—but those stories were mostly about Hugh Abernathy, of course, and Hugh Abernathy was in no shape to take charge of things anymore.

The gong downstairs rang again, making Toby's teeth vibrate. "It's a sign!" said Miss Price. "A portent of doom!"

"Actually," said Philip Elwood, "I think it's the dinner bell."

Either way, it seemed to rouse Mr. Peartree. He stood up, cleared his throat, and slipped into his usual calm, orderly manner as though it were a dinner jacket he'd misplaced. "Mr. Abernathy may not be here to host you all," he announced, "but I hope you'll let me attempt to perform his duties. Since there's nothing more we can do for him at the moment, may I suggest that we head downstairs for a hot meal? We'll all feel better with food in our gullets, and it will give us a chance to discuss what should be done next."

As the detectives left the Orchid Room, Toby hung back. "Are you all right?" Ivy asked. "You might as well come down to dinner. There's nothing more we can do for Mr. Abernathy now."

"It's not that," said Toby. "It's his case files." Toby couldn't bring himself to look at the body in the purple armchair, but he couldn't stop staring at the papers scattered across the rug. "Mr. Abernathy never got a chance to tell me what he'd learned about my parents, but if I can find their file—"

He never got a chance to finish his sentence. "Come along, children," said Mr. Webster, rattling a large ring of keys. "I'm afraid this room is a crime scene now. We've got to leave it just as we found it until the detectives have examined every inch of the place."

Ivy rolled her eyes. "We *are* detectives, Father."

"And we've got important work to do," Toby added.

But Mr. Webster wouldn't listen. Even as Toby and Ivy protested, he ushered them out of the Orchid Room and twisted one of his keys in the lock. Toby's heart twisted, too. "I've got to look at those files!" he whispered to Ivy. "If I don't find out what Mr. Abernathy learned, I'll never know what happened to my parents. What if they're still alive? What if they're in trouble, and they can't get home, and they need my help?" Finding Hugh Abernathy's body had been awful enough, but this was a disaster.

"Stay calm, Detective." Ivy spoke with such authority that Toby's heart began to untwist despite itself. "We'll figure out what to do. Have we ever lost a case?"

"We've never *won* a case," said Toby, but Ivy only sighed at him and pulled him down the stairs to dinner.

No one had much of an appetite. The soup was cold and green, with slimy bits floating in it. It reminded Toby of slugs and sludge and rainstorms, and he wondered if it was the thing that had killed Mr. Abernathy. Would it be more impolite to push the soup away or to taste it and die right there at the dinner table? He wanted to ask Ivy about this, but she was busy slipping chunks of brown bread to Percival under the tablecloth.

As Toby nudged his soup bowl farther away from him, Mrs. Webster swept into the dining room. "I've sent a message to Doctor Piper," she announced. "She'll be here as quickly as she can. I've also spoken to Cook, and she'll inform the rest of the servants of Mr. Abernathy's— situation. They're not to leave the house tonight."

"A wise idea, madam." Mr. Rackham, who had been brave enough to taste the soup, dabbed at his mouth with a napkin. "In fact, I think it would be prudent for all of us to stay put. If the murderer is among us, we can't allow him to escape."

"I agree," said Miss March. "We must all keep an eye on each other."

"Yes, we must." Philip Elwood looked from one end of the long table to the other, counting heads. "By the way, Toby, where in the world is your uncle?"

Five years ago, when Toby was only six and playing in the fields behind his house, a wasp had landed on his arm. He'd known right away that it was going to hurt him, but he hadn't been able to do anything to stop it; he'd only stood there, frozen, waiting for the sting. Now Philip's question hovered over Toby, buzzing in his ears, and he knew there was nothing he could do to stop what was about to happen.

Still, he tried his best. "Uncle Gabriel's upstairs," he said, just the way he'd rehearsed, "in the Marigold Room. He's really upset about what's happened to Mr. Abernathy, and he doesn't want any dinner. He probably won't come out of his room until it's time to leave."

"We can't allow that!" Mr. Rackham threw down his napkin. "We're all in this mess together now. What can Gabriel be thinking?"

"I imagine," said Miss Price, "that he's thinking about how relieved he is to be off the overnight ferry and on dry land in Gallis. Gabriel never has enjoyed ocean voyages. He gets frightfully seasick."

Toby, who had been reaching for his water glass, knocked it over instead.

"Gallis?" said Philip.

"Uh-oh," said Ivy.

As Toby scrambled to sop up the puddle of water on the tablecloth, Miss Price gave him an apologetic smile. "I'm sorry to ruin your story, dear, but considering the circumstances, I think it's best that everyone know the truth. Gabriel Montrose went abroad yesterday to follow a lead on a case. He's never set foot in Coleford Manor, as far as I know. And he certainly isn't here now."

For the second time that evening, everyone looked at Toby. He wasn't used to being the center of attention, and so far, it wasn't going well. The damp part of the tablecloth had started to drip onto his knees.

"So Gabriel doesn't have any new investigative methods after all!" Julia looked triumphant. "I wondered why I hadn't heard of them."

"I'm afraid I don't understand," Mrs. Webster said. "If your uncle is out of the country, Toby, what are you doing here with us?"

Toby sighed. He was tired of deceiving with confidence. "I wanted to be the world's greatest detective," he said. "I asked Uncle Gabriel to enter the contest, but he wouldn't, and I thought that if I came instead . . ." He looked quickly at Mr. Peartree, and then back at his knees. "I'm sorry I lied, sir, but we needed the money. You know what business is like back on the Row."

Ivy was leaning forward in her chair and staring at Miss Price the way another detective might stare at her hero—or her nemesis. "How did you know Toby was here alone?" she asked. "He's very convincing."

"He certainly is!" Miss Price said a little too kindly. Toby wondered if she meant it. "But we've known about Gabriel's trip to Gallis for ages. He told us about his plans when he came to our house for tea a few weeks ago, and Anthea and I poked and pried at him until we'd found out all the details. We like knowing what our neighbors are up to."

"Yes," said Miss March, "and we're good at it."

"You knew about Uncle Gabriel all this time?" Toby slumped down in his chair. For weeks, he thought he'd been getting away with something really clever, but at least two of the people he'd been trying to fool had known the truth all along. Had the others known, too? He hoped Ivy wasn't too upset: after all, this was a serious blow to the reputation of Inspector Webster's Detection Correspondence Course. "Why didn't you *tell* me?"

"We considered it," said Miss March, "but there didn't seem to be any harm in letting you enjoy yourself. Besides, we're fond of Gabriel. We decided that as long as you were here at the manor, we could watch over you for him, and we couldn't do anything of the sort if you were sent home."

"But he's got to go home at once!" Mrs. Webster rose from the table. "Toby's poor uncle doesn't have any idea where he is—or that he's at the scene of a murder! In fact, I'm thinking of sending my own daughters away to stay with their grandparents until Mr. Abernathy's case has been resolved."

"No!" said Toby and Ivy at once. Ivy rose out of her chair just like her mother, and Toby would have too if Percival hadn't been sitting quite so heavily on his feet.

Even Lillie spoke up, though she did it quietly. "I don't think that's a good idea, Mother," she said. "Didn't you hear Mr. Rackham say we must all stay put? I'm sure he wasn't only referring to the detectives in the house."

"I certainly wasn't," said Mr. Rackham. "The girl's right, madam. Now that a murder has been committed, we can't let anyone leave the grounds until the investigation is complete. That includes the children." He waggled a finger at Toby. "We've already learned that young Mr. Montrose isn't to be trusted. What other secrets might he be hiding?"

Normally, Toby would have protested that he really was trustworthy—most of the time, at least. But what if Mr. Rackham's distrust was the only thing keeping Toby from a long, humiliating carriage ride back to Detectives' Row?

He'd be in a world of trouble as soon as Uncle Gabriel got home—there was no way to avoid it now—but he absolutely wasn't going to leave Coleford Manor without finding out what Mr. Abernathy had learned about his parents. And he badly wanted to know who had killed Mr. Abernathy. A murder wasn't the sort of thing you could just forget about or ignore, especially if you had been the one to discover it in the first place. Even the worst detectives in the city would never stumble across a corpse, shrug, and go home for the weekend.

"I've got loads of secrets," Toby promised the others. "You'd better keep me around."

"I suppose we don't have a choice." Mrs. Webster frowned, but she sat back down. "I can't say I like the idea of spending the weekend locked up with a murderer, though. It can't be safe for any of us."

"I don't like it, either," Mr. Webster said. "You will track the culprit down soon, won't you, Rackham?"

All around the table, detectives bristled.

"Er," said Mr. Webster. "I mean, Rackham and the rest of you."

"I hope you do mean it," Miss March said. "When it comes to solving murders, Mr. Rackham isn't the only one who's up to the task. After all, we still haven't established who among us is the world's greatest detective."

"Well, we know Hugh didn't deserve the title," Julia

143

said darkly. "Surely the world's greatest detective wouldn't let himself get murdered."

"Please, Miss Hartshorn!" These were the first words Mr. Peartree had spoken since he'd sat down to dinner. "I hardly think we should be spending our time insulting poor Mr. Abernathy when we could be bringing his killer to justice. There are five world-renowned investigators at this table. I don't care which of you cracks this case, but someone's got to do it!" Toby had never heard Mr. Peartree speak so forcefully before—but then, he was the one person in the world who'd known Hugh Abernathy better than anyone. He'd spent years making sure his employer got whatever he needed, and what his employer needed now was a good detective. "Mr. Abernathy was going to give ten thousand dollars to the winner of his contest," Mr. Peartree continued. "The contest may be canceled, but the prize money is still in safekeeping at his office. I propose that we give it instead to the person who catches his murderer."

"That's an excellent idea," said Mr. Webster. "The news of Abernathy's death is bound to get out, and if it's not solved quickly and quietly, we'll have journalists and tourists swamping the house, poking their noses into our private affairs. Half the city will be lining up to take their turn at finding the killer! If one of you at this table can do the job, though, we might not have a scandal on our hands."

Mrs. Webster didn't look pleased. "And if one of them can't?"

"Then we'll have to alert the constable, scandal or not." Mr. Webster looked around the table. "I'll give you all until Sunday afternoon. If you don't find us a murderer by then, I'll bring in the police."

"Don't worry, my dear," said Miss March. She squeezed Mrs. Webster's hand. "I'm sure that won't be necessary."

The mention of the ten thousand dollars had been so invigorating that several of the detectives started to take tentative tastes of their dinner. Even Toby was feeling a little better. "With ten thousand dollars," he said to Ivy, "I could fix all the leaks in Uncle Gabriel's roof and keep Montrose Investigations in business."

"I could rent an office on Detectives' Row," Ivy said. "I could hang up a big bronze sign with my name on it, and a smaller sign for Percival."

"I could get a lifetime subscription to the *Sphinx Monthly Reader*," said Toby.

"I could pay Lillie to go away," said Ivy, "and to never come back."

Mrs. Webster had overheard them. "You won't do anything of the sort, Ivy," she said, "and neither will you, Toby. I want both of you children to stay well out of the way of the investigation."

"Oh, Mother!" said Ivy. "Don't be silly. Who ever heard

145

of a detective solving a case by staying away from it?"

Toby nodded. "Mr. Peartree said he'd reward anyone here who could find out how Mr. Abernathy died. What if 'anyone' is us?"

He was proud of this logic, but it wasn't enough to convince Mrs. Webster. "*No,*" she said in a voice Toby didn't want to argue with. "I won't allow you two to put yourselves in danger. Murder is not for children."

Ivy scowled at her mother. Then, deliberately, she rested both of her elbows on the table. Toby had guessed it already, but now he knew it for sure: Ivy Webster was the sort of girl who actually *liked* danger.

The dining room door opened, and Norton the footman limped through it. He handed a small paper card to Mrs. Webster. "I'm sorry to interrupt, madam," he said, "but I thought you'd want to know that the doctor is here."

CHAPTER 11

BERTRAM'S REMARKABLE DIGESTIVE TONIC

No one was allowed to bother Doctor Piper. While she examined Mr. Abernathy's body in the Orchid Room, the soup was cleared away and followed by roast lamb, which was followed in turn by sweet dessert cakes (which Toby liked) and bitter coffee (which he didn't). The minutes ticked by, and the detectives grew restless. One by one, they excused themselves from the dinner table to stretch their legs, explore the manor, or admire the Websters' collection of Gyptian artifacts, though Toby guessed they were all really trying to sneak a look at whatever Doctor Piper was doing upstairs. He would have liked to do the same, but Mrs. Webster wasn't letting him out of her sight. She herded him and Ivy into the parlor, where they played a halfhearted game of Snap and listened to Lillie practice her scales on the piano.

After a while, the others trickled in: first Julia Hartshorn with her crossword puzzle, then Mr. Rackham, who joined the card game and was promptly defeated by Ivy. Miss Price came in with her needlepoint and Miss March with her mystery novel; Philip Elwood even slipped his notebook into his pocket and banged out the low notes of a piano duet with Lillie.

When Mr. Peartree and Mr. Webster finally led Doctor Piper into the parlor, however, the music stopped. Toby threw down his playing cards in relief. He had been losing that round badly, and Ivy was getting more insufferable with every victory.

"Detectives," said Doctor Piper, setting down her black medical bag. Her voice was brisk, and she wore cloth gloves and sensible shoes; Toby guessed she was the sort of person who didn't put up with any nonsense. "I've completed a basic medical examination of the body, and I am prepared to share my early conclusions. Normally, I prefer to consult with the lead investigator on a case like this one, but the Websters tell me that you are *all* lead investigators, so I suppose you'll all need to hear my report."

"All except for the children," said Mrs. Webster as she gathered up the playing cards. "I'm sure it will be much too unpleasant for them. Shall I take them up to bed?"

"Please don't!" said Toby. He'd already seen a dead body that evening, and he was sure whatever the doctor had to say couldn't be more unpleasant than that. "We want to know what's happened."

"Yes, we do," said Ivy. "Toby discovered the murder, so he should be allowed to stay. And I don't want to go to bed, either. Doctor Piper knows I have a particular interest in medical anatomy."

Mrs. Webster looked more ready than ever to sweep them both upstairs, but Doctor Piper spoke first. "In my experience," she said, "children are very good at uncovering gruesome details, and even better at imagining the ones they can't uncover. It will be best for everyone in this room to hear the facts directly from me." She unzipped her medical bag and pulled out a green glass bottle—the same one Toby had seen on the purple table in the Orchid Room, wrapped in a stained paper label. "I believe," said Doctor Piper, "that Hugh Abernathy was deliberately poisoned with the liquid in this bottle."

It was a well-known fact that Mr. Abernathy relied on Bertram's Remarkable Digestive Tonic to keep his body as fit and nimble as his mind. He drank it three times a day— before breakfast, lunch, and dinner—and in the stories Toby had read, he was always complaining to Mr. Peartree about how foul it tasted. This hadn't stopped most of the would-be detectives in Colebridge from buying their very own supplies of Bertram's, though Toby had never seen a bottle anywhere in Uncle Gabriel's house. Uncle Gabriel probably believed that a lifetime of indigestion was preferable to drinking even one sip of Hugh Abernathy's favorite medicine.

Now, in the parlor, Mr. Peartree shook his head. "That's impossible. Mr. Abernathy has been taking Bertram's for years, and it's never killed him before. He had a glass at noon today and was perfectly healthy afterward!"

"Then someone must have added poison to the tonic after noon." Julia pulled on her own pair of gloves and picked up the Bertram's bottle. "May I borrow this for testing, Doctor?"

"Certainly," said Doctor Piper. "If I were you, Miss Hartshorn, I'd test first for Brandelburg acid. The effects are unmistakable."

Ivy nudged Toby in the ribs. "That's one of the three most popular poisons," she whispered.

"I know," Toby whispered back. "You said so in your lessons." Ivy had also said in her lessons that Brandelburg acid wasn't particularly difficult to find in Colebridge: it was in cleaning solutions, artists' paints, silver polish, and even the fluids photographers used to develop their pictures. Toby wondered whether Ivy had a jug of it hidden away somewhere in the Investigatorium.

"Mr. Abernathy died quickly," Doctor Piper said, "within

a few minutes of drinking this tonic. Do any of you know when that might have been?"

"It must have been his five-o'clock dose," said Mr. Peartree, knitting his fingers together and pulling them apart again. "He always drank his tonic at five precisely. The last time I spoke to him was at half past four."

"And we found him dead at a quarter past six," Toby volunteered.

The other detectives were all taking notes as quickly as they could write. "We know that someone added poison to Mr. Abernathy's tonic between noon and five o'clock," Philip said. He scratched his nose with the blunt end of his pen. "That should thin out the field of suspects. Who knew about Mr. Abernathy's habit of taking Bertram's?"

"Only everyone in the country!" said Julia. "You can't get through an issue of the *Sphinx* without knowing that." She looked meaningfully at Mr. Peartree.

Miss Price had stayed quiet while the doctor gave her report, but now she raised her hand. "I hope it won't distress anyone to hear this," she said, "but I believe all the people who are most likely to have poisoned Mr. Abernathy are gathered here in this very room."

"Surely not!" said Mr. Webster. At the piano, Lillie put a hand on the keys to steady herself, playing a chord so earsplitting it sent Percival leaping into Toby's lap. Toby didn't mind, though. He was glad to have a friend close by.

Percival certainly hadn't murdered anyone, which was more than Toby could say for anyone else in the parlor.

"I agree with Flossie," Miss March said. "No one else has been allowed in the house this afternoon except for the servants, and I can't imagine any of them would have a reason to want Hugh Abernathy out of the way." She looked around the room, and Toby pulled Percival a little closer. Who *did* have a reason to poison Mr. Abernathy? Miss March obviously knew—or thought she did—but Toby didn't think she was going to share that information with the others. As good as Miss March and Miss Price were at talking, they were even better at holding their tongues.

"Still," said Mr. Rackham, "the servants will have to be interviewed, and the Websters as well. We've got to do this thing properly. Newfangled tricks and potions will only get an investigation so far."

"They'll get it quite far enough," said Julia, "thank you very much."

Doctor Piper tapped one of her sensible shoes on the floorboards. Toby had been right; she didn't like nonsense. "I'll have to take the body with me," she said. "The county medical examiner will want to perform a more thorough investigation. Would a few of you please help me bring Mr. Abernathy down to my carriage?"

All the detectives stood up right away. So did Toby.

"Are you going to carry the body?" Ivy asked him. She wrinkled her nose. "You really do like to be helpful, don't you? You're a very strange person."

"I'm not the one who owns a human skeleton," Toby pointed out. "And anyway, I'm not being helpful—at least not right now. Everyone's going up to the Orchid Room, and I want to go, too. Mr. Abernathy's case files are in there, remember?"

"Right!" said Ivy. "Good thinking, Detective Montrose." She bounced out of her chair. "You're wrong about my owning a skeleton, though. I already told you: Egbert is on loan."

In the Orchid Room, Mr. Peartree held Mr. Abernathy's arms and Miss March held his legs while the other detectives crowded in on all sides to get a better view. "Poor Hugh," Miss Price murmured as Mr. Peartree staggered forward, hardly able to hold up his own arms along with Mr. Abernathy's. "First to be murdered, and then to be carried down the servants' stairs! He wouldn't have found it very dignified." She placed her hands on Toby's shoulders. "You're looking a little wobbly, dear. Are you feeling all right?"

Toby wasn't all right. From the doorway of the Orchid Room, he could see that Mr. Abernathy's dignity wasn't the only thing missing from the scene of the crime. On the floor in front of him, where all those folders and papers had been stacked a few hours before, was nothing but an old carpet woven in long rows of violet diamonds and lavender stripes.

"It's Mr. Abernathy's case files," Toby said. "I mean, actually, it *isn't* the files. They're gone."

There was only one lamp in the Investigatorium. It flickered earnestly in a corner and cast nervous shadows onto the old velvet sofa, where Ivy sat with her legs crossed under her. She'd let Toby sit down, too, so he could tell the situation was serious. No one knew who had taken Mr. Abernathy's files. The doctor swore she hadn't moved them, but they'd been in the Orchid Room when she'd arrived, and now they absolutely weren't.

"My god!" Mr. Rackham had said. "The murderer must have taken them!"

At this, Mrs. Webster had decided that enough was enough and that the children should be sent to bed before any more crimes could be committed. Toby and Ivy had protested, of course, but it didn't do any good. They were marched down the hall and into their bedrooms while the other detectives studied every floorboard and windowpane in the Orchid Room, searching for clues to Mr. Abernathy's death and to the whereabouts of the missing files. Julia had even mentioned something about taking fingerprints, and Toby wished he could have stayed to watch her do it. Instead, he crawled under his orange quilt, squeezed his eyes shut, and wondered how he'd ever be able to fall asleep in the same clothes he'd worn all day, with the buzz of detectives working just down the hall. Even if murder wasn't for children, he couldn't help feeling extremely left out.

Then Ivy had tapped on his door. She was draped in billowing pink flannel, with lace trim at the collar and all sorts of pockets in curious places. "Emergency meeting," she'd said in a low voice. "Meet me upstairs in five minutes. And don't you dare say a word about my nightgown."

Toby had promised not to. There wasn't much you could say about something that frightening.

Now, in the dim light of the Investigatorium, Ivy rolled up her sleeves. "I hereby call this emergency meeting to order," she said. "Our assistant is asleep downstairs, but we can bring him up-to-date in the morning. Right now, we've got to decide what we're going to do about this murder."

Toby hadn't realized there was anything to decide. "What about your mother?" he said. "She said we're not allowed to get anywhere near it."

"Oh, don't mind Mother." Ivy rolled her eyes. "She's always saying things like that. You've just got to ignore

155

her. You can do that, can't you, Toby? Or are you as well behaved as Lillie?"

When she put it that way, it sounded suspiciously like a dare. "I'm not *that* well behaved."

"Good," said Ivy, "because we can't leave this investigation up to the other detectives. You heard what Miss Price said: one of them could be the killer! For all we know, all five of them joined forces to poison Mr. Abernathy."

The lamp in the corner summoned up its enthusiasm and blazed brighter, making Toby squint. He didn't like danger anywhere nearly as much as Ivy did, but she was right: the others couldn't be trusted, not even the detectives Uncle Gabriel had known for years. Somewhere in Coleford Manor, right under their noses, a murderer was paging through Hugh Abernathy's case files—or, even worse, destroying them forever, along with Toby's last hope of finding out the truth about his parents. Toby could hardly stand to think about it. "You're right," he said. "We've got to investigate."

"I knew you'd think so!" Ivy clapped her hands. "Oh, Toby, I can see it now. Mr. Peartree will write about our adventures and publish them in the *Sphinx*! 'Inspector Webster and the Mystery of the Poisoned Sleuth'! Or maybe 'Inspector Webster in Peril at the Manor'! Or—"

"Um," said Toby. "Can't my name be in the titles, too?"

"Inspector Webster *and* Detective Montrose? It's sort of a mouthful."

"But we're partners." Toby hesitated. "We are partners, right?"

Ivy chewed her bottom lip. "Right. We're a team. We're . . . Webster and Montrose, Private Investigators." She said it again, trying out the sound of it. Then she looked up at Toby and grinned. "The sleuths who make criminals shiver."

PART III

SUSPECTS AND SECRETS

CHAPTER 12

MADAME ERMINTRUDE

It was morning in the Marigold Room. Daylight burst in through Toby's orange curtains, the local birds were in full-throated chorus outside his window, and Percival was sitting on his stomach.

"Good morning to you, too," Toby said. His mind was still cobwebbed over with sleep, but he was alert enough to guess a few things. "Did Ivy let you in?"

"Wrong!" Across the room, someone flung open the curtains. Toby squinted at her. She wore a long dress that looked like a lot of silk scarves sewn together, with even more scarves wrapped around her neck. Her hair was covered by a floppy straw hat, and her eyes were hidden behind a pair of motoring goggles. "I," she said, "am Madame

Ermintrude, the world-famous fortune-teller and race-car driver."

"Sorry, Ivy, but I'm not going to call you Madame Ermintrude." Toby wriggled out from under Percival's claws. "Isn't it too early for disguises?"

"It's practically seven." Ivy pushed her motoring goggles up onto her forehead. "And no time is too early for good detective work. But how did you know it was me? No one in the *Sphinx* ever guesses that they're talking to Hugh Abernathy in disguise."

"I don't think Madame Ermintrude was one of his disguises." Hugh Abernathy had been famous for playing hundreds of different roles during his adventures, and a few times he'd even fooled Mr. Peartree into believing he was a sausage vendor or a Gallian aristocrat. But Ivy was no Hugh Abernathy. "It's a good disguise, though," Toby said, "if you need to read someone's fortune or drive a race car. Do you?"

"Not today." Ivy frowned. "I'll keep working on it." She unwound a few of her scarves and sat down in the orange armchair, shoving aside the stack of pillows that had never really looked much like Uncle Gabriel. "I could hardly sleep last night, could you? I kept thinking about who the murderer might be, and about the three *M*s."

Toby hadn't slept much, either. Every time he'd closed his eyes, he'd seen Mr. Abernathy, cold and lifeless in that purple chair, and he'd jolted awake again. He guessed, though, that Ivy didn't allow herself to have nightmares. "What are the three *M*s?" he asked.

"Don't you remember? They're in lesson twelve of the correspondence course. What are the three crucial things any criminal needs in order to commit a crime?"

Toby rubbed his eyes and tried to picture the notes he'd taken months ago. "Well, there's means," he said, "and motive, I think. And opportunity."

"Exactly," said Ivy. "The three *M*s."

"But—"

"I know *opportunity* doesn't begin with *M*, but 'two *M*s and an *O*' is much harder to remember, don't you think? Anyway, in this case, we already know the means of Mr. Abernathy's murder. Someone put poison in his digestive tonic. That doesn't help us much, though. Poison isn't hard to get if you know where to look. Anyone in this house might have had the means to kill Mr. Abernathy."

"Right," said Toby. He might not have remembered the three *M*s right away, but he didn't want Ivy to think he was completely useless. "And the same goes for opportunity. The person who put the poison in the tonic had to sneak into the Orchid Room sometime yesterday afternoon. I don't think anyone outside the house could have gotten in without looking suspicious, but any of the detectives could have done it, or . . . well . . . any of your family. Sorry, Ivy."

"You don't have to apologize. You're only being logical. No one would have thought it was strange for Mother or Father to slip into a room in their own house, so they had the perfect opportunity."

"How about Lillie?" Toby couldn't even remember seeing her yesterday after lunch. Maybe she'd been too busy tampering with Mr. Abernathy's tonic to join the others playing badminton.

Ivy twisted one of her scarves around her wrist. "If Lillie were going to commit a murder, I'm sure she'd do it as wonderfully as she does everything else. But I can't even imagine what her motive would be."

"That's the third *M*," said Toby. "The most important one. If anyone in the house *could* have killed Mr. Abernathy, we need to figure out which person *wanted* to do it—and why."

"Good work, Detective," said Ivy. "That's exactly the conclusion I reached at three o'clock this morning."

Of course she had. Toby was starting to feel about as helpful to the investigation as Percival, who had jumped off the bed and begun scouting for mice under the wardrobe. "Don't tell me you've already worked out who the murderer is."

"Not yet," Ivy admitted. "I wish I had. Then I wouldn't have to be Madame Ermintrude. But today, Toby, we are going to find out exactly who in Coleford Manor wanted

Mr. Abernathy out of the way. You've practiced interviewing suspects, haven't you?"

"Sort of. At least, I've read the lesson about it. There weren't as many likely criminals on Detectives' Row as you might expect."

"Good enough," said Ivy. "The other guests seem fond enough of you, and so do my parents. I bet they'll tell you anything you want to know." She had twisted her scarves from her wrist all the way to her shoulder by now. "I don't know if they feel the same way about Madame Ermintrude, though. Most people don't like me very much."

"I'm sure that's not true," Toby said. Secretly, though, he wasn't sure at all. He liked Ivy now—or at least he thought he did, most of the time—but he hadn't felt that way before he'd gotten to know her a little, and Ivy wasn't easy to get to know. Especially not in her sun hat and motoring goggles. He tried hard to imagine the other detectives revealing their secrets to Madame Ermintrude. "Anyway, interviewing suspects isn't the only thing we need to do today. One of us should search for the missing case files. If we can find out who took them, it might tell us who the murderer is."

"Genius!" said Ivy. "It's the perfect plan." She climbed out of the orange armchair and pulled Toby off his bed. "I know all the best hiding spots in the manor. With you interrogating suspects and me finding Mr. Abernathy's files, we'll have this case cracked by lunchtime."

Ivy sounded so confident of this that Toby almost believed it himself. Maybe they really could catch the other detectives off their guard and solve the mystery before anyone realized what they were up to. If they could pull it off, Uncle Gabriel was going to be really impressed.

Ivy was studying his face. "You're looking funny," she said. "What's going on?"

"It's nothing," said Toby. "I mean, it's probably not important, but I just remembered how much my uncle hated Hugh Abernathy. If anyone had a motive to murder him, Uncle Gabriel did."

Ivy had been right: no time was too early for good detective work, and the other detectives at Coleford Manor had practically emptied out the breakfast platters by the time Toby reached them. Only Miss March and Mrs. Webster lingered at the table, chatting about a stone statuette Mrs. Webster was working to restore at the city museum. "We can't be sure yet," Mrs. Webster was saying, "but my guess is that it's an early representation of the Gyptian goddess of justice. We could certainly use her assistance here this weekend, now that— Ivy, what in heaven's name are you wearing?"

"I'm Madame Ermintrude," said Ivy, piling most of the remaining pastries onto her plate.

"Ah," said Mrs. Webster. "I wondered where my old motoring goggles had wandered off to."

Toby grabbed the last pastry before Ivy could get to it. "Where are the other guests?" he asked. He wanted to get started with his interviews. He hadn't seen any of the others on his way down to breakfast, but that wasn't too surprising; Coleford Manor was enormous.

"They've all come and gone," Miss March told him. She counted off detectives one by one on her fingers. "Miss Hartshorn has commandeered the kitchen for her chemical experiments, and Miss Price and Mr. Elwood are taking a stroll in the gardens. Mr. Rackham is interrogating the poor servants; he's probably frightening them to death as we speak. A lot of unnecessary bother, if you ask me, but Mr. Rackham didn't." Miss March double-checked her fingers. "As for everyone else, I believe they're in the parlor. Mr. Peartree is writing to the lawyers who handle Mr. Abernathy's affairs, and Mr. Webster is—"

"Amina!" Mr. Webster burst into the room and slapped a newspaper down on the table in front of his wife. "Look at this! Look what they've printed! How the devil did they find out?"

"—reading the paper," Miss March finished. She winked at Toby. "Is everything quite all right, Mr. Webster?"

Mr. Webster couldn't do anything other than sputter,

167

but Mrs. Webster had managed to keep hold of her words. "Oh dear," she said. She laid the paper flat in front of her. "It seems we've sprung a leak."

WORLD'S GREATEST DETECTIVE FOUND DEAD, the *Morning Bugle* headline shouted. And then, in more measured letters: *SCANDALOUS MURDER AT WEBSTER ESTATE*. Underneath that was a photograph of Hugh Abernathy that took up half the page, outlined in black. Toby set down his pastry and leaned forward to get a better look.

"Everyone in Colebridge will have seen this by now." Mr. Webster collapsed into a chair and glared at the photo of Hugh Abernathy, as if Mr. Abernathy himself were personally responsible. "They'll be on their way here with cameras and magnifying glasses. The police will want a crack at the case, and we'll have a plague of tourists, too, climbing over the fence posts and crawling through the hedge maze. We'll never have a minute's peace again!"

Toby was barely listening. He was halfway through the article now, and he didn't think the Websters were the only people who'd dislike it. "Oh no," he said quietly.

It hadn't been quiet enough for Ivy. She pounced. "What is it? Can you read it aloud?"

Toby glanced at Miss March. "I'd rather not."

"Well, I'd rather you did," Miss March said. "If the

Morning Bugle knows something about this crime that I don't, I'd like to hear it."

There wasn't any way out of it. "'Although several of the city's best-known detectives were present at the time of the murder,'" Toby read reluctantly, "'none of them showed any talent for crime solving, and they have already allowed important evidence to disappear from the scene. In fact, last night's performance suggests that no living sleuth is likely to measure up to Hugh Abernathy's standard of excellence. On Detectives' Row, only Mr. Abernathy stood out as a truly great investigator, and the future of the Row seems bleak without him.'" Toby's voice had gotten steadily quieter as he read, but that didn't make the words on the newsprint sound any nicer. "Sorry, Miss March."

Miss March stiffened. "There's nothing to be sorry about," she said, taking the paper from Toby and rolling it up tight, as though she wanted to use it to smack something. "It's all a bunch of flimflam and folderol if you ask me. No one will believe a word of it."

Toby hoped she was right. Otherwise, Uncle Gabriel wouldn't be the only investigator who'd soon be out of business. If the *Morning Bugle* printed more stories like this one, the Row would be as empty and desolate as Slaughter's Lane, and every detective at the manor would have to find a new line of work.

"Never mind all that," said Mrs. Webster. "I'd like to know how the paper got this information. I locked the gates myself yesterday afternoon. None of those journalists in the street could have heard anything that happened last night, and Doctor Piper promised to keep the whole matter quiet."

"Isn't it obvious, Mother?" Ivy waved her scarves in the air, narrowly missing Mrs. Webster's teacup. "One of *us* spoke to the journalists. Someone in this house is a double-crossing snake!"

Mrs. Webster rested her head in her hands. "Oh, Ivy. This isn't the time for dramatics."

"I don't see why not," Miss March said. "The child is right: it's clear that someone here is not to be trusted." She shrugged and pushed back her chair. "It's a shame, but I can't say I'm surprised. No secret lasts long in a city full of detectives."

CHAPTER 13

BRANDELBURG BLUE

Julia Hartshorn was washing glass jars in the kitchen sink, but she looked up when Toby knocked. "Raiding the pantry?" she asked cheerfully. "Don't worry; I won't tell a soul."

"Actually," said Toby, "Miss March told me you were doing things with chemicals. I wondered if I could watch."

Julia wiped the jars with a clean white cloth and laid them out on the big table in the center of the room. She'd transformed the kitchen into a sort of laboratory, sweeping recipe books and pie pans out of the way to make space for vials of jewel-colored liquids stopped up with corks, and industrial jugs stamped all over with warnings. This, Toby assumed, was the stuff of science. He hadn't expected it to look quite so deadly.

"Don't eat or drink anything Julia gives you," Ivy had warned him a few minutes earlier, before she'd snuck off to search for the missing files. "If she poisoned Mr. Abernathy and you find out about it, she might try to poison you, too."

Right now, Julia was frowning at him. That was dangerous enough. Toby had seen how upset she'd gotten with Mr. Abernathy yesterday, which was why she was at the top of his list of suspects to interview. "All right," she said at last, pulling on a pair of gloves. "I don't mind if you watch, but you've got to stand back. I'm not entirely sure what's going to happen." She uncorked the half-empty bottle of Bertram's Remarkable Digestive Tonic, sniffed at it, and made a face. "This stuff is horrible even when it hasn't been poisoned."

Toby stood by the sink and watched as Julia decanted the Bertram's into a clean jar. Then, carefully, she added a spoonful of powder from one of her vials. It looked almost like salt, but Toby didn't think it would improve the taste of the tonic. "We're testing for Brandelburg acid," Julia explained as she stirred the mixture. "If Mr. Abernathy's tonic contains it, it should glow blue—quite a nice shade, really, but not one you'd want to see in your digestive medicine. As far as we're concerned, blue is the color of death."

Toby thought of Mr. Abernathy's body, which had gone

right past blue and on to purple. If that was what science could do to people, he wasn't sure he trusted it, and he definitely didn't trust Julia. "Don't most detectives let the medical examiner test for poisons?" he asked.

"They do," said Julia, "but that's because most detectives don't have university degrees in chemistry. I don't know why not. Scientists are like detectives, in a way. They're always trying to discover the truth, and as far as I'm concerned, the truth is much easier to find in the swirl of a criminal's fingerprints than in the twists and turns of his mind." She struck a match and lit the kitchen stove. "Now that Mr. Abernathy's gone, though, I'm the only one on the Row doing my own chemical tests."

Toby remembered the long rows of doors he'd seen in Mr. Abernathy's house, and the room full of glass bottles and tubes. "Did you and Mr. Abernathy work together very often?"

Julia laughed. "We were neighbors," she said, "but the only times I spoke to him were when I had to ask him to clear his parade of clients away from my front steps. The only person Hugh Abernathy ever wanted to work with was himself. I'm surprised your uncle hasn't told you that." She'd taken a metal contraption out from somewhere and was busy assembling it over the flame. "They used to be investigative partners, did you know?"

At first, Toby thought Julia was joking. "They couldn't

have been!" he said. "Uncle Gabriel hated Mr. Abernathy! And besides, he's not in any of the stories in the *Sphinx*."

"Oh, it was ages before the *Sphinx*, and ages before I came up to the Row. I don't really know much about it, but I've heard the partnership didn't end well." Julia shrugged and balanced the jar full of chemicals on the metal frame, just a few inches above the hot stove. "Anyway, I'm not surprised your uncle didn't like Mr. Abernathy. Lots of people didn't."

Toby had a thousand more questions about Uncle Gabriel, but he couldn't ask them now, not when he had to find out if Julia Hartshorn had a motive for murder. "You didn't like Mr. Abernathy, either," he said, "did you?"

Julia looked up sharply from the stove. "What do you mean?"

"You were mad at him yesterday, during the badminton game." Toby tensed the muscles in his legs, just in case he needed to run. The long kitchen table stood between him and Julia Hartshorn, but Julia looked fast.

"Oh, *that*!" Julia sighed. She sounded almost relieved. "I've already told you that Hugh wasn't any good at working with other people. As it turns out, he wasn't any good at playing with them, either. Thank goodness Mr. Peartree came outside when he did. If I'd had to play doubles with Hugh for much longer, I might have broken my racquet over his head." She knelt down and stared into the warming jar. "But I didn't murder him, Toby, if that's what you're thinking. I promise you: no one cares *that* much about badminton."

The minutes ticked away on the kitchen clock, the mixture in its jar grew hotter, and Toby grew more frustrated. He wasn't getting very far with Julia Hartshorn. She had arrived at Coleford Manor just before ten o'clock the previous morning, eaten lunch with the others, and spent most of the afternoon winning all the points Mr. Abernathy would allow her on the badminton court. She'd run inside for a few minutes to fetch her sun hat, which would have given her more than enough time to tamper with Mr. Abernathy's tonic, and Toby was sure most of the things in her vials and jugs were poisonous. But Ivy had sent him to find out why Julia might have wanted Mr. Abernathy dead, and by the time she took the jar off the heat, he still hadn't managed it. If Julia Hartshorn had any secrets, she wasn't about to share them with Toby.

A thick brown sludge was starting to collect at the bottom of the jar, and Julia looked happy to see it. "We're almost done," she said as she reached for one of her large, dangerous-looking jugs. "If we've managed the experiment properly, the precipitate should turn blue when I add the acid. If we haven't . . . well, we might be in trouble." She peered at Toby. "You don't like trouble, do you?"

"No, Miss Hartshorn." The question was bewildering.

Who could like that slinking, shadowy thing? Did anyone actually enjoy the prickling burns at the backs of their necks, or the terrible twists in their stomachs? Toby had spent most of the past three years trying to get out of trouble's way; it had never occurred to him to *like* it. "I don't think anyone does."

"I do," said Julia. "Occasionally, at least. I've found that trouble can be very educational. If I never got into it, I'd never learn a thing." She collected a few drops of liquid from the jug inside a long thin tube. "Are you ready?"

The only thing Toby had ever learned from trouble was that the world would be much better off without it. He guessed it would be educational if the jar of chemicals exploded, or if the bottle of acid burned a hole in the kitchen floor, but he wasn't sure that was the sort of education he needed. Still, he didn't want Julia to think he was too small or too nervous to face whatever might happen. "I'm ready," he said.

"Good," said Julia. "Watch the jar."

Slowly, hardly moving her hand, Julia let the acid drip little by little into the jar. Toby stared at the brown sludge resting on the bottom. The first drop changed nothing. Neither did the second, or the third, or the fourth. With the fifth drop, though, the sludge began to glow, brilliant and deadly and blue.

"Presto," Julia said with a grin. "We've got our poison."

Toby hadn't expected it to be beautiful. It was summer-time blue, the blue that came just after sunset, before night crept in and pinned the world all over with stars. If Julia had told him she'd collected that color by climbing a ladder and scraping up the sky, Toby would have believed her. "Are you sure that's what killed Mr. Abernathy?" he asked.

"As sure as I can be. It wouldn't have taken much—no more than a few sips—and that awful tonic would have masked the taste of it. Our murderer must have known something about poisons." Julia shrugged as she picked up the jar and poured it down the sink. "Of course, Brandelburg acid is easy enough for anyone to find these days. There's no way of telling how it got into the bottle of Bertram's."

"Are you going to tell the other detectives?"

"That the tonic really was poisoned?" Julia frowned. "I suppose I'll have to. I'd like to be the first to solve this crime, but if I'm going to manage it in only two days, I'll need information from the others—and I'm sure they'll want information from me in return." Carefully, Julia peeled off her gloves. "I feel as though I'm trying to put together a puzzle that's missing half its pieces."

"So do I!" It was a relief to hear someone else say what Toby had been thinking all morning. "I mean," he added hastily, "that's probably how I'd feel if I were trying to solve the mystery."

He could tell right away that he hadn't managed to fool

Julia. She shook her head and laughed. "So you *are* snooping around after all! I thought you might be. Well, good for you. I'm all for it."

"You are?" Toby was surprised. "Don't you think murder isn't for children?"

"Mrs. Webster said that, didn't she?" Julia turned on the water tap, and Toby watched as she rolled up her sleeves to scrub her hands. "The Websters seem nice enough, but I don't think they understand a thing about—" Julia broke off. Her eyes followed Toby's. Then she yanked her sleeves back down to her wrists and turned off the tap so ferociously that Toby thought it might come off in her hands. "What did you see?"

"Nothing!" said Toby. "I don't know what you're talking about!"

All the laughter was gone from Julia's face. Toby had never seen a person's mood change so much in just a few moments. He backed away from her, knocking over a sack full of potatoes and making the whole disaster even worse. But Julia didn't seem to notice. She braced her arms against the kitchen table and looked down at the bottle of Bertram's instead of at Toby.

"If you want to be a detective," she said in a low voice, "don't start by investigating me. Investigate Philip Elwood. Yesterday afternoon, when I came inside to fetch my sun hat, I spotted Mr. Elwood standing outside the door to the

Orchid Room with his hand on the doorknob. He jumped a foot when he saw me coming down the hall. He might have been doing anything, I suppose, but if you ask me, he looked positively guilty. I wouldn't be surprised if he'd had a bottle of Brandelburg acid in his back pocket."

Toby stared at her. "Why are you telling me this?"

"Because you didn't see anything," Julia said, "and you won't say a word to anyone." Her voice was quiet, but so serious it made Toby shiver. "Do you understand?"

Toby nodded. Then he ran. He zigzagged around the rolling potatoes, kicking one under the table and another behind the stove, but for once in his life, he didn't even think of cleaning up. All he could think of was the thick, black line he'd seen etched into Julia's skin, starting just above her wrist and curling all the way to her elbow.

CHAPTER 14

A CROWD AT THE GATES

A lot of peculiar things lurked in the walls of old houses, and at Coleford Manor, one of those peculiar things was Ivy. As Toby stumbled out of the kitchen, she burst from a hallway cupboard and landed on her hands and knees on the floor a few inches in front of him. "Hey!" he shouted. "Look out!"

With great dignity, Ivy picked herself up. She was still dressed as Madame Ermintrude, but her hat was missing, and her hair was mostly cobwebs. "It's not my job to look out, Detective Montrose," she said solemnly. "My job is to teach you about the element of surprise." She looked Toby up and down. "From the way your knees are wobbling, I can tell I've been successful."

Toby's knees had actually started wobbling sometime during his encounter with Julia, but Ivy's flying leap hadn't made him feel any calmer. "I don't think I need any more lessons right now," he told her. "Have you found Mr. Abernathy's files yet?"

Ivy tugged a cobweb from her hair. "Use your powers of observation, Toby. Am I beaming? Am I holding a stack of papers? Have I told you that your parents are sailing around the world on a Gyptian yacht and they're due back next Tuesday?" She sighed. "I'm sorry. I've crawled through the attic, searched the broom cupboard, and ridden up and down in the dumbwaiter, but I haven't found anything except mice and spiders and leaky bottles of hair tonic. Did you learn anything from Julia?"

"A little," said Toby. He told her about the brilliant blue glow of the Brandelburg acid and about Julia's opinion of Hugh Abernathy, although he decided to keep what she'd said about Uncle Gabriel to himself. And he wondered whether he should tell Ivy about the marks he'd seen on Julia's arm. He'd promised he wouldn't say a word—but Ivy was his partner! Partners told each other everything, didn't they? Surely they weren't supposed to keep secrets from each other. "There's one more thing about Julia," he said quietly. "She's got a tattoo—a wavy black line that goes halfway up her arm—and she got awfully upset when I saw it. I don't know what it means, but I saw the same mark on my carriage driver's arm yesterday, and he turned out to be a thief."

"A thief?" said Ivy. "Are you sure?"

"I'd be a lot less sure if he hadn't stolen my suitcase."

Ivy wrinkled her forehead. "All right," she said, "but why would a detective and a criminal have the same tattoo? It doesn't make any sense. If Miss Hartshorn didn't want you to see that mark, though, it must mean something important. Maybe I can ask Father about it."

"You can't tell anyone else! I promised Julia. And she gave me something in exchange." Toby looked up and down the hallway to make sure no detectives were listening in the doorways. "Philip Elwood was trying to get into Mr. Abernathy's room yesterday afternoon while the other detectives were outside. Julia caught him in the act. She says he looked guilty."

Ivy began to smile. "And we caught him sneaking around in the broom cupboard! Oh, he's definitely up to something. You haven't spoken to him yet, have you?"

"I was just on my way to find him, actually," said Toby, "before we—um—ran into each other."

"Then I'll come with you." Ivy pushed her motoring goggles down over her eyes. "Despite what some people might think, a great detective can't spend all her life crawling around in the cobwebs."

Philip Elwood wasn't in his bedroom or the breakfast room or the library. In fact, he didn't seem to be inside the manor at all. Ivy was convinced they'd cornered him in one of the washrooms, but when the door swung open, only Lillie stepped out, clutching a damp ball of fabric to her chest. She gave a little gasp when she spotted them.

"Heavens!" she said. "What are you two doing lurking in the shadows? You startled me half to death!"

"It's not any of your business," Ivy informed her, "but we thought you might be Philip Elwood. Tragically, though, you're not." She looked hard at the bundle in Lillie's arms, and a rapturous smile grew on her face. "Oh, Lillie! Did you ruin your best dress?"

"Hush!" Lillie held the bundle tighter. Now that Ivy had mentioned it, Toby could see it was the same dress she'd been wearing yesterday afternoon. It was dripping wet now, though, and stained with an enormous brown splotch. "You can't tell Mother and Father. They'll be furious!"

Ivy looked positively gleeful. "What did you *do*?"

Lillie sighed. "I leaned against a fence in town yesterday, and it must have been freshly painted. I've been scrubbing for ages, but the stuff just won't come out! Please, Ivy, promise you won't tell."

"Hmm," said Ivy. "What will you give me if I don't?"

183

Lillie rolled her eyes. "I can tell you where Philip is. He's outside in the summerhouse; I just saw him through the window. Is that payment enough?"

Toby hoped it was. He felt sorry for Lillie; she looked desperately nervous. He didn't blame her, either; if he'd just ruined his nicest clothes, he would have felt exactly the same.

"All right," said Ivy at last. "I won't say a word to Mother."

"Or to Father!" Lillie said.

Ivy grinned at her sister. "We'll see," she said. "Come on, Toby. We've got work to do."

Outside the manor, Mr. Webster's prediction had already begun to come true. There was a crowd at the gates, and it seemed to Toby as though it was growing bigger by the minute, like an advancing army. On the front lines were the journalists, sticking their noses through the gaps in the iron bars and shouting out questions to anyone they spotted on the grounds. Behind them were the tourists—just a handful so far, in their best holiday clothes, pointing up at the manor and posing stiffly for the newspaper photographers. A quick-thinking florist had set up a stall where well-wishers could buy mourning bouquets to lay at the gates, and Toby knew that later, there would be candy vendors and street musicians, tour guides reciting the history of the manor, and painters selling hasty portraits of the unfortunate victim. At the very back of the crowd, looking as though they'd been unpleasantly interrupted from a good night's sleep, were half a dozen city police officers. Toby guessed they'd been last of all to hear the news about Mr. Abernathy.

"No," Mr. Webster was telling them through the bars, "you may not come in! Not the police, not the journalists, and certainly not the puppeteer or the toffee salesman. Our detectives have the matter well in hand, and I refuse to say anything more until the case has been resolved."

On the hill above them, Ivy gave Toby a nudge. "Father must be really angry," she murmured. "He normally adores toffee."

Toby was happy to let Ivy's father defend the manor. After all, they had more urgent business to attend to. Philip Elwood was sitting in the summerhouse, just where Lillie had said he'd be, absorbed in his little notebook. "I've spotted our suspect," said Ivy, narrowing her eyes behind her motoring goggles. "Follow my lead."

"I've done this before, you know," said Toby. "I just talked to Julia!" But Ivy was already halfway to the summerhouse. Toby sighed and ran after her.

Philip Elwood snapped his notebook shut when he saw them coming across the grass. "Mr. Montrose!" he said.

"Just the person I was hoping to speak to! And Miss Ivy, it's nice to see you again."

Ivy didn't look as though there were anything nice about it: Madame Ermintrude meant business. "You want to speak to Toby?" she said. "Then you can speak to me, too."

"If you'd like," said Philip. He sounded awfully cheerful for a murderer. "I've got a few questions, and I hoped Toby could come up with the answers."

"But we've got questions for you!" Toby said. The interview was already starting off badly. Murder suspects weren't supposed to be happy to see their interrogators, and they definitely weren't supposed to ask questions of their own.

"In that case," said Philip, "maybe we can all help one another. Why don't you both have a seat?"

Toby looked over at Ivy. He wasn't sure he wanted to give Philip Elwood any sort of help, and he couldn't imagine what Philip wanted to ask them. Did he already know they suspected him of murder? What would he do if he found out? Would the tourists at the gates have a whole new crime to gossip about the next morning?

If Ivy was having any of the same worries, she didn't show it. She only shrugged and sat down on the summerhouse bench, so Toby sat next to her, keeping his eyes on Philip. The detective leaned forward and smiled at him.

"I'll go first," he said. "I'd like to know about your uncle."

Toby would have been less surprised if Philip had pulled a pistol out of his coat pocket. "My uncle? What does my uncle have to do with anything?"

"He isn't even here," said Ivy. She tossed one of her scarves over her shoulder. "He's in Gallis. Weren't you paying attention last night?"

Somehow, Philip managed to ignore Madame Ermintrude. "He knew Mr. Abernathy well, didn't he?" he asked Toby. "They were partners once, many years ago."

"You knew about that, too?" Now Toby was really upset. It wasn't fair that everyone he met seemed to know more than he did about his own uncle. Why hadn't Uncle Gabriel told him the truth? What else was he keeping to himself?

Ivy looked as though she'd been kicked. "They were partners? And you didn't tell me?"

"I didn't have any idea!" said Toby. "I only found out this morning!"

"It's practically *afternoon*," Ivy muttered.

"But Uncle Gabriel's never said anything to me about working with Mr. Abernathy. He turns all sorts of awful colors whenever he hears Mr. Abernathy's name, and he calls him an ostrich."

"Interesting!" Philip drummed his fingers on the summerhouse bench. "They must have been friendly once, but something went wrong. Do you know what came between them? A failed case, maybe, or an argument about money?"

Toby glared at him. "I just told you I don't know anything about it. Even if I did, I don't see why I should tell you. Uncle Gabriel has nothing to do with this case."

"But he had something to do with Hugh Abernathy," said Philip, "and I want to learn everything I can about our victim. Who were his friends? Who were his enemies? What were his secrets? I'm certain that if we can answer these questions, we'll find the key to Mr. Abernathy's murder."

Ivy rolled her eyes. "You mean *you* will."

"Besides," said Toby, "we all know everything about Mr. Abernathy already. His whole life's been published in the *Sphinx*! He eats two poached eggs every morning for breakfast after tending to his topiary, his hair is as golden as a sheaf of wheat, he spent five years in the jungle searching for poison antidotes, he loves the opera and the harmonica, he doesn't like animals, his mother's name was Vivian, and he disguised himself as a merchant seaman and worked on a ship for seven months before anyone realized he didn't know a thing about the sea." Toby had to stop to take a breath. "I don't think Mr. Abernathy could have had any secrets."

"Oh, everyone has secrets," said Philip. "Detectives'

Row would never do any business if they didn't. Some of us just happen to be better at hiding our secrets than others."

Ivy pounced. "So you *do* have secrets! We thought so, didn't we, Toby? What were you doing in Mr. Abernathy's room yesterday afternoon?"

"And in the broom cupboard?" Toby added. He didn't want Ivy to ask all the questions before he'd gotten a chance to help. "We saw you there, so you can't deny it. If you've got something to confess, you'd better do it now."

"Confess?" Philip scratched his nose and looked over Toby's head, as though something much more interesting were happening just beyond them. "Is it against the law to go in search of a fresh bath towel? I didn't want to bother the servants, so I took the liberty of letting myself into the cupboard. I hope I didn't inconvenience anyone."

"Hmm," said Ivy. "And the Orchid Room?"

Philip shook his head. "That," he said, "you're right about. It's true that I spent the afternoon exploring the house, and I'll admit I did try to slip into Mr. Abernathy's room while everyone else was outside playing badminton. I thought I might be able to sneak a look at his plans for the contest."

"You mean you were going to cheat," said Toby.

"That's an awfully strong way of putting it—but all right, I suppose I was. In any case, it doesn't matter now.

Miss Hartshorn came down the hall just as I was about to open the door, and my nagging conscience got the better of me. I do have one, you know."

Ivy looked as though she doubted it. "Did you like Mr. Abernathy? Or were you jealous of him?"

"I didn't know him well enough to like him," said Philip. "We'd never met before, in fact. But I certainly wasn't jealous. I've got a good career, enough money to make ends meet, and a girl I'm going to marry. I didn't have a single reason to want Hugh Abernathy dead." He shrugged. "I'm sorry I can't be more helpful, but I've got no more idea of what happened to him than you do. Has Julia found out what's killed him yet?"

Ivy poked Toby in the ribs, but he didn't see the point of lying to Philip; everyone would know about the poison sooner or later. "Brandelburg acid," he said grudgingly.

Ivy buried her face in her scarves.

"The doctor was right, then," said Philip. "I'm told that's nasty stuff." He looked over his shoulder toward the manor gates, where the crowd was growing larger and louder. "Is that all you wanted to ask me? If it is, I'd better excuse myself. I'd like to solve this crime before the bystanders get restless."

Philip stood up to leave the summerhouse, but something about his story still poked at Toby, as if it were a pebble stuck in his shoe. He tried to think back to the

190

moment he'd bumped into Philip the day before. "There's just one more thing, sir," he said quickly. "Why do you wear your hat indoors?"

Philip gave Toby a strange, crooked smile. "You think I'm keeping something under it?"

In one grand motion, he pulled off his hat. Underneath it, to Toby's disappointment, was nothing more than a perfectly normal head of hair.

"My hat," said Philip, "is my trademark. I hope that, in time, it will become just as famous as Mr. Abernathy's poached eggs or his awful harmonica. Someday, with any luck, all those tourists in the lane will be clamoring for straw boaters of their own." He bowed to Toby and Ivy, stepped out of the summerhouse, and strode across the lawn toward the manor, tossing his hat in the air as he went.

When Philip Elwood was too far away to overhear them, Ivy pushed her goggles onto her forehead. "So?" she said to Toby. "What do you think?"

"He's lying about something. Maybe about lots of things." Toby was sure of it. He'd been dying to say so to Ivy for the past five minutes. "Did you see him scratch his nose? That's one of the telltale signs of a liar. And he looked over our heads when he talked to us; that's another."

Ivy grinned. "You've read lesson eight of my correspondence course," she said. "Well done, Toby. It's no wonder we hadn't heard of Philip Elwood or his silly old hat. If he were any good at being a detective, he'd know how to tell a fib."

"And he wouldn't have tried to cheat at Mr. Abernathy's contest," Toby pointed out.

Ivy's eyes lit up. "Maybe Mr. Abernathy found Philip snooping, and that's why Philip had to finish him off!"

Toby guessed things could have happened that way, but it didn't seem very likely. He'd caught his cousins cheating at checkers hundreds of times when he'd lived with Aunt Janet, and none of them had ever tried to poison him—at least, not that he knew about. "I don't see how killing Mr. Abernathy would have helped Philip at all," he said. "He wanted to win the contest, not get it canceled."

"Then it was a crime of passion!" said Ivy. "The two of them argued. Mr. Abernathy threatened to tell the world that Philip was useless at investigation, and Philip lost his temper. He ran to Mr. Abernathy's washstand and poisoned the tonic!"

"But that doesn't make sense, either," said Toby. "If Philip hadn't meant to kill Mr. Abernathy all along, why would he have brought poison with him to the manor? Most people don't pack bottles of Brandelburg acid in their luggage just in case they get into a fight."

Ivy frowned. "I bet Julia does."

"But Philip doesn't. He doesn't seem to know much about poisons at all. Besides, bumping off the world's greatest detective isn't something you do without a plan. Don't you think whoever killed Mr. Abernathy must have had the crime all worked out from the beginning?"

"Maybe." Ivy slumped down in her seat. "I still say Philip Elwood is suspicious, though."

"He's definitely not telling us the truth," Toby agreed. "But what about Julia and her tattoo? What about the other detectives, and your parents, and Mr. Peartree? What if they all turn out to be just as suspicious?"

"Everyone's got secrets," Ivy grumbled. "At least Philip was right about that."

"Then we'll uncover those secrets," said Toby, trying to sound more confident than he felt. "We'll keep doing interviews."

"And I'll keep crawling around in pantries and passageways, searching for Mr. Abernathy's silly old files." Ivy pulled off her goggles and unwound her scarves; Toby guessed even Madame Ermintrude was capable of being disheartened. "If only it was as easy to catch a criminal as it was to catch *you*, Toby—you know, with wires and tablecloths and things."

"Hey!" Toby sat up straight.

"Sorry," said Ivy, looking guilty. "I shouldn't have reminded you how easy you are to catch."

But Toby wasn't embarrassed, even though he guessed he should have been. Ivy had just given him the best idea he'd had yet. It was still green and tightly coiled in his mind, but as he looked down toward the crowd of shouting journalists, he could feel the idea beginning to unfurl. "I know what we have to do," he told Ivy. He couldn't believe they hadn't thought of it earlier. "We'll set a trap for the murderer!"

It was a brilliant plan—anyone could see it—but Ivy didn't seem to understand that right away. "With tablecloths?" she asked, wrinkling her nose. "I don't think Mother has any more."

"No, not with tablecloths," said Toby. He was talking faster now, but he couldn't slow down; he was too excited for that. "We'll set a trap with Mr. Abernathy's files."

"Oh, Toby." Ivy threw a scarf at him. "We don't *have* Mr. Abernathy's files!"

Toby grinned. "Exactly."

CHAPTER 15

THE RATTRAP

Before long, every detective at the manor had heard about the article in the *Morning Bugle*, and no one was happy about it. Toby could hear them complaining to each other in the parlor as he made his way downstairs, with Ivy a few steps ahead of him and Percival bringing up the rear. They had spent the last hour sprawled on their stomachs on the floor of the Investigatorium, preparing their trap—"a rattrap," Ivy had clarified, "to catch a sneaky, awful rat"— and now it was time to place the bait.

Ivy stopped near the parlor door, just out of sight of the detectives on the other side. She wasn't Madame Ermintrude anymore; she'd changed into a party dress so fluffy and sweet that anyone who didn't know better might think those words described her, too. "You haven't lost your nerve, have you?" she whispered. "It's all right if you have. I can probably set the trap myself."

"No," Toby said firmly. "It was my idea, remember? And I want to help."

"All right," said Ivy. "Just as long as you're sure."

"Why wouldn't I be sure?" Toby scrambled to keep up with Ivy, who had lifted her chin high in the air and walked into the parlor as though she'd already been named the world's greatest detective. How did she do it? Why couldn't Toby get his own chin to work that way? Maybe he wasn't as confident as Ivy was, or as smart, or brave, or rich, but he was starting to get a little tired of running after her. After all, he was clean, he was polite, and he was just as much of a detective as she was. When Percival nudged the backs of his ankles, he stood up a little straighter. This was his trap, and he was going to be the one to spring it.

"They've claimed my brain is filled with more cobwebs than facts!" Mr. Rackham, accosting Toby with the rolled-up *Morning Bugle*, came perilously close to knocking over one of the Websters' antiques. "Who would say such a thing? Would *you* say I'm a fool, young . . . er, young . . ." He narrowed his eyes.

"It's Toby," Toby reminded him.

"Of course! I know that perfectly well. And that's only one of the facts I've got in my brain."

"I'm sure it is," said Toby as he tried to squeeze by. Ivy was halfway across the room by now, and he was supposed to stay with her.

"For instance"—Mr. Rackham stepped directly in front of Toby, cutting off his only escape route—"I know that none of the servants in this house could have committed the murder. I interviewed them myself, every one of them. Could a witless fool do that?"

He seemed to expect an answer. "Probably not," Toby admitted. "But if you'll excuse me, Mr. Rackham, I've actually got something—"

"Precisely," said Mr. Rackham. "Servants must account for all their movements, you know, and each of them agrees that none of the household staff set foot in the guests' wing of the manor yesterday afternoon. It would have been highly irregular. They're still fond of the old ways at this house. Not like this newspaper journalist, this . . ." He unrolled the *Morning Bugle* and squinted at it. "Peter Jacobson!" he roared, making poor Lillie Webster slosh half her glass of lemonade at the noise. "Who in the world is that? I've never heard of him, so he can't possibly know a thing about me. And he's got no manners at all! I bet he'd sell his own mother if the price was high enough."

Toby felt sorry for Mr. Rackham, but he couldn't even see Ivy anymore. "I've really got to go!" he said. He ducked past Mr. Rackham, who continued complaining loudly to the wallpaper as Toby craned his neck to look for Ivy. Where was she? She hadn't stopped to chat with Miss March or sip lemonade with Lillie, and she certainly hadn't waited for Toby to catch up with her. They were supposed to stick together! Maybe she hadn't realized she'd lost him, Toby reasoned; maybe she'd just assumed he'd stayed behind her as she made her way through the crowd of detectives.

At least Percival was still underfoot. He whined a little, and Toby bent down to pet him. "Don't worry, boy," he said. "We've just got to find Ivy, and then we'll set our trap."

Percival looked doubtful.

From across the room, Ivy's voice rang out even more loudly than Mr. Rackham's. "Oh, Father!" she said, just the way they'd rehearsed it in the Investigatorium. "I'm so glad I've found you. I wanted to tell you about something I overheard this afternoon!"

Now that he could follow the sound of Ivy's voice, it didn't take Toby long to spot her. While he'd been fending off Mr. Rackham, Ivy had managed to pen her father into the far corner of the parlor, between the piano and an armchair, and turned herself slightly toward the rest of the crowd so they'd be sure to hear every word of her conversation. It was all exactly the way they'd planned it—except, of course, that Toby wasn't there with her. He was supposed to be standing on Mr. Webster's other side, not stranded next to the potted plant, trying to see over Miss Price's head. And, more importantly, he was supposed to deliver his lines. Should he squeeze past Miss Price? Shout his part from across the room?

Before he could decide one way or the other, though, Ivy decided for him. She didn't even pause. "I was sitting in the summerhouse this afternoon," she said, reciting the precise words Toby had spent half an hour learning by heart. "I know I'm supposed to be staying out of the way, but I couldn't help listening to those journalists at the gates. They were shouting up at all of us here at the house, and one of them said something that was really shocking!"

Toby tried to make his way around the edge of the parlor, but Mr. Peartree was sitting on the sofa with his long legs stretched out, blocking the way. Percival growled at Mr. Peartree's feet. "Excuse me," Toby whispered, but Mr. Peartree didn't seem to hear him. Everyone in the room had abandoned their own conversations and turned to listen to Ivy.

"You're very loud, my dear," said Mr. Webster. He touched his ear gingerly, as though Ivy was likely to damage it. "And you shouldn't be talking to those people at the gates or listening to anything they have to say. They certainly didn't listen to me when I asked them to go away."

Ivy sighed. "You're supposed to ask me what I heard, Father," she said more quietly. "Wouldn't you like to know what it was?"

"I'd like to," Julia Hartshorn put in.

Ivy beamed at her. "I'll tell you, then. A journalist wants to see Hugh Abernathy's private files. He says his paper will pay awfully well for a look at them, and even more if they're allowed to publish the contents." She did her best to look scandalized, although Toby thought she looked more pleased with herself than anything. Of course she was pleased; she'd laid the trap—*Toby's* trap!—all by herself. He might as well have been back on Detectives' Row, playing checkers with Mrs. Satterthwaite.

Mr. Peartree was looking a little more green than usual. "Perhaps it's fortunate after all that those files have disappeared," he said. "Mr. Abernathy would have hated for his private notes to be turned over to the press."

"Any of us would," said Miss March. "It's simply disrespectful. I'm surprised the man was bold enough to ask."

"No manners!" Mr. Rackham growled.

"You know what journalists are like," said Philip Elwood. "They'll do anything for a story. Did you ask for the fellow's name?"

For a moment, Ivy wobbled. The journalist only existed in Toby's imagination, after all, and they hadn't thought to come up with a convincing name for him. "I certainly didn't," Ivy said finally, putting on her scandalized look again. "You heard what Father said. I'm not allowed to speak to newspaper reporters."

When the others had all returned to talking about their own plans and theories, Ivy kissed her father on the cheek and hurried back across the room, scrambling right over Mr. Peartree's legs without bothering to apologize. "How'd I do?" she whispered, pulling Toby aside. She was bubbling madly, like one of Julia's potions. "Do you think they believed me? Oh, I hope they did. We've set the trap now, anyway, and all we have to do is wait for someone to spring it. I can't wait to see who tries to sneak outside with those files in their arms, can you?"

Toby didn't say anything. He hoped Ivy would stop bubbling before she boiled over and made a mess.

"Toby?" Ivy frowned at him. "What's the matter? Didn't I set the trap well? Aren't you excited?"

Toby couldn't understand it. How could a girl who thought she was the world's greatest detective have such a hard time seeing the things that were right under her nose? "You didn't wait for me!" he said. "You said my lines! You didn't even give me a chance to catch up!"

"Oh." At least Ivy realized that she was supposed to look apologetic. "I'm sorry, Toby, but I thought you were right behind me. Really, I promise I did. By the time I realized you weren't there, I'd already cornered Father, and . . . well, to be honest, I thought you might have lost your nerve."

"I didn't lose it! I told you I wouldn't. But Mr. Rackham

started complaining at me and waving his newspaper, and I couldn't get around him."

"Well, that's silly. Why didn't you just push him aside?"

Toby could feel himself bristling. He wasn't silly, and anyway, he hadn't spent half the day wearing his mother's old motoring goggles. "Because," he said, "that wouldn't have been *polite*."

"Honestly!" said Ivy. "I don't understand you at all, Toby. We've got a real, genuine murder to solve, and you're worried about being polite? Detectives aren't supposed to apologize; they're supposed to act! What if the criminal escapes while you're busy figuring out which fork to use at dinner?"

"Don't be ridiculous," said Toby. "That's definitely not going to happen."

"Oh, really? And why not?"

Toby blushed. "Because I had to memorize which forks to use when I worked at my uncle Francis's hotel."

"I knew it!" Ivy crowed. "I *knew* you were just as horribly well behaved as my perfect sister! Oh, Toby, if you're ever going to be any good as a detective, you can't be so afraid of making trouble now and then. Here; I'll give you a lesson." From the table at the back of the parlor, she picked up the tall glass pitcher of lemonade. Then, before Toby could stop her, she tipped it over.

Lemonade streamed from the pitcher and splashed down

near Toby's feet. It puddled on the floorboards, and its rivulets stretched toward the Websters' expensive-looking carpet, but Ivy didn't even seem to care. "See?" she said. "That's not so awful, is it?"

"Of course it's not awful for you!" said Toby. "Of course you're not afraid of trouble. It doesn't follow you around like it follows me!" Was he the one boiling over now? Well, he couldn't help it; he couldn't stand any more of Ivy's lessons. She didn't know as much about detection as she thought, and she didn't know anything at all about Toby. "When your parents find out you've spilled that lemonade, they're not going to pack up your suitcase and pass you from one relative to the next, are they?"

Ivy went perfectly still. The lemonade kept dripping. "No," she said quietly. "No, they're not. But—"

"I bet you could flood every room in the manor if you wanted," said Toby. "The whole thing could fall down around your ears, and you still wouldn't be sent to an orphanage." He snatched the pitcher from Ivy's hand and set it upright on the table. Then, although all his fingers itched to wipe up the puddle of lemonade, he made himself turn around and walk out of the parlor without looking back. Ivy could clean up the mess for herself.

CHAPTER 16

FRIENDS AND ENEMIES

A pair of moss-colored shoes clicked down the hall toward the Marigold Room, but Toby didn't notice. He was extremely busy being angry with Ivy, and coming up with reasons to be mad at her didn't leave much time to think about anything else. He counted those reasons on his fingers: she was bossy, and thoughtless, and more than a little strange, and—

"Excuse me, Mr. Montrose." There was a knock at the door. "May I come in?"

Toby got up from the orange armchair and opened the door to Mr. Peartree. "Is something wrong, sir?"

"Not at all—at least, nothing aside from the usual." Mr. Peartree stepped into the room and squinted. "Good gracious! What a lot of orange. I don't feel as though I really fit in."

It was true. In most rooms, despite his unusual clothing, Mr. Peartree tended to fade into the background—to become part of the room itself, Toby thought, like a wallpaper pattern or a crack in the ceiling plaster. In the Marigold Room, however, he was as noticeable as a caterpillar on a pumpkin, and he settled himself in Toby's armchair as though he intended to stay awhile. "Can I help you, sir?" Toby asked.

"As a matter of fact," said Mr. Peartree, "I was wondering if *I* might be able to help *you*. I couldn't help noticing that you tore out of the parlor as though all the hounds of the hunt were after you, and I thought I'd come see if everything was all right." He took off his green gloves and tucked them into his pocket. "If you don't mind my making a deduction, I suspect that you and Miss Ivy might be doing a little sleuthing of your own. You haven't learned something . . . unpleasant, have you?"

"No, sir; it's nothing like that." Since Mr. Peartree had taken the only chair in the room, Toby sat cross-legged at the end of the bed. "We haven't learned much of anything, actually. I don't think we're even working together anymore." Ivy hadn't followed him out of the parlor, and she certainly hadn't come to apologize, so as far as Toby could tell, Webster and Montrose, Private Investigators were officially out of business. He wished he felt happier about it.

"Ah," said Mr. Peartree. "There's been trouble with Miss Ivy?"

That was one way of putting it. "She's impossible!"

"Most detectives are," Mr. Peartree agreed. "Hugh Abernathy certainly was. No one else on the Row could stand to work with him. It was convenient, actually, because he couldn't stand to work with any of *them*."

"Except for you," said Toby.

Mr. Peartree shrugged. "I, Mr. Montrose, am not a detective. I was only Mr. Abernathy's assistant. It was Hugh who made the plans, and Hugh who solved the cases. I merely wrote about them."

"Didn't that bother you?" Toby asked. "Didn't you want to become a detective, too?"

"Heavens, no." Mr. Peartree looked mildly horrified. "I hope I never gave anyone that impression. I'm sure some people think I was jealous of Hugh, but I've always been more content to stay behind the scenes. Besides, I'm fairly hopeless when it comes to detecting. If I'd gone off and tried to start my own investigative business, I'd have lasted a week at most. And anyway, I wasn't interested. As I've been reminded this weekend, I find writing about murder far more enjoyable than experiencing it firsthand." Mr. Peartree shrugged. "Hugh could be difficult, but we were good friends, and I'm immensely sorry he's gone."

Out of all the people at the manor, Toby realized, Mr. Peartree was the only one who'd known Mr. Abernathy well, and the only one who seemed truly upset. Losing a friend didn't make Mr. Peartree an orphan, exactly, but maybe it didn't feel all that different. "What will you do now?" Toby asked.

"Retire, I suppose." Mr. Peartree examined the dirt underneath his fingernails. "Go abroad to the south of Gallis, where no one knows me and I can sit by the ocean in peace. I'll have to wrap up Hugh's affairs—sell the house, move out of the Row. I don't suppose there's another detective here who'll want a secondhand biographer."

Toby wondered what Uncle Gabriel would think of having his most recent investigations written up in the *Sphinx Monthly Reader*. Not even Mr. Peartree was talented enough to turn the case of Mrs. Lee's lost jewels (found behind her dressing table) or the case of Mr. Sergi's midnight visitors (a family of barn owls) into a really thrilling tale. And Uncle Gabriel would have been horrified by the idea; he would have marched through the house in his dressing gown, waving his spatula and shouting about that puffed-up old ostrich's assistant. "Mr. Peartree," said Toby, "I was wondering—is it true that Mr. Abernathy and my uncle used to work together?"

Mr. Peartree looked up. "Where did you hear that?"

"From Julia Hartshorn," said Toby, "and from Philip

Elwood. I think everyone knows about it, sir, except for me."

"Well, it was a long time ago," said Mr. Peartree, "before I came to Detectives' Row. Hugh didn't like to talk much about it, but if I remember correctly, he and your uncle were school friends. When they were old enough, they opened an agency together—Montrose and Abernathy, it was called. For a while, they were quite successful."

"But they fought," said Toby.

"It's just as I said before, Mr. Montrose: detectives are impossible. Your uncle and Hugh couldn't stand to share the spotlight; they each wanted all the fame and fortune for themselves. Still, they managed well enough until Lord Entwhistle recruited them to track down the Colebridge Cutthroat."

Toby sat up straight. "Uncle Gabriel didn't have anything to do with that case. Hugh Abernathy solved it alone. That's how he became famous!"

Mr. Peartree shook his head. "Your uncle was there, too, Toby, though not many people know it. When Mr. Abernathy hired me to write that first story for the *Sphinx*, he asked me to leave Gabriel Montrose out of it, for Gabriel's own sake."

"What do you mean?" said Toby. "Did Uncle Gabriel do something wrong?"

Mr. Peartree considered his words. "I wasn't there that night," he said at last, "but I've been told that your uncle's jealousy nearly cost Lord Entwhistle his life. Montrose and Abernathy were supposed to be guarding Entwhistle House, but Gabriel thought that Hugh was trying to take over the case, and he started an argument about it. I believe he even punched Hugh in the nose."

"I've heard about that part," said Toby. It wasn't hard for him to imagine how the argument had gone. He wondered if Mr. Abernathy had been anything like Ivy, always eager to take charge and give orders. And he wondered if Uncle Gabriel had once been anything like Toby himself, small and nervous and always tagging along. This seemed to be so exactly the opposite of Uncle Gabriel's personality that Toby almost laughed—but then again, Mr. Peartree had said it all happened a long time ago.

"In any event," said Mr. Peartree, "the two men were so distracted by their own disagreements that they didn't notice the Cutthroat sneaking into Entwhistle House. If Mr. Abernathy hadn't realized their mistake and run to the rescue, all three men might have been killed on the spot."

Toby cringed. No wonder Uncle Gabriel had never mentioned his role in the case. If anyone else had found out the truth of the matter, his career would have been ruined. "Uncle Gabriel must have felt awful," Toby said.

"I'm sure he did," said Mr. Peartree. "Lord Entwhistle was furious with both detectives. The next day, Hugh dismissed Gabriel from their partnership. He didn't have a choice in the matter, you understand, but Gabriel took it badly."

"He still hates Mr. Abernathy," Toby said. "I don't think he ever got over their argument."

"Perhaps not." Mr. Peartree paused and studied Toby's face. "Since we're speaking of your uncle, I hope you won't mind if I ask you a question about him. Is he training you properly?"

"To be a detective?" Toby shrugged. "I'm in charge of answering the door, taking clients' coats, and getting tea for them if they want it. I dust Uncle Gabriel's desk twice a month and organize his files on Tuesdays and Thursdays."

"Hmm," said Mr. Peartree.

"They need a lot of organizing."

"Well, if that's what makes you happy, Mr. Montrose, then *I* am happy for *you*." Mr. Peartree pulled his gloves back on and got up from the armchair. "Enough about your uncle. I'm very sorry to hear about your spat with Miss Ivy, and I'm sure you'll go on to do remarkable things, with or without her. But I hope you'll feel comfortable coming to me if you have any more trouble. I know more than a little about dealing with difficult detectives."

"Thank you, sir," said Toby. He remembered how Mr. Abernathy had smashed Mr. Peartree's pocket watch against the floor, and how Mr. Peartree had only sighed. That, Toby thought, was the sort of detail you never read about in any of the Hugh Abernathy stories. In fact, it reminded him of something he'd been wondering about earlier, before the rattrap and the lemonade and the fight. "Mr. Peartree?" he said. "Could you tell me something about Mr. Abernathy?"

"Certainly."

"Did he have any secrets?"

Mr. Peartree paused in the doorway. There was a soft tapping sound as he drummed his green-gloved fingers on the doorknob. "I'm sure he must have," he said at last, "and I knew him better than anyone, but even I can't tell you what his secrets might have been. I'm afraid only the world's greatest detective could possibly tell you that."

CHAPTER 17

THE NIGHT WATCH

Night had settled over Coleford Manor. Outside the house, murder tourists yawned and turned toward home, while the hardiest journalists crawled inside tents they'd pitched and tried to scribble by firelight. Inside the house, servants lit the lamps and drew the curtains, and all the detectives trudged away to sleep, still muttering theories about poisons and blackmail and escaped convicts. "Only one day left before the coppers take over," Mr. Rackham said on his way up the stairs. "Heaven knows we'll need all the time we've got left."

No one had gone out of the manor all afternoon, with Mr. Abernathy's stolen files or without them. That made sense, though: if Toby had been a criminal, he wouldn't have wanted to risk being spotted by taking the papers outside in the daylight. He would have waited until the household had gone to bed, until he was the only one awake in the huge old house, with its echoing corridors and ancient beams that made him jump every time they creaked. Even Percival had fallen asleep on the hallway rug.

Toby didn't know whether Ivy was awake, and he told himself he didn't care. He'd hardly even seen her since he'd stormed out of the parlor. He'd spent the rest of the day trying to do as much detecting as he could without her help, but it hadn't exactly been easy. When he'd attempted to interrogate Miss Price and Miss March, they'd dragged him into a long and tangled skein of gossip instead: Lillie Webster had been humming cheerfully on the staircase that morning; did Toby think she was likely to be in love? Had Toby heard how Mr. Peartree had shouted at poor little Percival when the dog had tugged on the laces of his moss-colored shoes? And wasn't Julia Hartshorn looking ill this afternoon, as though her lunch had turned her stomach? Was Toby feeling all right? What had he been doing that day? By the time he escaped from the white-carpeted Daisy Room, Toby hadn't learned a single thing about the murder, but Miss March and Miss Price had learned practically everything there was to know about Toby. He wished he knew how they'd done it. At least he'd avoided telling them about the trap.

Julia Hartshorn didn't look all that ill to Toby, but she had been acting strange. She'd spent the afternoon rummaging through the manor's cupboards and storerooms for anything that might contain Brandelburg acid, but she kept stepping out of rooms whenever Toby stepped into them, and he'd seen her three different times in the conservatory, staring out the window at the crowd beyond the gates. Was she planning to meet someone? Was she trying to escape? Toby still hadn't managed to find out.

He also hadn't managed to interview Mr. Rackham, but this wasn't entirely his fault, since Mr. Rackham had disappeared for most of the afternoon. He'd set off to search the farthest reaches of the manor, and everyone had been worried when he hadn't returned by the dressing gong. Mrs. Webster finally found him half an hour later, pacing back and forth in one of the attics. "Got turned around pretty badly up there," Mr. Rackham had explained as he brushed the cobwebs from his clothes. "I blame the builders. There's no good reason at all to construct a house with so many rooms! Only three things live in attics like those: bats, ghosts, and murderers." After hearing this, Lillie had announced that she wouldn't go up to the attics ever again, and Ivy had tormented her by making ghostly noises all through dinner. They'd been awfully funny noises, actually, and Toby had tried hard not to laugh.

Now, in the darkness, the idea of ghosts didn't seem

214

quite so funny. Toby hadn't been frightened of the dark since he was small, and of course he knew ghosts weren't real, but what was making the pipes clang in the ceilings? Why had a floorboard creaked in the empty hall? Had those been footsteps? He'd probably only imagined them. Still, crouched near the long, heavy curtains, with a draft from the conservatory window prickling his neck, Toby couldn't help realizing the truth: he was entirely alone in a strange house at midnight, looking out for a murderer. He hadn't even thought to bring along a weapon to defend himself. Would the person who'd killed Mr. Abernathy hesitate to kill Toby, too? If he wasn't extremely careful, *he* was going to end up as the ghost of Coleford Manor.

That was when the howling began.

It started low and grew louder: a thin, unearthly noise, the sound of loneliness and danger, of empty moors and people lost at sea. It echoed in Toby's bones; it seeped into his heart. He knew he was supposed to stay quiet, and he tried as hard as he could, but there was no way to avoid it: he started to scream.

Then a black-clad arm reached out from the shadows, and a black-gloved hand clamped over his mouth.

"Toby!" said Ivy. "Hush! Do you want the murderer to hear you?"

"Mmph," said Toby. It was hard to say anything at all through the glove.

"Don't worry; *I'm* not the murderer." Ivy pulled her hand away from his mouth. "It's me! Ivy!"

"I *know*," said Toby. Now that his eyes had adjusted to the darkness, he could see her more clearly. She was dressed all in black, with her hair tied back and a mask over her eyes, as though she were auditioning for the role of a burglar in a country play.

"Why did you scream?" Ivy asked. "Did I frighten you?"

Toby glared at her. "You didn't have to howl like that."

"Howl?" Toby couldn't see Ivy's face very well in the darkness, but she sounded genuinely confused. "Oh! You must have heard Percival. He's a wolf in his dreams, you know. He once frightened Cook so badly that she locked herself in the linen cupboard and refused to come out until morning."

Toby was glad Ivy couldn't tell exactly how mortified he looked. What sort of detective was frightened of small brown dogs? Now Ivy would tease him the way she'd teased Lillie. "Could you stand somewhere else, please, Inspector Webster?" he said before she could start. "I'm trying to look out for a murderer, and you're blocking my view."

Ivy drew back as though she'd stepped on a snake. "Well, all right, then. I'm looking out for a murderer, too, as it happens, but I'll do it over here." She stalked over to the opposite side of the window and sat down on the floor. "How's your view now, Detective?"

"Wonderful," said Toby through his teeth.

"I suppose you learned a lot during your investigations this afternoon."

"Heaps," Toby agreed.

"And you didn't need any help?"

"That's right," said Toby.

"Good," said Ivy. "I didn't, either."

The room was horribly quiet.

"Toby?" Ivy whispered after a while. "Are we still partners?"

Toby hugged his knees to his chest. "I don't think so."

"Oh," said Ivy. "Are we still friends?"

Toby hadn't thought about this. Ever since he'd left the farmhouse, he hadn't lived in one place long enough to have friends—not real ones, the kind you laughed and ran wild with and trusted with your most important secrets. He wasn't even sure he remembered how to make them. "I don't know," he told her.

"All right." Ivy leaned forward and rested her chin in her hands. They sat like that for a very long time, Toby at one end of the window and Ivy at the other, with the whole night stretched out between them. Sometimes, in the darkness, Percival howled.

"If we'd been friends," Ivy said eventually, "Mother would have been happy. She worries about me. She says I spend too much time by myself, even though half the time

I'm with Percival and the rest of the time I'm with Egbert—but that's not the sort of company that makes Mother feel any better. I know because I overheard her and Father talking once, when I was practicing my eavesdropping technique. 'I never worry one bit about Lillie,' Mother was saying, 'but Ivy is such an unusual child. There are times when she's a complete mystery to me.' Then Father agreed with her—and you know how awful they both are at solving mysteries."

Ivy's chin wasn't pointed toward the ceiling any longer, and her confident air seemed as thin and flimsy as one of Madame Ermintrude's scarves. How hadn't Toby noticed it earlier? He'd spent all day trying to dig up people's secrets, but he'd never even thought of uncovering Ivy's. "What did you do after that?" he asked.

"I tried to be more like Lillie and less like myself, of course, but it didn't stick. Not the piano lessons, not the charity work, and definitely not the manners." Ivy pulled off the burglar's mask and tossed it onto the rug. "I've got fifty different costumes in the Investigatorium, but none of them turns me into a girl who fits this family. You were right that Mother and Father would never send me away; they do love me, and I don't have any idea what it's like to lose your parents. But I know what it's like to feel that you don't quite belong anyplace, and that's what I wanted to tell you, although I don't think I've done it very well." Ivy squirmed. "And I'm sorry I called you well behaved."

"I didn't mind that part so much," Toby admitted. "I *am* well behaved."

"Well, it's not your fault." Ivy sounded like she might be smiling. "We can't help who we are."

Somewhere, not so very far away, something creaked.

Toby froze. "Did you hear that?" Ivy whispered.

Toby nodded. "I hope it's not ghosts again."

"It's the squeaky floorboard on the front stairs," Ivy said. "If our criminal had ever tried to raid the pantry for midnight snacks, he'd have known to step over it."

"We don't know yet that it's a criminal," Toby whispered. "Maybe it's someone who walks in their sleep, or—"

"Shh!" said Ivy. "Listen."

Soft footsteps hurried down the hall, and a tall, thin shadow passed the conservatory door. For all Toby could make out in the darkness, it might have been anyone. His heart felt as though it might spring out of his chest at any moment. Had that shadow been the person who had killed Mr. Abernathy?

A door squealed open farther down the hall, and Ivy held up a hand in warning. Then there was a scrabbling sound, like someone fumbling with a window sash, and Toby knew that the rat had sprung its trap.

"Come on!" Ivy whispered, but Toby was already half-way to the door. They ran down the hall, looking into each room they passed along the way. The dining room was empty and undisturbed. So was the music room. But in the front parlor, a breeze billowed the drapery, and the moonlight illuminated a figure with a sheaf of papers clutched to his chest and one foot already out the window.

"I knew it!" Ivy shouted.

Philip Elwood froze. He put his foot back down on the floor. He looked at Toby and Ivy.

Then he dropped the papers and ran.

CHAPTER 18

ANSWERS AND QUESTIONS

Philip Elwood was out the back door of the parlor before Toby and Ivy had a chance to blink. They tore after him across the ground floor of the manor, startling Percival awake and making Mrs. Webster's ancient artifacts quiver.

"He's too fast!" said Toby. "We'll never catch up to him!"

"Don't worry," Ivy said. "This is the perfect time to follow lesson eighty-three of Inspector Webster's correspondence course."

"Lesson eighty-three?" Toby's elbow collided with the dressing gong as they ran past it, and the boom echoed through the manor.

"Yes," said Ivy. "'Three Rules for Pursuing a Criminal on Foot.'"

"I don't think I've seen that lesson yet."

"Of course you haven't!" said Ivy as they skidded through the kitchen doorway. "It doesn't exist!"

Philip had stopped to catch his breath in the kitchen, but when he saw Toby and Ivy, he pushed over a shelf and sent stockpots and saucepans crashing into their path. Toby ducked as an eggbeater flew over his head. "It doesn't *exist*?" he shouted.

"I mean that I haven't written it yet," said Ivy. "I know what the rules are, though. They're very helpful." She counted on her fingers. "One: run as fast as you can. Two: don't lose sight of the suspect."

"We're doing both those things already," said Toby, clearing a path through the pots and pans, "but I don't think they're helping."

"And three," said Ivy, "control the route. Force your suspect to run to a place where he can't get away."

Philip was fumbling with the locks on the servants' entrance to the manor now, but he couldn't seem to get the door unstuck. Ivy ran toward him, brandishing a rolling pin she'd grabbed from the kitchen counter. "Halt, villain!" she shouted, sounding very much like a hero from a story in the *Sphinx*. In any case, Philip didn't halt. He pushed Ivy aside and made a break for the servants' stairs. Ivy swung her rolling pin in his direction, but she only clipped his knee; he winced and kept running.

Toby had been thinking about Inspector Webster's third rule of pursuing a criminal on foot. "We've got to get him up to the third floor," he told Ivy, "and make sure he heads toward the Investigatorium."

"The Investigatorium?" Ivy frowned. "Oh! Of course!" She crashed up the staircase after Philip. "I wouldn't try the second-floor landing if I were you, Mr. Elwood!" she shouted. "That whole hallway is full of detectives. If you wake them up, they'll catch you in a second!"

Philip must have realized she was right, because he ran straight past the door that led to the second-floor hallway. Toby took the stairs two at a time behind him. When they reached the third-floor landing, Philip darted into the hallway and stopped for a moment, looking around. It was too dark to see much of anything, but Toby knew that the Investigatorium was to his right. To his left were the attic rooms—the ones full of bats and ghosts, where Mr. Rackham had gotten lost and a murderer would feel right at home. They absolutely couldn't let Philip turn left.

Toby and Ivy burst out of the stairwell, blocking the left side of the hallway. "Well, Mr. Elwood?" said Ivy. "Aren't you going to keep running?"

"Or would you like to stay here and confess?" Toby asked.

Philip drew in his breath, wiped the sweat from his brow, and ran in the only direction he could.

"One . . . ," counted Ivy under her breath. "Two . . . three!"

At the far end of the hall, there was a wiry twang, a dull thud, and the sound of a tablecloth landing on someone's head.

"That," said Ivy happily, "is how you trap a rat."

No one had slept through the commotion. In a matter of minutes, the other detectives had all gathered around Philip in their robes and slippers. "You say he's the murderer, dears?" Miss Price asked, shining her lantern in Philip's face. "Are you entirely sure?"

Philip groaned and pulled the tablecloth around him like a blanket. "I've told you already, I'm not a murderer. The children are pretending to be detectives, and they've let their imaginations run away with them. They've also bruised my left kneecap and nearly broken my neck."

"Really?" Miss March looked impressed. "How bloodthirsty of them."

"We wouldn't have hurt Philip if he weren't a criminal," said Toby. "Ivy and I caught him sneaking out a window with Mr. Abernathy's files. When he saw us, he tried to run away. Why would he run if he weren't guilty?"

"An excellent question," said Mr. Rackham. "I myself take great care never to run. The world moves too quickly as it is."

Julia was shining her own lantern up and down the

hallway. "Toby," she said, "where are Mr. Abernathy's files now? I don't see them anywhere."

"Philip dropped them in the parlor," said Toby. He'd been itching to go downstairs and retrieve them, but there hadn't been any time. "I'll get them now."

"No, you won't," said Julia firmly. "Stay here and watch Philip, please. I'll find the files."

"And I shall come with you," said Mr. Rackham. "It would be unfortunate if those files happened to wander away under your watch, Miss Hartshorn."

Julia glared at Mr. Rackham, but she didn't protest as he followed her down the stairs.

Ivy leaned against the Investigatorium door, studying Miss March and Miss Price. "Don't you both want to get a look at Mr. Abernathy's papers, too?"

"They're not Mr. Abernathy's papers," Philip said mildly.

"Whether they are or they aren't," Miss March said to Ivy, "Flossie and I shall find out what's in them soon enough."

Miss Price nodded. "There's no point in exhausting oneself by running up and down staircases at two o'clock in the morning," she said. "I have to say, Philip, that table-cloth suits you. You must wear it more often."

While Miss March and Miss Price poked at Philip's bruises and prodded his excuses, Ivy nudged Toby in the ribs. "Do you realize what this means?" she said. "We caught the murderer! We're the world's greatest detectives! We'll be rich and famous, and you won't have to go to the orphanage! Isn't it wonderful? Wherever criminals lurk, Webster and Montrose will track them down!" She froze. "I mean, unless you don't want to. I know you'd rather not be partners anymore, and you probably don't need my help."

"But I do need your help!" said Toby. It was a relief to admit it. Being Ivy's enemy all afternoon had been exhausting, especially when he would have much rather been her friend. "I had an awful time trying to investigate the murder alone, actually. I didn't learn anything at all."

"Really?" said Ivy. "Oh, Toby, thank goodness! I didn't learn anything, either. I felt so guilty about making you upset that I couldn't do an ounce of detecting. I never would have caught Mr. Elwood by myself."

"Neither would I," said Toby. "I would have been too busy apologizing to him as he squeezed out the window."

"Maybe." Ivy grinned at him. "Can you forgive me for being so thoughtless? You can set all our traps from now on, and I'll get you some disguises, and your very own skeleton—I'm sure Doctor Piper must have another stashed away somewhere—and you can be polite whenever you'd like to, or rude if you'd rather be that." She took hold of both Toby's hands. "What do you say? Can we be partners again?"

Toby hesitated.

"Do you not want a skeleton?" Ivy's face fell. "I was afraid that might have been too much."

"It's not that," said Toby. "Of course I want to be partners again. But Mr. Peartree says detectives are impossible, and they hardly ever get along. We're always arguing, Ivy. What if we really start to hate each other someday? What if I punch you in the nose?"

Ivy shrugged. "Warn me first," she said, "so I can duck."

Julia appeared at the top of the stairs, followed by Mr. Rackham, Mr. Peartree, and the rest of Ivy's family. "Stay back, my dears," Mr. Webster said grandly. He put his arm around Lillie, who'd gone pale in the lantern light. "That man is a murderer, and you mustn't go anywhere near him."

"Don't be nonsensical, Robert!" said Mrs. Webster. "He's not likely to slay anyone right here in the hallway." She gazed down at Philip. "Besides, he's wearing my table linens. How murderous can he be?"

"I'm not murderous at all," said Philip.

"Yes, he is," Ivy said fiercely.

"He's not!" said Lillie. "He can't be!"

"May I get a word in edgewise?" said Julia. She held up a sheaf of papers in her hand. "Mr. Rackham and I found these on the parlor floor. They were just where Toby and Ivy told us they'd be."

"Ha!" said Ivy. "You see, Lill? Those are Mr. Abernathy's missing case files."

"Actually," said Julia, "they're not."

The back of Toby's neck began to prickle, and he thought he heard the trouble snickering in the shadows. "That can't be right," he said. "They've got to be Mr. Abernathy's files. What else would anyone want to run off with?"

"Love letters!" said Miss Price. "Or valuable maps, perhaps, or government secrets, or blackmail. . . ."

"Well, it's nothing as exciting as all that," said Julia, "but I can certainly see why Mr. Elwood didn't want to be caught with these papers." She cast the light from her lantern over the pages. "'Hugh Abernathy,'" she read aloud, "'was a man with intelligence to spare and an ego to match. He kept his secrets as well as his grudges, inspiring fear in his enemies and devotion in his admirers. In short, he was a legend.'"

Mr. Peartree dabbed at his eyes with the sleeve of his green pajamas. "It's true," he said. "Every word of it."

Julia ignored him. "'The same,'" she read, "'cannot be said of the idle blatherers, unimaginative bores, and hapless children who are attempting to take Mr. Abernathy's place as the world's greatest detective. As the investigation at Coleford Manor stretches into its third day, we continue to reveal the upsetting truth about the state of modern detection and the questionable talents of the men and women who practice it.'" Julia stopped reading. "If we'd only waited a few hours longer," she said, "we would have seen this charming story on the front page of the *Morning Bugle*. Isn't that right, Peter Jacobson?"

"Jacobson?" Mr. Rackham looked bewildered. "There's no one here named Jacobson. Jacobson is a reporter!"

"So *that's* who you are." Miss Price bent down to look Philip Elwood—or Peter Jacobson, Toby supposed—in the eye. "I do wish you'd told us earlier. We all could have saved ourselves a good deal of exercise."

Mr. Peartree raised his hand. "Excuse me, Miss Price. Do you mean to say that this gentleman isn't actually a detective?"

"That's right, dear." Miss Price beamed at him. "I'm sorry Anthea and I didn't say anything about it, but we didn't see the harm in keeping a few little facts to ourselves."

"We've met the real Philip Elwood, you see," Miss March explained. "We ran into him last year when we vacationed in Gyptos. This man looks nothing like him, except for that ridiculous hat he favors." She frowned at Peter Jacobson, who cringed under the tablecloth. "I wondered if you'd written that newspaper report we were all forced to digest this morning. If I'd known for sure, I wouldn't have kept my mouth shut. What do you have to say for yourself?"

"You don't all need to glare at me like that," said Peter. The bruise he'd gotten from Ivy's rolling pin must have still been bothering him, since Toby saw him wince as he got to his feet. "It's true that I'm a reporter, but I didn't murder anyone, and I certainly don't plan to in the future."

"You'll only kill our careers, then?" asked Julia. "How kind of you."

"It's not my job to be kind, Miss Hartshorn," Peter said. "I came here to report on Mr. Abernathy's competition. The whole city's been dying to know what he'd planned for this weekend, and when a friend of mine offered to help me get inside the manor during the contest, how could I resist? I knew all the other papers would have reporters clamoring on the other side of the gate, and I'd be right here on the spot! I didn't know Mr. Abernathy would get himself murdered, of course."

"But you had no concerns about reporting the news when he did," said Miss March.

"Why should I?" said Peter. "Doesn't everyone deserve to know the truth?"

"*Truth*," said Miss Price, "is rather a generous word for it."

"Excuse me, everyone." Mr. Peartree raised his hand again. "If this man is an impostor, then where in the world is the real Philip Elwood?"

"Still chasing after criminals on the Continent, I assume." Peter shrugged. "Once my friend told me about the contest, I called in a favor with a postal worker I know, and he got ahold of Mr. Elwood's invitation. The real Philip has no idea what he's missing. I assumed I'd be caught out by one of you as soon as I set foot on the manor grounds, but I was delighted to learn that almost no one in this house had met Philip Elwood before! Even Hugh Abernathy had never laid eyes on the man."

"I hope he's a better detective than you are," said Ivy. "You're just awful."

"Ivy!" said her mother. She sounded rather halfhearted about it, though.

"Is that why you wanted to know about Uncle Gabriel?" asked Toby. "Were you writing about him for one of your articles?"

Peter nodded. "I've been working on a story about Mr. Abernathy's early life. A tribute, you might say. It's at the bottom of that stack Miss Hartshorn is holding on to. I was on my way to deliver today's work to my newspaper colleagues on the other side of the gate when you and Ivy startled me. Be careful with that story, please, Miss Hartshorn; I spent half the night polishing it."

"Really?" Julia smiled. "It won't take me anywhere near that long to rip it up."

Peter groaned.

"I'll keep it safe for the moment, though," Julia told him. "As far as I'm concerned, these papers might still be evidence."

"That's right!" said Mr. Rackham. "Nothing this fellow

231

has said proves that he's innocent of murder. In fact, his story makes him more suspicious than ever."

"Yes!" said Ivy. "What if Mr. Abernathy found out Peter's true identity, and Peter poisoned him to keep it secret? Or what if he committed the murder to make his newspaper stories more exciting?"

"*Ivy!*" her mother said again.

"But, Mother, Miss Hartshorn said she saw Peter poking around near Mr. Abernathy's room on Friday afternoon! And Toby and I saw him acting suspicious, too." Ivy crossed her arms. "Can anyone here prove that Peter Jacobson isn't a murderer?"

Miss March looked at Miss Price, Miss Price looked at Julia, Julia looked at Mr. Rackham, Mr. Rackham looked at Ivy's parents, Ivy's parents looked at Mr. Peartree, and Mr. Peartree looked right back at them. Toby and Ivy both stared at Peter, but his eyes were fixed on someone else.

"That's enough!" Lillie Webster squirmed free from her father's arms and ran to Peter's side. "You may think you're as clever as the grown-up detectives, Ivy, but you're not. I know Peter didn't poison Mr. Abernathy. He couldn't have done it! I was with him all afternoon on Friday."

"You were with *him*?" Ivy wrinkled her nose. "For goodness' sake, Lillie, *why*?"

"Um, Ivy," Toby whispered. "Remember how Peter told us there was a girl he wanted to marry?" Lillie had grabbed Peter's hand now, and for once she looked even fiercer than Ivy, as though she might burn Coleford Manor to the ground and stomp across the flaming fields in her nightgown. "I think Lillie might be that girl."

"I am," Lillie said grandly, "and you might as well all know it. I'm sick of keeping secrets, and I won't keep one that sends Peter to prison."

Maybe the attic ghosts were real after all, Toby thought, because Mrs. Webster looked as if she'd seen one. "Married?" she said. "But you don't even know this man. He's an utter stranger!"

"And he's a *journalist*!" Mr. Webster sounded so appalled that Toby wondered if he might take a rolling pin to Peter Jacobson's knees himself.

Ivy, on the other hand, was practically bouncing with glee. "Oh, Lillie," she said, "you do have secrets after all! Awful ones!"

"Peter's not a stranger, Mother," Lillie said. "I met him last year when I went into town for my music lessons, and we've become friends. He's a very talented reporter, but he doesn't get the recognition he should, and when you and Father told us about Mr. Abernathy's competition, I gave Peter the news right away, before any of the other papers could beat him to it. It seemed like the perfect chance for him to make a name for himself. We decided that Peter would pose as one of the detectives, and if he could get away with it, I'd help him gather facts for his articles."

"That's what we were doing on Friday," said Peter, "while the rest of you were playing badminton. Lillie let me into the guest bedrooms, and I tried to learn as much as I could about each of you."

Mr. Peartree's eyebrows shot up. "You went through our private things?"

"I only took a quick look, I swear! I didn't even make it into all of the rooms. Miss Hartshorn came along as we were trying to get into Mr. Abernathy's; she scared us half to death. Lillie had the presence of mind to hide, but I wasn't nearly as quick. We gave up on breaking and entering after that. Lillie listened at doorways for me and told me what she'd heard, but since we couldn't let on that we knew each other, we had to meet in the broom cupboard to make our plans."

Lillie blushed violently.

"A mop and a dustpan," Mrs. Webster said sternly, "are hardly suitable chaperones. What if someone had caught you? What in the world would they have thought?"

"Toby and I *did* catch them," Ivy said. It didn't seem to make her mother any happier. "Well, we caught Peter coming out of the broom cupboard, at least. We must have just missed Lillie."

"I was sure you two knew what we were up to," Lillie said. "I'd knocked over that awful bottle of brown hair tonic in the cupboard and ruined my dress. When you found me washing it out, and then you asked if I knew where Peter was, I was so nervous that I thought my heart would stop beating."

"Hair tonic in a broom cupboard?" Miss Price murmured. "How odd!"

"It's not half as odd as my daughter's behavior." Mr. Webster looked thunderous. "We never should have given Lillie those music lessons, Amina. Just look what that infernal piano has done to her!"

"All of this is beside the point," Mr. Peartree said briskly. "Ruined dresses and secret betrothals might make for an entertaining story, but they don't tell us whether this man poisoned Mr. Abernathy."

"That's true," said Mr. Rackham. "What we need to hear is an alibi. Miss Webster, do you swear you didn't leave Mr. Jacobson's company from noon to five o'clock on Friday?"

"I do," Lillie said solemnly.

"And I swear the same for Lillie," said Peter. "We never left each other's sight, and I hope we never will again." He unburdened himself of Mrs. Webster's tablecloth and tucked it gallantly around Lillie's shoulders.

Ivy buried her face in her hands. "I can't bear to watch," she whispered to Toby. "It's too revolting."

"I suppose that settles it," said Julia as the clock chimed

three. "Philip Elwood isn't Philip Elwood after all, but he's not likely to be a murderer, either." She sounded awfully disappointed about it.

Mr. Rackham was disappointed, too. "The next time you're tempted to drag us all out of bed," he said to Toby, "please make sure that you've caught the right criminal first. The rest of us have a lot of important work to do, and we can't afford to waste any more time on mere hunches."

"Yes, sir," Toby mumbled. "Sorry, sir."

Julia and Mr. Peartree marched Peter Jacobson back to his bedroom with strict orders not to let him out until morning. The Websters did the same with Lillie, and the other detectives drifted back to their own rooms, leaving Toby and Ivy alone in the deserted hallway. "So much for our trap," said Toby. "All we caught was a fake detective, and we still don't have Mr. Abernathy's papers."

"Cheer up!" said Ivy. "For once, I'm the golden Webster daughter! And at least we know Peter didn't poison anyone. That's more information than we had before, isn't it?"

It was, but Toby didn't see how it could possibly be enough. "We only have one day left before your parents let the police in," he said. "We've got too many suspects and not enough clues, and we still don't know why anyone here would have wanted to kill Mr. Abernathy."

"We'll stay up the rest of the night, then," said Ivy,

stifling a yawn. "We'll wait for the real criminal to spring our trap."

"It's no use," said Toby. "The whole house is awake now. No one else is going to sneak outside tonight."

"Then we'll come up with a new plan in the morning," said Ivy. "A better plan. The sort of plan Hugh Abernathy would make." She picked up the lantern Miss Price had left in the hallway and began to make her way down the stairs. "You'll see, Toby. Things are bound to improve soon."

Toby hurried after her before the light from her lantern got swallowed up in the shadows. No matter how close he stayed to Ivy, though, he could feel the trouble nipping at his ankles. It was quick, it was hungry, and Toby was almost sure it was growing.

PART IV

INTO THE MAZE

CHAPTER 19

THE VANISHING CORPSE

The front page of Sunday's *Morning Bugle* stared defiantly at the detectives from its place on the breakfast table. The detectives stared back. They could do nothing else.

ABERNATHY BODY DISAPPEARS! the headline screamed. *MEDICAL EXPERTS BAFFLED! DETECTIVES MYSTIFIED!*

"They've finally got one thing right," said Miss Price, peering over her marmalade-heaped toast. "We are all mystified, aren't we, dears?"

"It can't be possible," said Julia. "I refuse to believe it. That man was completely dead! We all saw him; I checked his pulse myself."

"Lying on a table in the mortuary sounds deathly dull to me," Miss Price said. "I'm sure Mr. Abernathy thought so, too. What if he picked himself up and strolled away? Is that the sort of thing your late employer might do, Mr. Peartree?"

"I don't know!" Mr. Peartree's hands were trembling, and half the cream he'd intended for his coffee poured into his lap instead. "Mr. Abernathy has never been dead before! This whole situation is outside my area of expertise."

"It's well within mine," Julia told him, "and I can promise you that even the world's greatest detective can't bring himself back to life."

Toby knew Julia was right, but he couldn't help feeling that Hugh Abernathy was exactly the sort of person who wouldn't let mere death stand in the way of his adventures. Even Doctor Piper didn't have a better explanation for the corpse's disappearance. She'd told the newspaper that she'd delivered Mr. Abernathy to the county mortuary herself and locked the doors behind her before going to fetch the medical examiner. When she returned with the examiner an hour later, the doors were still locked, but the body was nowhere to be found.

"I bet it was thieves," Ivy said darkly. "Mr. Abernathy's got to have the most valuable bones in Colebridge. Whoever stole him will chop him up and sell the bits to the murder tourists. They'll ask five dollars apiece for his teeth, and fifty each for his kneecaps."

"That's awful!" Toby pushed away his half-eaten breakfast. "I don't think I'm hungry any longer."

Ivy shrugged and helped herself to a sausage off Toby's plate. "I guess you won't be wanting this, then."

"Is something the matter, Toby?" Mrs. Webster had come in from the hallway. She wore a straw sun hat and thick brown gloves, and a wicker gardening basket dangled from her elbow. She must not have heard the news about the vanishing corpse, Toby guessed, since she was the only one of them who actually looked happy.

"I'm afraid Mr. Montrose isn't the only one who has lost his appetite," said Mr. Peartree. "Mr. Abernathy's body has disappeared from the mortuary, and we're all extremely perturbed." He narrowed his eyes at Ivy. "At least, most of us are."

"Oh dear." Mrs. Webster's smile faded. "What's to be done? Can any of our sleuths go over there to investigate?"

"There's nothing I'd like more," Miss March said, "but we can't leave the manor. I hate to think of that dreadful police squad tearing apart the scene. If there are any clues to be found, they'll be destroyed before any of us get a chance to see them."

"It's all right, Anthea." Miss Price squeezed Miss

243

March's hand. "At least we know that no one in this house could have pilfered the body. We've all remained present and accounted for this weekend—even that strange Peter Jacobson."

Mrs. Webster drew in her breath at the mention of Peter's name. He was still under Mr. Webster's guard in the Delphinium Room, from which every last scrap of writing paper had been removed. "I don't mean to be an ungracious hostess," Mrs. Webster said, "but I'll be happy to see the last of this weekend. A murderer is on the loose, a corpse is floating about somewhere, my servants' nerves are shattered, my older daughter is threatening to run away with that journalist, and my younger daughter refuses to stay out of the whole mess. In fact, she seems to be thoroughly enjoying it." She threw up her hands. "I give up! I'm going to weed the rose garden. If anyone else gets engaged or poisoned, please come let me know."

"Poor Mother," Ivy said as Mrs. Webster left the room. "I haven't seen her make such a grand production since one of her dusty old artifacts was stolen from the museum. Mother is lovely, but she can be a very dramatic person." She aimed her fork at Toby's breakfast. "Are you going to eat that boiled tomato?"

Toby wasn't. It had gone as cold as the murderer's trail, and he couldn't see how Webster and Montrose, Private Investigators would ever catch up. It had taken him ages to fall asleep the night before, with the trouble scratching at his bedroom door; when he finally did sleep, he dreamed that he was chasing a rat through the hedge maze on the Websters' lawn. Whenever he came close to grabbing the rat by the tail, he made a wrong turn in the hedges and ended up even more lost than before. "You didn't hear anyone else trying to sneak outside last night, did you?" he asked Ivy as they got up from the table. "Or early this morning?"

Ivy shook her head. "I didn't even hear Percival growl at anyone."

"Me either." Toby hadn't expected her to say anything different, but he still wished his trap had caught something worth keeping. "The only person who's left the house is your mother, and she didn't look much like a creeping criminal."

"Mother would never creep!" Ivy laughed as she headed up the stairs toward the Investigatorium. "She's not a crime expert like we are, Toby. If she were a murderer, she'd have no idea how to behave properly. Can you imagine it?"

Toby tried, but it wasn't easy. Amina Webster wasn't much like the criminals Hugh Abernathy chased down each month in the *Sphinx*. "She might not know about wiping her fingerprints off the things she'd touched," he said, "or about coming up with a good alibi."

"Exactly," said Ivy. "She'd probably try to carry those stolen files out of the house in plain sight, right under everyone's noses."

Toby froze. "Would she put them in a gardening basket?"

"Maybe," said Ivy, "or—oh!" She sat down on the staircase and stared at him. "Oh, no. Not *Mother*!"

If she said anything after that, Toby couldn't hear it. He was already halfway down the staircase, running as fast as he could toward the front door.

The crowd outside the manor had grown larger than ever. Worse yet, it was loud. The murder tourists had shown up that morning with dozens of harmonicas—the instrument Hugh Abernathy had so famously played—and in the hours since dawn, performing wheezy laments to the great detective had become something of a trend. The police officers at the scene had resorted to pressing their hands to their ears and yelling at one another over the din. Toby could hardly hear his own footsteps as he ran toward the manor gate. His legs were churning recklessly downhill, going much faster than the rest of him, and he could tell he was in danger of tumbling tail over teakettle, as Aunt Janet would have said. But his eyes were on Mrs. Webster in her huge straw sun hat, with her gardening basket over one arm, leaning forward to speak to the journalists on the other side of the fence.

She must have heard Toby coming over the swarm of harmonicas, because she set down her basket and wheeled around, putting her hands out to stop him from crashing into her. "Good heavens!" she said. "What's happening, Toby? Is something wrong at the house?" He could feel her fingers tighten a little on his shoulders. "Is Ivy all right?"

Toby gulped the air. Furrows of worry had gathered around Mrs. Webster's eyes; could she really be a murderer? "I thought you said you were going to weed the roses," he said.

"Well, yes, I did." Mrs. Webster's fingers relaxed, and she offered Toby the same kind smile she'd given him when he'd turned up at the manor on Friday with no idea what to do next. "When I saw all these people at the gate, though, I thought I'd give them a scolding first. It's only eight o'clock in the morning," she said in a confidential tone, "and they're already howling like hounds in search of a fox. I've asked them to leave us alone, but I'm afraid they haven't taken my words to heart."

As if to prove her point, one of the journalists rapped his pen against the iron bars. "You said you had some business to conduct with us, ma'am?" he asked.

"That's right." Mrs. Webster flattened her smile. "I want to request that you leave my family and our guests in peace. We won't be granting any interviews, so I think you'll be happier if you pack up your tents and return to wherever you came from."

It was as if Mrs. Webster's words had dissolved into

the air. None of the journalists budged. "What about that boy?" one of them called, pointing at Toby. "Has he got any secrets to share?"

"He certainly doesn't," Mrs. Webster snapped. She turned her back on the journalists and bent down to face Toby. "I'd feel much less worried if you ran back to the house," she told him. "I'm not sure it's safe for you out here."

Toby wasn't sure, either. If Mrs. Webster *was* a murderer, the question he was about to ask her was extremely dangerous. He wished Ivy were there with him, but she hadn't followed him out of the manor, and neither had Percival. All Toby had was his embroidered junior detective badge, a little battered from the night before but still pinned securely to his shirt. "Before I go," he said to Mrs. Webster, "may I look inside your gardening basket?"

The harmonicas swelled as Mrs. Webster plucked up the basket from the ground. The worry had come back to her eyes. "What a strange request," she said, laughing a little. "There's nothing at all to see, I promise you. Just ordinary trowels and hedge clippers and things."

"Then you won't mind if I look at them," Toby pointed out. Before Mrs. Webster had any time to realize what was happening, he reached out and flicked the lid off the gardening basket. Mrs. Webster sprang for it, but she moved too quickly; the basket slipped out of her hands and overturned on the drive. Dozens of pieces of crisp white paper spilled onto the ground. Toby looked down at the page that had fallen near his foot: it was covered from top to bottom with Hugh Abernathy's bold handwriting.

"Bother!" cried Mrs. Webster. She got down on her hands and knees, staining her dress with dirt as she scrambled to gather the files.

"Oh, Mother," said Ivy. She had come up behind Toby so quietly that he hadn't noticed her, and her face was grim. "What in the world have you done?"

CHAPTER 20

THE GYPTIAN STATUETTE

Mrs. Webster had barely spoken as Toby and Ivy marched her up to the Investigatorium, but now, as she looked from the shelves of detectives' tools to the racks of disguises, she seemed to be searching for words. "What is all this?" she asked at last.

"We're the ones asking the questions, Mother," Ivy snapped. "Sit down, please. And don't try any funny business."

Mrs. Webster wasn't behaving like a mother any longer. That worried Toby. Instead of scolding Ivy for her rudeness, she only nodded and took a seat on the old velvet sofa. Egbert the skeleton stared down at her—or he would have if he'd had eyes in his skull to stare with. Every time a breeze blew through the cracked-open window, his bones rattled together, and Mrs. Webster flinched.

There was a sharp click as Ivy locked the Investigatorium door. "Do you have all the papers?" she asked Toby.

Toby was still holding Mrs. Webster's gardening basket, filled with the pages covered with Hugh Abernathy's handwriting. "I've got everything that was on the ground," he said, "and everything that stayed in the basket, but there might be more we don't know about." He pulled the papers out and stacked them on the desk as neatly as he could. "These are Hugh Abernathy's stolen files, aren't they?" he asked Mrs. Webster.

"Of course they are," she said, "and there aren't any more. I should know, since I'm the one who took them in the first place."

"I can't believe this." Ivy turned away from her mother and started sorting through the tangle of disguises on the clothes rack. She grabbed a yellow rain hat and threw it on the floor. "My mother's a murderer!" A mangy fur cape, three skirts, and a pair of lederhosen flew through the air to join the rain hat. "Tell me, Mother, what does a murderer's daughter wear? A gold tiara? A pair of handcuffs?"

"Ivy, wait!" Toby tried to gather up the disguises on the floor, but Ivy only threw more at him. "Shouldn't we give our suspect a chance to explain herself?"

"Explain herself?" A pink ballet slipper whizzed past

Toby's left ear. "What's there to explain? You heard what Mr. Rackham said as well as I did. Whoever stole those files must have poisoned Hugh Abernathy." Ivy glared at her mother. "And we know exactly who stole the files."

Mrs. Webster stood up. "Has it occurred to you," she said in a voice just as fierce as Ivy's, "that Mr. Rackham might be wrong?"

Ivy narrowed her eyes. She held a wadded-up wool cardigan in one hand and looked eager to throw it. "What do you mean?"

"I didn't poison anyone," Mrs. Webster said calmly, "and I'm not a murderer. My goodness, Ivy! I hoped you knew me better than that." She took the cardigan from Ivy's hand, shook it out, and folded it. "Then again, I can see now that there are a few things I should have known about you—and about Lillie, too." She sat back down and sighed. "I always told your father this house was much too big."

"I don't see what the size of our house has to do with anything," said Ivy. At least she wasn't throwing disguises anymore, Toby thought. "If you really didn't murder anyone, why did you want Mr. Abernathy's files?"

"And why were you trying to sell them to those journalists?" Toby asked. This had been bothering him ever since he'd seen Mrs. Webster at the gate. His trap had finally worked, but he couldn't understand why. "You're rich! You don't need the money."

Mrs. Webster laughed at this—a sad laugh, like the one Uncle Gabriel gave whenever another day went by without a client at his doorstep. "We *were* rich," she corrected Toby. "Now we've barely got enough to last the rest of the year. Almost every penny we've earned has gone into Hugh Abernathy's pockets."

Toby had known that Mr. Abernathy charged handsomely for his services, but he hadn't expected they'd be expensive enough to drain the Websters' fortune. "You hired him to solve a crime?" he asked. "I didn't know that."

"Neither did I," said Ivy. She sounded suspicious.

"We did hire him," said Mrs. Webster. "At least, that's how it began. A while ago, there was a theft at the city museum. The stolen artifact was a statuette of an ancient Gyptian goddess of justice. I'd just acquired it on a dig, and Robert and I had loaned it to the museum. When the police had no luck tracing the thief, we decided to obtain the services of a private detective. I needed the very best, and everyone knows that's exactly what Hugh Abernathy was."

"Did he find the statuette?" Toby asked.

"Oh, he had no trouble with that. Some second-rate burglar had tried to sell it to half a dozen pawnshops in the city, and Mr. Abernathy retrieved it within a week. But when we went to his office to pick it up, he told us that he'd been even busier than we'd thought. Over the course of his investigation, he'd learned that we hadn't been entirely truthful about the statuette's origins."

"You mean you lied," Ivy said flatly.

"Yes," said Mrs. Webster. "I didn't find the goddess of justice on a dig. It had been stolen from a tomb near our excavation site, and your father and I purchased it from the thieves. It was a magnificent piece—truly one of a kind—and if you could have seen the way those criminals were mishandling it . . ." Mrs. Webster shook her head. "There's no point in making excuses, though. We knew perfectly well that we were buying stolen property and that it would ruin our careers if anyone ever found out. Hugh Abernathy knew it, too. When we begged him to keep our secret, he told us cheerfully that he'd never tell a soul—as long as we paid him a fair price in return. If we refused, he'd have his assistant print our story in the *Sphinx* for the entire world to read."

"He blackmailed you?" Toby had believed Mrs. Webster's story until now, but the idea of Mr. Abernathy betraying his own clients was too awful to imagine. It certainly didn't sound like the Hugh Abernathy he'd read about. "He wouldn't have done that," Toby insisted. "He was a detective! Detectives are supposed to help people!"

"All Mr. Abernathy helped us out of was our savings,"

Mrs. Webster said. "We'd been paying him much more than we could afford to keep him quiet. He even demanded to host his charming little contest here. Robert and I couldn't stand the thought of letting him into our home, but we couldn't possibly say no!"

"Oh, Mother!" said Ivy. Toby wondered if she was going to start throwing things again. "That's an awfully good motive for murder. Are you *sure* you didn't poison him?"

"Of course I'm sure!" Mrs. Webster sat up straight on the velvet sofa. "I don't know how I can possibly prove it to you, Ivy, but I would never do such a horrid thing, and neither would your father. We didn't have any idea that Mr. Abernathy was going to pass from this world to the next in our purple armchair. Once he did, though, I realized that we had to destroy whatever evidence he'd collected against us before someone else could find it. I brought Doctor Piper upstairs to examine the body, and while she was busy with that, I picked up all of his files and hid them in my dressing table. It didn't take more than a moment. And in any case, it didn't help. None of those papers had anything to do with us. As soon as I realized it, I thought I might as well sell them and make back a little of the money Hugh Abernathy took from us." Mrs. Webster sighed. "I can't imagine what you children must think of me. I feel like an awful fool."

"You *are* a fool!" cried Ivy. "You should have told me

what Mr. Abernathy was doing to you and Father all this time. I could have helped!"

"Oh, darling, I don't think there was a thing you could have done. And you shouldn't be burdened with your parents' troubles. Theft and blackmail and murder—why, you're only a child!"

"I'm a *detective*!" Ivy was really shouting now. She looked as though she were fighting back tears, although knowing what Ivy was like in a fight, Toby didn't think the tears stood much of a chance. "I guess I must not be very good at my work, though," she said, "because detectives are supposed to *know* things, and I don't even know what's happening in my own family. Do you realize that no one ever tells me anything? You don't, Mother, and neither do Father or Lillie. Is it because you think I'm unusual? I know you do, so don't deny it. I heard you saying so to Father."

"Darling!" Mrs. Webster flew to her daughter. Toby had never seen anyone attempt to hug Ivy before—he hadn't been sure it was possible—but Mrs. Webster took Ivy in her arms as though she were as delicate as a baby bird. Even when Ivy tried to wriggle away, Mrs. Webster held fast. Mothers, Toby remembered, could be like that.

"You are a very unusual person, Ivy," Mrs. Webster said firmly, "and that is precisely why all of us love you. I had no idea you were feeling so lonely. I should have been paying much better attention. In fact, I wish you would teach me how you manage to notice so much about the people around you. I do try, but I'm sure you can see I have plenty to learn about being a good detective."

Ivy stepped back from Mrs. Webster's embrace. She wiped her eyes with the sleeve of her dress. "Luckily for you, Mother," she said, "I've got a correspondence course."

CHAPTER 21

MR. ABERNATHY'S SECRETS

No one had ever taught Toby what the polite thing to do was when a detective and her mother were sniffling all over each other, passing handkerchiefs and apologies back and forth. For a few minutes, he tried standing in the corner and staying out of the way, but that didn't seem right at all. He was a detective, not a coatrack, and Mr. Abernathy's case files were still stacked on the Investigatorium desk. The corners of some of the pages were bent upward, as if they were beckoning him. "I'm going to look through these papers," Toby announced to the room, though only Egbert really seemed to hear him.

The files were clipped together into five tidy bundles—one for each of the cases Mr. Abernathy had been investigating,

Toby assumed, though none of the bundles were labeled. He picked up the thickest one and scanned the first page, looking for the words *Montrose* or *seashore* or *rowboat* or *alive*. But this bundle didn't seem to have anything to do with Toby's parents. He flicked through it impatiently, tossed it aside, and moved on to the second bundle, then the third and the fourth. There were letters and doctor's reports, handwritten notes from Mr. Abernathy himself and typed documents from the police, but nothing looked familiar to Toby. He could feel his skin prickling all over with heat and worry as he grabbed the final bundle of papers. He'd forgotten all about trying to keep things tidy. *I have discovered that Toby Montrose's parents are alive and well and living near the seashore*, the papers were supposed to say. *When their rowboat capsized, they swam to safety, but the trauma of the incident caused them to forget to return from their holiday. Now that I have reminded them of their loving family (particularly their brave son, Toby), however, they are eager to come home. I will tell the boy at once. Another case happily solved!*

Toby looked down at the last bundle. There was the word *Montrose*, so bold it practically leapt off the page. But these files weren't about accidents by the seashore, and they didn't even mention Toby or his parents. All of these papers seemed to be about Uncle Gabriel.

Toby dropped the whole bundle back on the desk. Uncle

Gabriel didn't have anything to do with Toby's parents' accident. Where was the information Mr. Abernathy had promised him? "It's not here," he said. "It was supposed to be here!"

He hadn't meant to interrupt, but Ivy overheard him. "What's not there?" she asked.

"The notes about my parents' case!" Toby shuffled through the papers again, praying that a new bundle would appear on the desk. "Mrs. Webster, are you sure these are all the files Mr. Abernathy had? Did you see anything about a mother and father in a rowboat?"

Mrs. Webster shook her head. "I'm sorry, Toby. I only glanced at most of the papers, but I don't think I saw anything like that."

"Maybe the information about your parents is back at Mr. Abernathy's house!" Ivy jumped up from the sofa and ran to Toby's side. "I'm sure that's where he kept all his most important files. We'll ask Mr. Peartree to find them for you."

"All right," said Toby, even though he didn't feel all right at all. If Mr. Abernathy had wanted to talk about Toby's case, why hadn't he brought the files with him? Come to think of it, why had he agreed to take the case in the first place? He'd said that Toby could repay him somehow at the manor, but he'd gotten himself murdered before Toby had

had a chance to do anything in return. Meanwhile, Toby's parents might still be out in the world somewhere, missing Toby and needing his help. . . .

A low, steady scratching noise came from the doorway. Toby grabbed Ivy's arm. "Do you hear that?" he whispered. "I think someone's trying to get in."

Ivy cocked her head. The noise grew louder, and Ivy looked around the room. "Percival!" she said. "We forgot to brief our assistant!" She sighed and went to unlock the door. "He'll never let us hear the end of it."

Percival stalked into the Investigatorium with his nose in the air. He walked straight past Ivy without acknowledging her at all, gave Toby's shoes a cursory sniff, settled onto his stomach, and began to chew indignantly on the carpet fringe.

"Oh, don't act so offended," Ivy told him. "You really didn't miss very much. Mother's a criminal, and we've got Hugh Abernathy's files, but we haven't read them yet. In fact, we were waiting for you." She picked up half the papers from the desk and handed them to Toby. "I know these aren't about your parents, but they might help us learn more about Mr. Abernathy, and *that* might help us guess why someone killed him. You can take one half, and I'll take the other."

Toby wrinkled his nose at the stacked pages. They

didn't look very useful to him. Still, he had to admit he was curious to read all those notes about Uncle Gabriel. "Which half does Percival get?" he asked.

"He can guard Mother," said Ivy. "I don't want her sneaking out and doing anything else shocking while we're not paying attention."

"I *was* going to speak to Cook about dinner," said Mrs. Webster, "but if that behavior is too suspicious for you, I suppose I can stay here for a while longer." She picked up one of Ivy's stray *Sphinx* issues and began to leaf through it.

Toby and Ivy lay on their stomachs on the Investigatorium floor with Mr. Abernathy's files spread out between them. The pages at the top of Uncle Gabriel's bundle seemed to be a record of all the cases he and Mr. Abernathy solved together long ago, when they were partners. The cases weren't anywhere near as glamorous as Toby had expected: together, Montrose and Abernathy had located a missing child, returned a stolen necklace to its rightful owner, and escorted seven different escaped convicts back to Chokevine Prison. Still, they had solved each case swiftly and without much fuss. Within months, some of the most influential men and women in the city were asking Montrose and Abernathy for assistance. *Received a summons from Lord Entwhistle today*, Mr. Abernathy had written in the case record. *Gabriel and I paid him a visit. He wants us to capture the Cutthroat whose murders have enthralled the city. Naturally, we leapt at the opportunity. If we succeed, our firm will be the best-known detecting operation in Colebridge—and beyond!*

This was where the case record ended. The rest of the bundle consisted of a very long, very angry missive from Lord Entwhistle, written in bright purple ink with many splatters and cross-outs. It didn't take long for Toby to figure out that although Hugh Abernathy had caught the Colebridge Cutthroat, Lord Entwhistle had been furious. *You tell me that Mr. Montrose's carelessness nearly caused the Cutthroat to slip through your fingers*, Lord Entwhistle wrote. *I would like to suggest that you press those fingers together tightly, curl them into a fist, and deliver a blow to Mr. Montrose that will remove him from your company forever. I can tell you are a capable fellow, Abernathy, but Montrose is worse than useless, and I place the blame for this calamity squarely on him. I promise you that no one of consequence in this town will ever entrust Gabriel Montrose with their private affairs while I am living to warn them of his dangerous incompetence.* Lord Entwhistle went on to call Uncle Gabriel a nincompoop, a flibbertigibbet, and several other words Toby wasn't sure were real. All of them sounded very unflattering.

As Toby read, he grew even more upset than Lord Entwhistle. The real adventure of the Colebridge Cutthroat had been a disaster—that much was certain—but Toby *knew* Uncle Gabriel, and Uncle Gabriel wasn't anything close to useless. Why had Lord Entwhistle been so convinced that the disaster was entirely Uncle Gabriel's fault? Why had Mr. Abernathy kept this awful, yellowing letter all these years, and why had he brought it to Coleford Manor? Whatever his reasons had been, Toby decided, he didn't need the letter anymore. Toby picked up the last page of it—the worst page, about nincompoops and flibbertigibbets—and started tearing it carefully into pieces.

"What are you doing?" Ivy grabbed the torn-up sheet out of his hands. "That's evidence, Toby!"

"No," said Toby, "it's awful, and it's all about Uncle Gabriel. It's a good thing your mother didn't manage to sell it to the journalists. If they printed it, Uncle Gabriel would never have any clients ever again!"

"Does he have any clients now?"

"Well, this would make things worse!" Toby pulled the paper back. "No one else can see this letter, Ivy. I mean it."

Ivy was too busy frowning at her own stack of papers to argue with him. "Are all the notes in that bundle about your uncle?" she asked.

Toby nodded. "Are yours?"

"No." Ivy chewed the ends of her hair. She looked like she was thinking hard. "The first set of papers in my bunch is all about Philip Elwood—the real Philip Elwood, I mean, not the one downstairs who wants to marry Lillie.

Some of the notes are written in Gyptian, so they're hard to make out, but the grand sum of everything is that Mr. Elwood's been mixed up in some awfully seedy business. Mr. Abernathy thought Mr. Elwood was actually working with some of the criminals he helped to capture." Her mouth twitched. "I guess the real Philip Elwood isn't much better at being a detective than the fake one is."

"I didn't know Mr. Abernathy was investigating Philip Elwood," Toby said. "Why would he be doing that?"

"Why would he investigate Mr. Rackham, either?" Ivy asked. "That's the other set of papers I've got. They're all Mr. Rackham's medical records, and they say he can remember only half of what he's told. The doctor doesn't think he'll be able to work for much longer. Our attic isn't the only place he's been lost in the past few months."

"Poor Mr. Rackham." Toby thought of all the times Uncle Gabriel had gone to help Mr. Rackham feed his chickens or make a pot of tea. Had he known Mr. Rackham's secret, too? "I don't think these are case files, Ivy. I think Mr. Abernathy was keeping notes about his competition guests."

"But your uncle's not a guest," Ivy pointed out.

"He was supposed to be. Mr. Abernathy didn't know I'd lied about that." Toby couldn't help feeling a little bit proud as he said it. "And the real Philip Elwood was supposed to be a guest, too."

Ivy's eyes widened. "Then you've probably got notes about the others—about Miss March and Miss Price, I mean, and Julia. What did Mr. Abernathy think of them?"

"I haven't looked yet." Toby moved Uncle Gabriel's bundle aside and examined the next set of papers. These weren't Mr. Abernathy's notes; they were letters addressed to him, handwritten on a few sheets of soft lilac stationery. The old-fashioned script looped across the pages like tendrils of a vine, and there were lots of words Toby couldn't read at all. Only a few phrases were legible, really, because the writer had printed them in tall capitals and underlined them for emphasis. *WE WILL NOT STAND FOR IT*, one said. Another said *I AM WARNING YOU* and a third said *YOU WILL BE SORRY*. Each of the letters ended in the same way, as though the writer's pen had torn across the paper in a powerful rage as she scrawled her signature: *Flossie*.

Toby put the letters down and shoved them toward Ivy; he didn't like holding them. "These are from Miss Price," he said. "She was sending threatening notes to Mr. Abernathy."

"Miss Price?" said Ivy. "But she's so sweet! Are you sure she knows how to threaten people? Did she swear she'd tickle Mr. Abernathy's nose with a feather duster?"

"Just read the letters," said Toby. Honestly, he couldn't imagine Miss Price writing them, either. She and Miss

March had been really kind to Toby ever since he'd moved to the Row, and they were Uncle Gabriel's closest friends. Could their charming smiles and the fresh cinnamon buns they made every Saturday be disguising something more sinister? Why had Miss Price been so angry with Mr. Abernathy—and what had that anger driven her to do? Thinking about the possibility made Toby feel sick to his stomach. Uncle Gabriel had told him once that a certain queasiness in the gut was one of the unfortunate side effects of being a detective, and Toby was starting to understand what he'd meant.

"Oh dear," said Ivy. She recoiled from the sheets of lilac stationery. "I guess we know what Miss March and Miss Price thought of Mr. Abernathy. What do you think he *did* to them?"

But Toby had already moved on to the final set of papers. It was slim, just a few pages typed on official letterhead from Chokevine Prison. "This is a letter to Mr. Abernathy from the prison warden," Toby told Ivy. "A prisoner went missing from Chokevine ten years ago, and the warden wanted Mr. Abernathy's help to find her and bring her back."

Ivy shrugged. "People are always escaping from Chokevine, aren't they? I wonder why Mr. Abernathy kept that letter."

"Maybe the missing person was someone he'd sent to

Chokevine in the first place," Toby said, "or someone he knew a lot about." He frowned and read the letter more closely. "Whoever she was, she must have done something awful. She'd been sentenced to prison for life. The warden says here that she might be wearing a disguise or using a different name, but— Oh no." The letter started to shake in Toby's hands.

Ivy reached for it. "What's the matter?"

"Lots, I think," said Toby. "The warden told Mr. Abernathy that every criminal who's spent time in the prison can be recognized by the chokevines tattooed on their forearms."

Ivy sat bolt upright. "Julia Hartshorn!" she shouted.

Toby nodded. The curling tendrils around the Chokevine Prison insignia looked exactly like the strange mark he'd seen on Julia's arm. No wonder she'd panicked when Toby had noticed it. "She's an escaped convict," he said.

On the sofa, Mrs. Webster put her magazine aside. "Surely not!"

"She might even be a murderer," said Ivy. "What if she's a murderer Mr. Abernathy helped to catch? And what if she killed him in revenge?" Her eyes were wide. "What if Julia is the Colebridge Cutthroat?"

"She can't be!" Toby's mouth felt dry. "Can she?"

"Of course not," said Mrs. Webster, but she didn't sound convinced.

"Well," said Ivy, "whoever she is, Mr. Abernathy knew about it." She handed the warden's letter back to Toby. "And now Mr. Abernathy is dead."

In the hallway beyond the Investigatorium, something shuffled and creaked.

The trouble began to prickle its way up Toby's neck. "What's that noise?" he whispered.

Ivy sighed and got to her feet. "Just Percival again. He's always wandering off."

"Ivy?" Toby's whole face was prickling now. "Percival's over there. He's chewing on Egbert."

Ivy froze. She stared at Percival, who was gnawing happily on the skeleton's ankle. Then she ran to the Investigatorium door and flung it open, making the whole room shake.

"There's no one here." Ivy stuck her head out the doorway and looked both ways. "I'm sure we've just spooked ourselves. We've got nothing to worry about."

Toby looked again at the thick, poisonous chokevine. He really hoped Ivy was right.

CHAPTER 22

THE THIRD M

"The third *M*," said Ivy as she paced the Investigatorium. "The motive for Mr. Abernathy's murder. At first, we didn't have any idea what that motive could be." She spun dramatically on her heel. "But now we've got too *many* motives. Did Julia kill him for revenge? Did Rackham murder him to keep his secrets quiet? Did Miss March and Miss Price finally put their sinister warnings into action? Or was it someone else"—here she spun again, to face her mother—"someone who couldn't afford to pay Mr. Abernathy another cent?"

"I've told you fifty times, Ivy—"

"I know, Mother; you swear you're innocent. And we've got plenty of other suspects who might have killed Mr.

Abernathy instead; the house is crawling with them." Ivy stopped suddenly, as though something had just occurred to her. "Mother, didn't you say you had to go talk to Cook about dinner?"

"Well, yes," said Mrs. Webster, "I did, but I'm sure that can wait a little longer. Actually, children, I've gotten awfully intrigued by your investigation, and I'd love—"

"—to leave us alone? How thoughtful of you." Ivy took her mother by the elbow and lifted her off the sofa before Mrs. Webster could do anything about it. "Toby, would you help me show Mother out the door? We'll need to hurry: Cook hates to be kept waiting, and she's got an enormous number of knives."

Toby didn't know quite what Ivy was up to, but he could recognize the urgency in her voice when he heard it. "Of course, Inspector!" he said, taking hold of Mrs. Webster's other elbow. Between the two of them, it wasn't that hard to carry her across the room and out the door. "Thanks so much for your help with the case, ma'am. I'm sure Ivy will let you know if she has any more questions for you."

"But what about Miss Hartshorn?" Mrs. Webster said as they deposited her in the hallway. "Do you think she's really a convict? And that dear Mr. Rackham; shouldn't we try to help—"

"Good-*bye*, Mother." Ivy pulled the Investigatorium door shut. Then she turned back to Toby and dusted her hands together. "There. I hope poor Mother isn't too flustered, but I couldn't see how we could possibly continue our investigation and look after her at the same time. She'd only tell us to be careful and behave ourselves, and if we follow advice like that, we'll never get anything done."

"I thought you wanted to keep an eye on her," said Toby.

Ivy shrugged. "I did, but we've got too many suspects to worry about now. We can't possibly watch them all. If Mother tries anything funny, we'll know where to find her, but for now, we've got work to do."

Toby was already gathering the scattered files from the floor and stacking them back into neat piles. "I still don't understand what Mr. Abernathy was doing with all these papers," he said. "Why would he have brought them with him to the manor?"

"It's like you said earlier." Ivy stretched out on the sofa. "He wanted to learn more about the detectives who were entering his contest."

"But that doesn't make sense!" said Toby. He hadn't meant to speak so loudly, but even Percival jumped at the noise. Toby wondered if this was a side effect of spending so much time with Ivy. "Mr. Abernathy'd had some of these documents for years," he explained. "He probably learned all about the detectives' secrets a long time before he invited them to the manor. If he knew such awful things about them, why did he want to give each of them a chance to be his successor?"

"That's a very good question, Detective Montrose. I hadn't thought of things that way." Ivy wiggled her toes. "Do you think he was being kind? No, never mind; that doesn't sound like Mr. Abernathy at all."

"Oh, Ivy, he wasn't *that* awful—"

"He blackmailed my parents." Ivy's voice was icy. "Who knows what else he might have been up to while Mr. Peartree was busy writing all those nice things about him in the *Sphinx*? Hugh Abernathy had a lot of secrets, Toby— his own, and other people's. I'd like to know exactly what he was planning to do with them."

Downstairs in the parlor, the detectives were in a tizzy. Hugh Abernathy's body was still mysteriously absent, according to the telegram Mr. Peartree had just received from Doctor Piper, and now poor Mr. Peartree himself was practically pulling his hair out with frustration as the investigators argued about what should be done. Julia Hartshorn wanted to ask volunteers to comb the woods around the mortuary, Mr. Rackham advocated for a pack of hunting dogs, and Miss Price even dared to murmur that perhaps the police should be enlisted to search for the corpse. That was when everyone started shouting at Miss Price.

"I only said *perhaps*," Miss Price protested. "If we

weren't all locked up in this house for the rest of the day, I'd begin the search myself."

It didn't seem like a particularly good time for interruptions, but Toby didn't have much of a choice. He could already hear the toes of Ivy's tall buttoned boots tap-tap-tapping with impatience in the hallway (she was dressed as Madame Ermintrude again), and he'd promised her that he could handle this assignment by himself. Only two people in the world knew more about secrets than Mr. Abernathy did, and fortunately or dangerously, both of those people were in the parlor.

"Miss Price?" he said, tapping the detective on the shoulder. "Miss March? I'd like to speak to you both."

Miss Price's cheeks flushed as pink as red currant jam, and she smiled at Toby. "Hello, dear," she said. "Of course you can speak with us. Can't he, Anthea?"

"It'll have to be in private," Toby added. There was that new voice of his again—the louder, firmer one that made him swallow with surprise. "Will you come with me?"

"I'm sure there's nothing you can't ask us right here, Toby," Miss March said. "We're very busy at the moment. We've got theories to discuss, evidence to organize, a corpse to find, and only a few hours left to solve this case before the police arrive."

"I know," said Toby. "That's why I need to talk to you

right away. My partner and I want to know the truth about Hugh Abernathy."

Miss Price blinked at him. "What in the world do you mean?"

"You wrote him threatening letters," Toby said quietly enough to keep the others from hearing. "I've seen them, so there's no point in denying it. What did Mr. Abernathy do to you, and why did he keep those letters?"

Miss March and Miss Price exchanged a look. Neither of them was smiling anymore.

"Oh, my dear." Miss March put her hand on Toby's shoulder. Her fingers were thin and stiff and cold. "What have you gotten yourself into?"

The afternoon sky had darkened and grayed. The smell of thunder hung in the air, and even the sun didn't dare to show its face as Miss March and Miss Price directed Toby and Ivy briskly out of doors. "We mustn't be overheard," Miss March commanded, steering them across the lawn. The crowd at the gates had grown since the morning; it was overflowing the road, and more than a few bystanders were trying to scale the iron fence. Miss March headed resolutely in the opposite direction. "What do you say, Flossie? Shall we go into the maze?"

"The maze will do nicely," Miss Price agreed.

Toby wasn't sure there was anything nice about the hedge maze. It looked dark and close and shadowy, like it had spent a long time waiting for a chance to swallow up a few detectives. Toby had been planning to take Miss March and Miss Price back to the Investigatorium, but it was obvious that he and Ivy weren't in charge of this interview any longer. For all he knew, Miss March and Miss Price were planning to strand them inside the maze and leave them for packs of wolves, escaped convicts, or hungry reporters from the *Morning Bugle* to find. "Do you go into the maze a lot, Ivy?" he asked. "I mean, Madame Ermintrude?"

The wind whipped a scarf across Ivy's face. "Mother won't allow it," she said grimly. "We've lost three gardeners and a house cat inside it, and only the cat ever made its way out again."

"It's a lucky thing we're not gardeners, then, isn't it, Anthea?" Miss Price sounded positively cheerful as she squeezed through an opening in the tall hedges. "A shame we aren't cats, but there's nothing to be done about it. Come along, children! We haven't got time to waste!"

Inside the maze, the wind died abruptly and the noises of the crowd faded away. The hedges' thick branches pressed against Toby, and their needles whispered old, earthy secrets to one another as he brushed past. He had to hurry to keep up with Miss March and Miss Price. They were surprisingly quick, and Toby wasn't about to let either of them out of his sight.

The path diverged in two directions, left and right, and Miss March paused at the fork. She licked her fingertip, held it in the air for a moment, and turned down the left-hand path. Ivy looked awfully skeptical behind her motoring goggles, but she followed Miss March anyway, and Toby did the same. He hoped the detectives knew what they were doing.

When they had rounded several more corners and buried themselves so deeply in the hedges that Toby could no longer tell which way they'd entered, Miss Price suddenly stopped walking. She cupped a hand around her ear and listened. "Good," she said. "We're quite alone, my dears, so let's get down to business. You say you want to know the truth about Hugh Abernathy, but I'd like to know: are you absolutely sure that's what you want?"

"Of course it is," said Ivy. "Why wouldn't it be?"

"The truth can be a tricky thing," said Miss March. She was walking again now, quickly, and her curls flapped at her temples like a nest of fledglings. "Our clients hire us to search for the truth, but more often than not, they're unhappy when we find it. It's not their fault, poor things; it's human nature. If facts comforted us in the same way

fictions did, we'd all spend cozy evenings reading our encyclopedias around the fire."

"Just think of the wonderful stories Mr. Peartree writes,"
Miss Price said. "Everyone in the city loves to read about
Hugh Abernathy's adventures. Wouldn't you like to keep
thinking of Mr. Abernathy as the man in those stories?"

Toby thought about all the lazy mornings he'd spent
sprawled on his stomach with the newest issue of the
Sphinx spread in front of him, and all the nights he'd spent
dreaming about Mr. Abernathy's adventures, each more
remarkable than the last. But he hadn't been a detective
then. "I think it's too late for that, ma'am," he told Miss
Price. "I'd rather know the truth, even if it's awful. It's a lot
better than not knowing anything at all."

Miss Price nodded. "So you're your uncle's boy. I'm
glad." She rounded a corner of the maze, and her words
floated back to Toby over the hedge. "All of us on the Row
prefer to know the truth about things. Actually, I think
Hugh Abernathy preferred it most of all. He loved finding
out absolutely everything there was to know about the uni-
verse: its animals, its substances, its secrets. That is what
made him an excellent detective."

"Among other things." Miss March's voice was dry as
sand. "Flossie, are you sure you haven't missed a turn?"

"Quite sure." They had reached what looked to Toby
like a dead end, but Miss Price ran her hands nimbly along

the wall of branches in front of her. "You're right, though, Anthea. Mr. Abernathy loved the truth not only because it showed him the nature of things, but because it gave him power—and there's nothing he adored more than that." Her fingers slipped through an overgrown gap in the hedge, and she smiled. "This way, dears. I think we've reached the heart of it all."

Toby squeezed through the gap. The center of the maze was small and silent, a little square clearing of root-ridged dirt just large enough to fit the four of them. Toby was glad he couldn't see the remains of the three lost gardeners anywhere in the clearing. It felt like the sort of place that kept its secrets close.

"Your uncle Gabriel noticed right away that Hugh Abernathy was a hard worker," said Miss March. "When the two of them were partners, Hugh spent every waking moment investigating their clients' cases. Sometimes he solved mysteries the clients didn't even know they had. But Gabriel noticed something else, too. Hugh had an unfortunate habit of using his clients' secrets against them."

"He blackmailed them." Ivy looked thunderous.

"To put it bluntly, yes. Hugh never could keep his hands off a juicy scandal or a shocking truth, particularly if it put money in his pocket. Gabriel was furious when he found out. He tried to convince Hugh to stop, but Hugh swore if he said a word to anyone, he'd destroy Gabriel's career."

"And he nearly did," Miss Price said. "Has anyone told you the true version of the adventure of the Colebridge Cutthroat, Toby?"

Toby squirmed under Miss Price's gaze. "I've heard it," he said. "Uncle Gabriel was jealous of Mr. Abernathy, and he started a fight that almost cost them the case."

Miss Price looked bewildered. "Oh, my dear," she said, "that's not what happened at all!"

"Your uncle's not a fool," Miss March agreed. "By the time Montrose and Abernathy took on the case at Entwhistle House, Gabriel knew Hugh was blackmailing their clients, but he tried not to let his concerns interfere with the job he'd been hired to do. He stood guard outside Lord Entwhistle's bedchamber while Hugh Abernathy kept watch in Entwhistle's study. When the hour came to switch posts, however, Gabriel walked into the study and found his partner reading through all of Entwhistle's private papers. Hugh had even tucked some government documents away in his pockets."

"That," said Miss March, "was when Gabriel lost his temper. They had the most enormous argument. Gabriel shouted at Hugh to return the documents at once, and when Hugh refused, Gabriel hit him."

"Not hard enough, if you ask me," said Miss Price. "Unfortunately, the men were so caught up in their fight that they nearly missed the Cutthroat's entrance, and

I'm sorry to say that Hugh Abernathy was first to Lord Entwhistle's bedchamber door. He blamed the whole mess on Gabriel."

"And everyone believed him?" Toby asked.

"You met Mr. Abernathy," said Miss March, "so you know how charming he could be. Besides, who could doubt the word of a man who'd just captured the city's most dangerous criminal? Hugh Abernathy became the world's greatest detective that night, and he'd been happily manipulating his clients away from their money ever since." She pursed her lips. "I'm not at all sorry that someone finally put a stop to his schemes."

"Are you?" Ivy crossed her arms. "If you wanted to stop Mr. Abernathy, why didn't you do it yourself? You could have sent him to prison ages ago!"

Ivy was stubborn, but Miss March was stubborner. "What makes you think we didn't try?" she asked. "When Gabriel came to us and told us the truth of what had happened at Entwhistle House, we hoped we could set matters straight immediately."

"But we didn't have proof," said Miss Price, "not the kind the police or the courts would accept. All we had was Gabriel's word, and it wasn't worth much, particularly against Mr. Abernathy's."

"Flossie did write Hugh some wonderfully nasty letters," Miss March said, smiling a little. "I understand you've read them. Honestly, I'm surprised he saved them all these years. I would have tossed them in the fire long ago."

"Mr. Abernathy wouldn't have." Toby felt sure of this. "I bet he never threw anything away. He just collected information and waited for it to be useful to him. He had files on all the detectives here this weekend!"

"Really?" said Miss March and Miss Price in unison.

"You didn't know?" said Toby. "But you know everything!"

Ivy groaned. "Lesson five of the correspondence course, Detective Montrose," she said. *"Keep your mouth shut."*

Toby clamped his lips together—too late, he knew, but it was better than nothing. "Sorry," he mumbled.

"Don't worry, Ivy, dear." Miss Price squeezed Ivy's hand. "Whatever there is to know about the other detectives on the Row, I can assure you we already know it."

This didn't seem to make Ivy feel any better. "Well, then," she said, "there's something *I'd* like to know. If you and Mr. Abernathy disliked one another so much, why did he invite you to his competition this weekend? And why did you accept his invitation?"

"I'm afraid I can't answer your first question," said Miss March. "I have no idea what the man was thinking. But as for the second—well, we were curious! We *are* detectives, after all. We wanted to find out what Hugh thought he was playing at."

"Gabriel told us we were being foolish," said Miss Price, "but Anthea and I never could resist a good murder. Apparently, at least one of the other guests felt similarly."

Toby's mind was racing. He thought of Uncle Gabriel, covered in pancake batter and shouting about that puffed-up, self-serving old ostrich. If Toby had been Uncle Gabriel, he would have thought of something a lot worse to call Mr. Abernathy. How could Uncle Gabriel live on Detectives' Row all those years, watching half the city of Colebridge stream to Hugh Abernathy's door while his own door was practically falling off its hinges? Why hadn't anyone seen the truth? Even Toby had missed it. He'd scurried off to Mr. Abernathy's office as soon as he could. He'd even *hired* Mr. Abernathy!

"I think I'm glad," said Toby, "that my uncle punched Hugh Abernathy in the nose."

Miss March burst out laughing. "I'm afraid your uncle has a number of regrets," she said, "but I'm absolutely sure he never regretted that."

CHAPTER 23

THE END OF THE ROPE

"I'll bet he was planning to blackmail them all!" said Ivy. "Julia Hartshorn, and Mr. Rackham, and maybe your uncle, too, and— Oh, I *hate* this maze!" Two of her scarves had gotten snagged on its branches, and she thrashed around like a hooked fish until Toby was able to untangle her. Miss March and Miss Price had vanished into the greenery far ahead of them, and it didn't seem likely that they'd waited to lead Toby and Ivy to the exit. "That's why Mr. Abernathy had all those papers with him," Ivy continued. "He didn't invite the detectives here to reward them; he invited them here so he could threaten them! Wring them dry! Squeeze them like a sack of lemons!"

"Lemons?" asked Toby.

"It's something I heard Father say once." Ivy shrugged. "Anyway, it's pretty clear one of the lemons didn't like being squeezed." She frowned at Toby. "Why do you look so happy, Detective Montrose?"

Toby grinned at her. Ivy was making deductions so rapidly she was practically glowing, but even she hadn't managed to spot everything. "Look over there," he said. He pointed to his left. "I found the exit."

"Thank goodness!" Ivy flew out of the maze with her scarves streaming behind her, and Toby stayed at her heels. "The next time I see one of the gardeners, I'll ask him to chop the whole thing down. Though now that Mother and Father don't have any money, we might not have any more gardeners, either."

"Do you think Mr. Peartree knew?" Toby asked as they hurried across the lawn. "About the blackmail, I mean?"

"Maybe he was a victim, too!" said Ivy. "Maybe he was forced to write all those nice things about Mr. Abernathy in the *Sphinx*, week after week, until he simply couldn't take it anymore, and *snap*!" She pantomimed wringing someone's neck.

Toby wasn't sure about this. "Mr. Peartree and I found the body together," he said. "He was really upset, Ivy."

"Then he's a good actor."

"Mr. Abernathy was the actor, not Mr. Peartree. Besides," Toby said, thinking of how miserable Mr. Peartree had looked on that awful night in the Orchid Room, "that's the kind of sadness I don't think you can fake."

Ivy nodded. "All right; I believe you. Anyway, I still think Julia Hartshorn should be at the top of our list of suspects. You know how dangerous those escaped convicts can be. Father once told me—"

Before she could explain exactly what Mr. Webster knew about convicts, Percival ran out the manor door and down the steps toward them, barking as noisily as a dog twice his size and refusing to let Ivy get a word in edgewise. She had to shout over him instead. "Yes, Percival," she bellowed, "I know. We left you behind again, and I'm very sorry. If you'll only stop making a ruckus, Detective Montrose and I will be happy to tell you everything we've learned."

But Percival didn't stop barking. If anything, he grew louder. Toby had to cover his ears. "Does he do this a lot?" he shouted at Ivy.

"Never! I don't understand it." Ivy put her hands on her hips and glared at her assistant. "Percival Webster, if you can't behave yourself, I'm going to have to remove you from this case."

In the next moment, several things happened almost at once. On an upper floor of Coleford Manor, a hand reached out from a window. A shadow passed overhead—*the trouble*, Toby thought; he was sure of it. And an enormous stone bird plummeted from the sky, shattering into pieces on the pavement in front of them.

Somebody shrieked. Toby didn't think it was him, but it was hard to be certain. He'd been knocked off his feet by the collision; now he sat up gingerly and looked around at the wreckage. The whole world seemed to him to be covered in dust. Chunks of stone the size of his fists were strewn across the lawn, and Percival was growling at the badly damaged remains of a carved griffin that had, from the looks of it, taken its first and final flight from the side of the manor. Next to one of the griffin's broken talons, Ivy was sprawled on the grass. Her scarves had flown in every direction when she fell, and Toby couldn't see whether her eyes were open behind the cracked lenses of her motoring goggles.

"Ivy?" He sat up and shook her. "Ivy, are you all right?" He tried to remember how to check for a heartbeat—Cousin Celeste had taught him that once, at the hospital—but his own heart was beating so loudly in his ears that he wasn't sure he could find anyone else's. "You're all right, Ivy, aren't you? Oh, please say something!"

The dust was starting to clear, and Toby could make out Miss March and Miss Price running toward them. "Good gracious!" Miss Price cried. "Are you hurt, dears? We'd just stepped inside when we heard the most awful crash! Anthea let out a shriek that could curdle your blood."

"I think it was a perfectly reasonable reaction under

the circumstances." Miss March knelt down by Toby and pressed a cool hand to his forehead, as if being narrowly missed by a falling statue might have given him a fever. "Hello there, Toby. Can you stand up?"

"I think so." Toby scrambled to his feet. "But Ivy's not talking. I don't think she's moving, either." It wasn't right the way she was lying there, perfectly still. Ivy was always running into rooms or out of them, bursting with so much energy that Toby wondered how the whole manor hadn't fallen down around her sooner. "Maybe she wants us to call her Madame Ermintrude?"

"Madame Ermintrude," said Ivy, "is dead."

Her lips barely moved, and her voice sounded more like a croak, but it was *hers*, and it was glorious. Slowly, she lifted her head and pulled the cracked motoring goggles from her eyes. "I'm going to need a new disguise, Detective Montrose. What do you think of Mitzi, the world-famous trapeze artist and spy? There's no need to hug me so hard, Detective; you're going to break my ribs. And could you please ask my assistant to stop licking my face?"

The other detectives came running as Miss March and Miss Price helped Toby and Ivy toward the house. "What in heaven's name is that?" said Mr. Rackham, staring at the remains of the griffin. "It looks like some sort of monster. Where did it come from?"

"It fell from the manor wall." Toby pointed at the bare

spot below a third-floor window where pieces of stone and mortar were still crumbling away. "It almost squashed us."

Julia squinted up at the wall. "You're both lucky to be alive," she said. "What a horrible accident."

"Oh," said Ivy, "it wasn't an accident. It was the murderer."

The others stared at her.

"He tried to kill us," Ivy explained. "Or she did," she added, glancing at Julia.

"Now, Ivy," Miss Price said soothingly, "you've had a frightening experience, but you mustn't let your imagination run away with you."

"It's not running anywhere!" said Ivy. "Tell them, Toby. That griffin didn't fly off the wall by itself."

Toby nodded. "It didn't seem like an accident to me, either," he said. "Percival knew something awful was going to happen, and he ran outside to warn us. He saved our lives!"

Mr. Rackham dismissed this with a wave of his hand. "Nonsensical!" he said. "Why would a murderer want to kill two children? It seems like such a waste of time."

"Isn't it obvious?" said Toby. "We're close to finding out the truth!"

"Closer than *you*, at least," Ivy snapped at Mr. Rackham.

"Ivy! Toby! My dears!" Mrs. Webster ran out of the house, followed by her husband and Mr. Peartree. After that, there was an enormous amount of hugging and weeping, and Toby found himself being carried up to his bedroom in Mr. Webster's arms, no matter how loudly he tried to explain that he was perfectly capable of walking.

"You both need rest after a fright like that," Mr. Webster said, setting Toby down in front of the door to the Marigold Room. "I can't think how that griffin managed to fall from its perch. Not a brick has shifted out of place in all the years we've lived here. Still, I'd better have some harsh words with the mason." He opened the bedroom door and blinked. "Er, Toby," he said, "it's none of my business, I suppose, but did our furniture do something to offend you?"

The Marigold Room looked as though it had been through a hurricane. Pillows and blankets were everywhere, and Toby's few belongings were scattered around the room. The orange drapes lay in heaps on the floor, the water pitcher was shattered, and even the armchair was overturned. It lay on the carpet like a toppled giant.

"I didn't do this, sir!" said Toby. "I swear I didn't! Someone's been in my room!" It was the most enormous mess Toby had ever seen, but for once in his life, he didn't even think of trying to clean it up. Instead, he squeezed past Mr. Webster and ran back down the hall, hollering for Ivy.

She was standing in her own bedroom doorway, and she didn't look surprised to see him. "Did they search through your things, too?" she asked. "They turned mine entirely inside out, but I don't think they found anything. It helps that there wasn't anything to find." Her room was twice as disastrous as Toby's, and Toby couldn't help feeling bad for Mrs. Webster, who stood aghast over the wreckage of Ivy's closet. "It's just party dresses and dolls and things," Ivy said with a shrug. "If the murderer wanted to find out what we were up to, those wouldn't have helped at all. All my really *good* stuff isn't in here, anyway; it's in—"

"The Investigatorium!" said Toby. "We left Mr. Abernathy's papers inside!"

They took the stairs two at a time, wheeling around corners and leaping over the tripwire at the end of the third floor hallway. In front of them, the Investigatorium door gaped open. "I locked it behind me," Ivy said. "I know I did. I never forget to lock the door."

The storm that had passed through each of their bedrooms had been here, too. Books and disguises littered the carpet. The ceiling trap had crashed down to the floor, but it hadn't caught anything except Ivy's binoculars and a few of Egbert's ribs. The rest of Egbert was scattered in all directions; his fingers had rolled under a bookcase, and his skull rested on the velvet sofa. The window near the desk had been pushed wide open. Toby couldn't see Mr. Abernathy's files anywhere. Only Ivy's collection of *Sphinx*es remained untouched.

Ivy ran to the window and leaned halfway out of it. When she pulled her head in again, she looked grave. "The griffin statue fell from right below this window," she said. "The spot where it used to be is all crumbling away. Do you realize what that means?" She didn't even wait for Toby to answer. *"The murderer must have been standing in this room."*

"And they've got Mr. Abernathy's files." Toby sat down on the sofa next to what remained of Egbert. The skull grinned eerily up at him. "I can't believe it."

But Ivy was grinning, too. Toby couldn't imagine what she possibly had to grin about, or why she was lying down and wriggling into the small space under her desk. There was a soft click and a rustle of papers. Then Ivy crawled back out into the open, waving Mr. Abernathy's files in one hand.

"Secret compartment," she said as she got to her feet. "Every good detective has one. The murderer might be clever, but that won't keep Webster and Montrose from cracking this case!"

"No," said Toby, staring over her shoulder, "but your parents might."

Mr. and Mrs. Webster stood in the Investigatorium doorway. They wore identical expressions that made Toby think no one would be cracking anything for a very long time. "I don't know exactly what you children have been doing," said Mr. Webster, "but whatever it is, it ends now."

"Your father and I have reached the end of our rope," Mrs. Webster agreed. "You both could have been killed today, and it's obvious that not a single detective in this house was able to do anything to prevent it. Yes, Ivy, I know you're a detective, too, but you are also my daughter. I won't allow you to put yourself in danger."

Mr. Webster nodded. "Enough is enough," he said. "We're calling in the police."

CHAPTER 24

CONSTABLE TROUT

George P. Trout, chief constable of the Colebridge City Police, did not like to be kept waiting. Toby knew this—in fact, everyone within shouting distance knew this—because Constable Trout had bellowed several hundred words to this effect as Mr. Webster escorted him through the manor gates, as Mrs. Webster led him into the parlor, and as Cook prepared his tea. "Thirty hours I stood in that road!" he said, pulling off his boots and holding his damp socks to the fire. "Thirty hours surrounded by fools with harmonicas, and the last fifteen minutes in the rain. Do you know how I feel about rain, child?"

"You don't like it?" Toby guessed. The air began to fill with the odor of well-warmed feet, and Toby wished he could hold his nose without seeming impolite. Could you be arrested for offending a police officer? He didn't want to risk it.

"That's right!" said Constable Trout. "I don't like rain, I don't like harmonicas, and I don't like to be kept waiting." He glowered at the empty room. "Where are my suspects?"

"They're on their way, sir." Mrs. Webster carried a steaming teapot into the parlor and poured out a cup for the constable. "I did ask them not to dawdle."

"Detectives!" said Constable Trout. "First-class dawdlers, every one of them. If you don't mind my saying so, ma'am, you should have called me in as soon as this whole murder business began. Those swindlers haven't done anything but waste your time."

Mrs. Webster grimaced. Toby guessed she was also trying hard to be polite. "Speaking of swindlers," she said, "here they are now."

The residents of Coleford Manor filed into the parlor. Julia Hartshorn shot the constable a scathing look and chose the chair farthest away from his. Mr. Rackham, looking no less disdainful, sat next to her. Miss March and Miss Price took up their positions on the love seat, and Mr. Peartree bowed slightly to Constable Trout as he settled himself by the window. Ivy squeezed into the chair next to Toby, and Percival jumped up onto her lap. "He still thinks he's protecting us," she whispered. "I'm hoping he'll be inspired to bite the officer's ankles."

The servants filed in next and stood straight-backed and silent along the parlor walls. If they were frightened, Toby thought, they'd done a good job of hiding it. Mr. Webster had been given the unpleasant task of dragging Peter Jacobson into the room, planting him at one end of it, and keeping Lillie safely at the other. Peter didn't look any happier to see Constable Trout than Julia Hartshorn had. "I wonder how many people the constable will take to prison," Toby whispered to Ivy. "I hope he's brought a big enough carriage."

"Is this everyone?" Constable Trout put his boots back on and surveyed the crowd. "You all look like criminals to me. Give me one good reason why I shouldn't put the pack of you in handcuffs and send you off to Chokevine."

"Excuse me, Constable," said Mrs. Webster. "Several of our guests have spent the weekend investigating Mr. Abernathy's murder. Before you arrest anyone, wouldn't you like to be informed about the evidence they've collected?"

Constable Trout grunted. "I suppose that might be useful," he said. "All right, detectives. Let's have it. I want to hear each of your theories about who killed Hugh Abernathy, and I don't want any cheek. You, in the back." He pointed a thick finger at Julia Hartshorn, who shrank back slightly in her chair. "You'll go first. What have you got to say about this case?"

Julia got to her feet. She wore a long, thick sweater over her dress, and Toby noticed that she'd tugged the sleeves down past her wrists. Was Ivy right? Could she be the Colebridge Cutthroat? Whatever crimes she'd committed, she'd escaped from prison and lived on a street full of detectives for years without getting caught. What else could she get away with?

"You arrived several hours earlier than we'd been told to expect you, sir," Julia said, staring at the wallpaper over Constable Trout's head. "I didn't have time to run most of the tests I'd planned—"

"Excuses!" huffed the constable.

"—but I do have some preliminary results," Julia said firmly. "Mr. Abernathy was poisoned with Brandelburg acid, which was added to a bottle of his favorite digestive tonic at some point on Friday afternoon. I found at least two different sets of fingerprints on the bottle—possibly three, though the prints are so smudged that it's hard to make them out. One set is mine, and the second is most likely Mr. Abernathy's."

"Then the third set belongs to the murderer?" Trout asked.

"Not necessarily," said Julia. "As I told you, I'm not sure there *is* a third set. Our murderer might have taken care not to touch the bottle as he poured in the poison. And any number of other people must have held the bottle at some point—a pharmacist, for example, or Doctor Piper, or a housemaid. Anyway, the prints aren't clear enough to be useful."

"In that case," said Trout, "you've wasted my time."

Julia pulled her sweater sleeves down over her knuckles. "I also searched the house for common sources of Brandelburg acid," she said. She was talking more quickly now, and Toby could understand why: the sooner she finished, the sooner the constable would focus his glare in someone else's direction. All Toby could do was hope that direction wouldn't be his own. "In the waste bin near Mrs. Webster's desk, I found an empty canister of metal polish. I also found a half-empty canister in one of the desk drawers. As I'm sure you're aware, constable, metal polish contains more than a small amount of Brandelburg acid."

"Really!" Constable Trout's eyebrows crawled up his forehead. "You have plenty of household staff, Mrs. Webster. Don't they polish the silver for you?"

"I am an archaeologist, Constable," Mrs. Webster said coolly. "I restore and preserve ancient artifacts. In my work, I occasionally use a polishing compound to clean the metal tools and housewares we uncover. Surely that isn't a crime."

"Archa-ma-whatsis! Sounds suspicious to me." The

constable looked back to Julia. "Are you accusing Mrs. Webster of murder, then?"

"I don't think that would be responsible, sir. I'm not ready to accuse anyone at all. There's just not enough evidence."

Constable Trout glowered. "Another excuse." He jabbed a finger in the air once more, this time toward Mr. Rackham. "Next!" he said. "Have you got anything useful for me?"

Mr. Rackham cleared his throat. "I don't put any stock in these new techniques, sir. In my years of experience, I have found that when you want to get to the heart of a case, it's necessary to ask only one question: *Where is the money?*" He looked around the room at each detective in turn, letting the question hang in the air. "Mr. Abernathy, as you'll recall, had a great deal of it—but what happens to it now that he's passed away? Who stood to benefit most from his death?"

Miss Price shrugged. "Why don't you tell us, dear?"

"I will!" said Mr. Rackham. "Ladies and gentlemen, I suggest to you that the person who killed Hugh Abernathy was his only friend, his closest companion, and the very person who now owns his vast fortune: Mr. Peartree!"

No one in the room looked more surprised to hear this than Mr. Peartree himself.

"I'm afraid there's been a mistake!" he stammered. "I didn't inherit any of Mr. Abernathy's money. In fact,

I witnessed his will. Apart from the money he'd set aside for this contest, Hugh left every cent of his fortune to the Colebridge Home for Ailing Detectives."

Mr. Rackham squinted at him. "Are you sure?"

"*I* am," said Constable Trout. "Do you think my deputies haven't been to see Abernathy's lawyer? It's just like the little green man said: the funds go to charity, and no one named Peartree gets a penny." He stared hard at Mr. Rackham. "Another waste of time."

"Oh dear." Mr. Rackham sat down unsteadily, and Julia patted his hand.

"Who's left?" said Constable Trout. "Just the two of you, isn't that right?" He pointed at Miss March and Miss Price. "Don't tell me you're as hopeless as the others."

The women exchanged a look. "I'm very sorry, Constable," Miss Price said kindly, "but we have no information to give you."

"None at all?" Trout's eyes narrowed. "Aren't you those batty old ladies who always have their noses in other people's affairs? Do you really expect me to believe that you know nothing?"

"That's exactly what we expect," said Miss March. "I can tell you, though, that you'll be wasting your time digging into the backgrounds of every person in this room. Flossie and I are quite convinced that Mr. Abernathy's murderer was an outsider—a person who slipped in, poisoned the digestive tonic, and left the grounds before anyone even knew a crime had been committed."

"Yes," said Miss Price. "There are so many escaped convicts roaming the countryside these days, you know. It's a wonder more people aren't poisoned every day!"

Ivy was chewing on her lip. "That can't be true," she whispered to Toby. "The murderer couldn't have been an outsider, and they know it! Miss Price was the person who said so in the first place!"

Toby nodded. He was sure Miss March and Miss Price were lying to the constable, but he wasn't sure why. "Maybe they don't want Trout to solve the case," he whispered back. "Or maybe they're protecting someone."

"Maybe," said Ivy, "but who?"

"You two!" said Trout. Now his finger was pointing at Toby and Ivy. "I don't like whispering, and I don't like children. This is a serious criminal investigation. Isn't there some sort of nursery you can be sent away to?"

"*Nursery?*" Ivy was livid. She flew out of her chair and faced down Constable Trout. Toby wondered if she realized he was three times her size. "How dare you! I'm a detective!"

For a horrible moment, Toby thought Ivy would take a swing at the constable—and for a moment after that, he wondered whether he should let her. Before anyone's fists could start flying, however, there was a flurry of knocks at the front door and a rush of footsteps down the hall.

"Pardon me, Constable," said a harried-looking police officer, "but this lady demanded to be let inside. She says she's looking for a missing child." He turned to the woman behind him—silver-haired, stern-faced, and very, very clean. Toby jumped to his feet. "What did you say the child's name was?" the officer asked.

"*Toby Montrose!*" said Aunt Janet.

Not even the offer of a hot cup of tea could quell Aunt Janet's fury. "Thank you, but I won't be staying," she informed Mrs. Webster. "I've only come to collect Toby and bring him safely home." She kept one efficient hand on Toby's shoulder so he couldn't run away—not that he had any idea where he might run to. "If I'd known earlier that he'd invited himself to your house without permission, I would have retrieved him at once. I can't apologize enough for his behavior."

"That's really not necessary," Mrs. Webster said. She gave Toby a sympathetic sort of look.

"Oh, but it is! Do you know what you've put me through, Toby? When I went to Detectives' Row and found you weren't there, I almost fainted from worry."

"I'm sorry," said Toby, even though he didn't think Aunt Janet had ever been in real danger of fainting from anything. "I didn't want anyone to worry. I left a note!"

"And it's lucky I found it," Aunt Janet said, "or you'd still be missing."

"I wasn't missing!" Toby protested. "I knew exactly where I was the whole time."

But Aunt Janet was already guiding Toby toward the doorway. "Come along," she said. "We have a lot to discuss, but we won't do it here. We've already disrupted these poor people's weekends quite enough."

Ivy stepped in front of them. "Toby can't leave!" she said. "This is a crime scene, and he's got to stay here until the crime is solved."

"That's right," said Toby. Surely even Aunt Janet wouldn't dare to interrupt a murder investigation. "We still haven't figured out who killed Mr. Abernathy."

"I'm sure the constable can do that without any help from you," Aunt Janet told him. "Isn't that right, sir?"

Constable Trout nodded. "The last thing I need is another child getting underfoot."

"He's a *detective*!" said Ivy, but no one listened.

"You'll come back to Colebridge with me," said Aunt Janet, "and you'll stay there until we've decided what's to be done with you. After all that's happened this weekend, I can't risk losing you, too."

Toby stared up at her. The corners of her eyes were glistening in a way he'd only seen once before, three years ago, when the police officer had come from the seashore and

303

knocked on her door. "What do you mean?" he asked her. The words felt brittle and stale at the back of his throat. "Who else have you lost?"

"Oh, Toby." Aunt Janet's voice wavered. "I've gotten a message from Gallis. It's about your uncle Gabriel."

PART V

WHODUNIT?

CHAPTER 25

A VISIT TO MR. PEARTREE

In the days since Aunt Janet had hustled Toby out of Coleford Manor and back to her house in the city, Toby had hardly left his bedroom. Aunt Janet knocked on his door every few hours to bring him thick bowls of oatmeal, and a cousin or two came by every so often to ask if he wanted to talk, but Toby couldn't see what there was to talk about.

He especially didn't want to talk about Uncle Gabriel, who hadn't been heard from for a week now. After stepping off the ferry in Gallis, Uncle Gabriel had told the proprietress of his shabby hotel that he was a detective working on the most important case of his career. If he didn't return to the hotel the following evening, he told her, it would mean he was in trouble. When that evening had come and gone with no sign of Uncle Gabriel, the hotel proprietress had contacted the police, and an apologetic young sergeant had shown up to make contrite, worried faces on Aunt Janet's doorstep. Aunt Janet kept telling Toby through the door, although he didn't want to talk about it, that Uncle Gabriel was a persistent sort of person, and that he could wriggle his way out of a sticky situation if anyone could. As the days trudged past, however, she said this less and less.

Every morning, Toby read the newspaper, searching for stray bits of information about the investigation at Coleford Manor. Sometimes Constable Trout's face leered up at him from the front page, but the constable hadn't yet made any more progress than the detectives had in solving Mr. Abernathy's murder, and Toby couldn't help feeling pleased. Every afternoon, he studied the notes he'd taken that weekend, looking for clues he might have missed the first hundred times through. And every evening, he lay in bed while the trouble howled around him, keeping him awake.

On Friday morning, while Toby was reading in the *Morning Bugle* that Constable Trout had sent all the guests home from the manor but come no closer to solving the case, a thin, bloodless man from the Colebridge Children's Home came to see Aunt Janet. They spoke in low voices in the hallway, and every so often the thin man would look over in Toby's direction, though he never spoke to Toby once. Under the table, by Toby's ankles, the trouble shrieked with delight. "I'm very sorry," Aunt Janet told Toby after the thin man had left, "but with Gabriel gone, there's nothing more I can do. The Children's Home can take you in on Monday."

Over the past three years, Toby had been packed up and passed around more times than he could count. He'd never argued; he'd never complained; he'd never once tried to do anything about it. This time, though, was different. Maybe it was that boys of eleven were really nothing like boys of ten, or maybe it was that Toby was a detective now, but the more he thought about it, the more sure he felt. Uncle Gabriel wasn't coming home—that much seemed almost certain—and Toby was no closer to winning ten thousand dollars than he had been a week ago, but there was still one more thing he could do to stay out of the orphanage, even if it wasn't likely to work. He tried to ignore the sound of the trouble. "Excuse me, Aunt Janet," he said. "I need to send a letter."

The sun had just risen over the city rooftops when Toby turned into Detectives' Row two days later. It hadn't been easy sneaking out of Aunt Janet's house that morning, and he still felt guilty about the coins he'd slipped from her purse to pay for the carriage driver, but he promised himself that he wouldn't be gone long enough for anyone to miss him, and he'd pay Aunt Janet back as soon as he could. There, on the corner of the High Street, a girl was waiting for him. She wore a deep blue leotard and pink tights, and she was balanced on one leg, clutching a frilly parasol in one hand and holding her dog's leash in the other. Every time the dog tugged on it, the girl hopped and wobbled. For the first time in days, Toby could feel a smile creeping across his face. "Hello," he said to the girl. "Are you Mitzi, the world-famous trapeze artist and spy?"

"*There* you are!" Ivy put her foot down and folded up her parasol. "Thank goodness. I had to turn over three weeks' pocket money to the most frightening carriage driver in order to get here, and if I hadn't threatened to let Percival bite him, I think he would have asked for even more." She shuddered. "Now that I've followed the instructions in your letter, Detective Montrose, I'd be grateful if you'd tell me what we're doing here."

For the first time since Toby had moved to Detectives' Row, there was no long and winding line of clients outside the shiny black door to Mr. Abernathy's house. A few floral bouquets and framed illustrations from the *Sphinx* lined the sidewalk, but a small sign on the front steps read *NO VISITORS, PLEASE*, and the detective's loyal admirers seemed to be respecting its wishes.

Other things had changed, too. The last time Toby

had been to this house, he'd been small and worried, with trouble at his heels, so nervous he'd barely remembered his own name. Hugh Abernathy had been the world's greatest detective: a man who could answer any question, untangle any knot, and find a solution to any problem. Now, though, Toby knew there had been much more to the truth about Hugh Abernathy than he'd realized. He was beginning to suspect there was more to the truth about Toby, too. "We're solving a mystery," he told Ivy. "An important one."

"I don't see what we can do to solve Mr. Abernathy's case now that the police have taken over," Ivy said. "With that awful Trout person in charge, I don't think anyone will ever find out who murdered him."

"That's not the mystery I mean," said Toby. "Do you remember when you said we could ask Mr. Peartree to help us find the notes Mr. Abernathy took about my parents' disappearance?"

Ivy nodded.

"Well, I'm being sent to the Colebridge Children's Home tomorrow morning. Maybe my parents are still alive, and maybe they aren't, but this is the last chance I'll get to find out what happened to them." Toby took a long breath. "If they *are* alive, I won't have to go to the orphanage. And if they're not—"

"Don't even think it," said Ivy. She looked deadly serious. "I'm glad you asked me to come with you, Detective.

Webster and Montrose, Private Investigators are on the case."

It took almost two minutes for Mr. Peartree to appear, but when he did, he was as crisp and precise as ever. He was almost as green as ever, too, except for his hands, which were missing their gloves. It was a good thing Aunt Janet wasn't with them, Toby thought; she would have taken a scrubbing brush to the grime under Mr. Peartree's finger-nails.

"Mr. Montrose!" he said, reaching out to clasp Toby's hand in his. "Miss Webster! What a nice surprise. Is there something I can do for you?"

"We're here on official business," said Ivy. "Toby hired Mr. Abernathy to find his parents, and he's come to inquire about the status of the investigation."

Mr. Peartree raised his eyebrows.

"I was hoping I could look at my parents' case file," Toby explained.

"Ah." Mr. Peartree nodded. "Of course. Come in, both of you—but, please, Miss Webster, leave that wretched creature outside." He looked pointedly at Percival.

Ivy bristled, but she tied Percival's leash to the railing. They followed Mr. Peartree across the chessboard hallway, up the spiral staircase, past the door that said SKULLS, and through the tall double doors into Mr. Abernathy's study.

The shelves that had once been stuffed with books were half-empty now, and sturdy brown cartons were stacked along the walls.

"I apologize for the state of things," Mr. Peartree said, pulling his gloves back on. "I've been packing up Mr. Abernathy's belongings. The Colebridge City Museum has offered to purchase them, and I've got to send them along to the curator before I leave. The house goes up for sale next week, and I depart for sunny Gallis straight afterward." He ran a wistful finger across the spines of half a dozen *Sphinx*es. "But you children didn't come here to listen to me reminisce. May I get you something to drink? I've just poured a cup for myself." On a table near Toby's elbow stood a thin porcelain mug, filled to the brim with cream and coffee.

Toby and Ivy said they'd both like tea, if it wasn't too much trouble, and Mr. Peartree clattered down to the kitchen to see what he could do about it. "What a strange place," Ivy whispered once he was out of earshot. "Did you see that room full of bottles and vials? Julia Hartshorn would probably pay a fortune to get inside. Ooh, do you think Mr. Peartree would let me get a look at Hugh Abernathy's collection of disguises? It's got to be around here somewhere, and I bet it's fantastic."

Toby nodded, but he wasn't really paying attention. Something sticky and brown had gotten smudged on his palm when he'd shaken hands with Mr. Peartree, and he couldn't stand the idea of letting it stay there. "I hope Mr. Peartree won't mind if I use the washroom," he said. "I've got something on my hand."

"Oh, you and your *neatness*!" cried Ivy. "Honestly, Toby Montrose, sometimes I'd like to toss you into a mud puddle just to see what you'd do about it." She looked hard at Toby. "Something's wrong—wronger than mud, I mean. What is it?"

"It's this brown stuff," said Toby. "It's paint or something, I think, and it's gotten on me before. It smells just the same as the stuff in that leaky bottle in the broom cupboard back at Coleford Manor. Do you remember? It got all over Lillie's dress, and she had to wash it. Now Mr. Peartree's got some on his hands."

"Hair tonic!" said Ivy. "It leaked all over me, too, when I searched the manor. That's funny, though; I didn't know Mr. Peartree dyed his hair brown."

"He doesn't," Toby said. "At least, I *thought* he didn't. His hair was already brown to begin with, wasn't it?"

"He probably wants to hide his age," Ivy said knowledgeably. "Grown-ups are always trying to do that, you know. Mother says she started getting five gray hairs a minute after I was born."

She kept chattering away, but the smudge on Toby's hand still bothered him—and it wasn't just the smudge.

Other things were untidy, too, or strangely out of place: Mr. Peartree's gloves, his fingernails, the cup of coffee. Outside on the front steps, Percival howled. What had Mr. Peartree called him? A wretched creature?

Toby grabbed Ivy's arm so suddenly that even though she was Mitzi, the world-famous acrobat and spy, she still almost lost her balance. "Listen to me," he whispered, hoping against hope that the double doors weren't about to swing open. "I have to tell you something. It's about the man we just talked to."

Ivy frowned. "You mean Mr. Peartree?"

"That's just it," said Toby. "That's not Mr. Peartree."

CHAPTER 26

THE WRONG MURDER

"Of course that's Mr. Peartree." Ivy spoke slowly, as if Toby had just told a joke she didn't understand. "Who else could it be? Who else has a mustache like that? Who else wears so much green?"

"Anyone can wear green," said Toby, "and anyone can wear a false mustache. But did you see Mr. Peartree's fingernails? They were dirty, Ivy. I noticed it back at the manor, too."

Ivy groaned. "Everyone's fingernails are dirty, Toby."

"Not Mr. Peartree's! He's a very neat person—even neater than I am. Besides, he always wears gloves. How could he have gotten dirt and hair tonic on his hands if they're always covered up?"

"He's been packing boxes," said Ivy. "That must be awfully difficult to do in gloves. He probably took them off for a few minutes."

"Okay," said Toby, "but it's not just his hands that are wrong. Look at what Mr. Peartree was drinking."

Ivy stared at the mug on the table. "It's coffee."

"Right, but what else?"

Ivy shrugged. "Cream, I guess."

"Exactly!" Toby had to work hard to keep his voice at a whisper. "Do you remember my first day at the manor, when we snuck into the kitchen and observed the servants? They were making soup for dinner, and Cook shouted out that they couldn't put any cream in the soup, because *Mr. Peartree can't tolerate cream*. I wrote it down in my notebook."

"Are you sure?" said Ivy. "I brought Mr. Peartree extra cream for his coffee last Sunday morning. He asked for it specifically."

"Then that's even more evidence that something is wrong." Toby was sure of it now; he had to be right. All the questions that had fogged up his thoughts for days were beginning to burn away, leaving only a clear, bright truth behind them. Was this how Uncle Gabriel felt when he cracked a case? Toby hoped he'd have a chance to ask him someday. Right now, though, there wasn't any time to worry about Uncle Gabriel. "Ivy, this is really important.

Do you know if Mr. Peartree likes dogs?"

Ivy wrinkled her forehead. "I think he does. He scratched Percival behind the ears when he and Mr. Abernathy first came to the manor. I noticed particularly because Mr. Abernathy *didn't* say hello to Percival himself, and I thought that was rude."

"Mr. Abernathy hated dogs. He didn't like any animals, actually—at least that's what it says in 'The Adventure of the Kidnapped Greyhound.' He and Mr. Peartree were hired to find a valuable racing dog, and he complained about it the whole time."

"I read that story," said Ivy. "Poor Percival. No wonder that awful Mr. Abernathy wasn't kind to him."

"When I first met Mr. Abernathy," Toby said, "he called Percival a wretched creature. That's exactly what Mr. Peartree called him today, too. But why would Mr. Peartree say that if he doesn't hate dogs? Think about it, Ivy: the dyed hair, the dirty fingernails, the cream, the way Mr. Peartree acts around Percival. None of it makes sense—unless that man isn't Mr. Peartree at all."

Ivy sat down on a packing carton. "Hugh Abernathy was a master of disguise," she said quietly. "He once dressed up as a merchant seaman and worked on a ship for seven months before anyone realized he didn't know a thing about the sea." She folded her hands under her chin and looked up at Toby. "Hugh Abernathy isn't really dead, is he?"

"I don't think so," said Toby. "I think he's downstairs in the kitchen, making our tea."

"And what about the real Mr. Peartree?"

Toby thought back to that awful first evening at Coleford Manor: the purple corpse in the purple room, its hand stretched toward the glass of poisoned digestive tonic, its face contorted almost beyond recognition. It had been wearing Mr. Abernathy's clothes, but anyone could wear those. Had any of the detectives taken a really good look at the body? No one was likely to get a chance now, of course, since it had gone missing.

"Oh no." Toby sat down next to Ivy. "Inspector Webster, we've been investigating the wrong murder."

A pair of moss-colored shoes clicked down the hall toward Mr. Abernathy's study, and a green-gloved hand turned the doorknob. Toby and Ivy were prepared for this. After more than a little arguing, they'd finally agreed on what to do. They'd thank the man in green for the tea, explain that they really couldn't stay, and leave as quickly as they possibly could without looking suspicious. After that, they'd go straight to Miss March and Miss Price with their theory. Toby wasn't sure whether the women would believe that

Mr. Peartree was dead, and that Hugh Abernathy had poisoned him, but considering their opinion of Mr. Abernathy, he thought they might at least be willing to listen. Toby was certain of one thing, though: if Mr. Abernathy really had murdered Mr. Peartree, it was much too dangerous for Toby and Ivy to confront him on their own. Ivy had wanted to, of course, but she'd finally given in and admitted that Toby's plan was the only sensible one, even if it wouldn't bring any fame and glory to Webster and Montrose, Private Investigators. "Fame and glory," Toby had told her, "aren't as important as staying alive. And remember: don't drink that tea!"

Now the man in green set down the tray he'd been carrying. "I'm sorry to have kept you waiting," he said. He really did look almost exactly like Mr. Peartree, Toby thought—but was the bridge of his nose the slightest bit crooked, as though someone long ago had punched it? "The kitchen stove has a mind of its own, I'm afraid. Now, Mr. Montrose, let me see if I can find the information you're looking for. It should be on this shelf right here, under the letter *M*."

The man in green turned his attention to the bookcase. He didn't seem to notice that Toby's hands were trembling a little or that Ivy was glowering at him from beneath her parasol. "Actually, sir," said Toby, "we promised my aunt that we wouldn't be late for Sunday lunch, and we'd better leave before she starts to worry. I'm sorry to have bothered you."

"Leave?" The man in green turned to look at Toby. "What about your parents' case, Mr. Montrose? I'm sure it will take only a few moments for me to find Mr. Abernathy's notes."

"That's all right," Toby said quickly. "I can come back for them later."

"I can write an apology to your aunt—"

"No," said Toby, "that would only make things worse. She hates apologies." He didn't feel as if he was lying with much confidence; could the man in green tell how nervous he was? Some people said Hugh Abernathy could spot a lie from three hundred yards away, and Toby was less than three. He lifted his chin a little higher. "Come on, Ivy," he said. "We shouldn't waste any more time."

"Wait!" The man in green moved toward them. "What about your tea?"

"Thank you," Ivy said sweetly as she followed Toby toward the doors, "but we wouldn't want to spoil our appetites."

"It's not poisoned, you know," the man in green called after them.

Toby froze. It seemed to him that the room had gone quiet around them. The floorboards stopped squeaking, the pipes stopped clanging, and even the books on their shelves held their breath. "Poisoned?" he said. "Why would it be poisoned?"

The man in green let out a spring drizzle of laughter. "Don't look so worried, Mr. Montrose. It's just that I know how much you children enjoy playing your detective game. Interviewing suspects, setting traps, avoiding suspicious-looking cups of tea—it's all very charming. I thought you might be playing your game again this afternoon." He glanced at Ivy, who was looking daggers at him and clenching her jaw. "Now, of course, I can see you're not. My apologies."

But Ivy had had enough. "A *game*?" she shouted. She threw her parasol to the floor and marched back toward the man in green. "I'm tired of your games, Hugh Abernathy. You think everything's a game, don't you? You think blackmail is a game! You think murder is a game! You invited a crowd of detectives to a party where you poisoned your own assistant! Toby didn't want me to confront you—and honestly, Toby, I'm sorry—but I can't stand here for one more second letting you think that you're the world's greatest detective, when anyone can see you're as false as your mustache!"

Toby sighed and picked up the remains of the parasol, which had splintered into pieces when it landed on the floor. Why couldn't Ivy ever stick to the plan? She really was impossible! At this rate, she was going to get both of their heads preserved for eternity in Mr. Abernathy's room full of skulls. Even so, as he watched her rail at the man in green, Toby couldn't help hoping they'd end up next to each other on the shelf.

"You might as well know that Webster and Montrose are the *new* greatest detecting team in town," Ivy told the man in green, "and the first thing we do will be to expose your crimes. It's about time the world found out the truth about Hugh Abernathy." She held out an open hand. "Now, my colleague and I would like our ten thousand dollars, please. We've won your contest, haven't we?"

Slowly, carefully, the man in green walked to the far end of the room and sat down in Hugh Abernathy's leather chair. "I suppose you have won," he said—not in Mr. Peartree's voice, but in his own. "Congratulations, detectives. I didn't think anyone would crack this case, but I should have remembered that even when nothing is likely, everything is possible." He shrugged. "Before you try to slap me in hand-cuffs, however, may I offer you both a piece of advice? It was once given to me when I confronted an adversary during 'The Adventure of the Catacombs,' and I think you might find it useful now."

Ivy frowned at him. "All right."

"Excellent," said Hugh Abernathy. He reached one hand into the pocket of his green twill pants. When he pulled it out again, it held a small silver pistol. "I suggest you run."

CHAPTER 27

THE TRUTH AT LAST

Toby didn't need to be told twice. Before Hugh Abernathy could get up from his chair, both he and Ivy were out the tall doors and down the chessboard hallway. Toby had never run so fast in his life. "Did you see that pistol?" Ivy said. "I'm almost sure it's the same one he swiped from the villainous jewel thief in 'The Adventure of the Yellow Diamond'! Do you think it still fires?"

"I'd really rather not find out," said Toby, "if it's all the same to you." He flew around the curves of the spiral staircase and raced toward the front door. The iron knob felt cold under his hands. When he tried to turn it, nothing happened. "Ivy," he whispered, "it's locked."

"Let me try." Ivy elbowed him aside and tugged at the

doorknob. It didn't budge. Then they both tried pulling at once, but even the two of them couldn't break through Mr. Abernathy's locks and latches. On the other side of the door, Toby could hear Percival whining.

"You shouldn't waste your energy on that," Mr. Abernathy called down to them. He stood at the top of the staircase, twirling his pistol around one finger as if he had all the time in the world. "I double-bolted the door after I made your tea, and the only keys are in my pockets. I know this doesn't put me in the best light as a host, but then again, you two haven't been particularly gracious guests. I'm not accustomed to being shouted at in my own study."

"You'd better watch out," said Ivy, "or I'll shout some more." She gave the doorknob one last useless tug. "I'm so sorry, Toby. This is all my fault. I should have followed the plan."

"That doesn't matter now," said Toby. Mr. Abernathy was halfway down the stairs now, and so was his pistol. "Come on! We've got to find another way out."

They hurried across the hall, ducked into the kitchen, and took cover behind a stove. Toby's heart pounded in his ears, but he could still hear Mr. Abernathy's footsteps coming closer. "What does the correspondence course say about being chased by a criminal?" he asked.

"Nothing," Ivy muttered.

"You mean you haven't written the lesson yet?"

"I mean I haven't even thought about it! I didn't think it would be relevant! Everyone knows chases like that only happen in Hugh Abernathy stories. I never imagined we'd actually be *in* one." Ivy was breathing faster now, and sweat was glistening on her forehead. Was she starting to panic? Toby couldn't let that happen. He looked around the kitchen. In front of him was the door that opened out into the hallway; behind him was another door that stood halfway open, and a dark flight of stairs leading downward to the cellar.

"All right, Inspector Webster," he said, trying to sound calmer than he felt. "Here's the plan. We've got to split up." The idea of separating from Ivy made Toby feel sick, but he didn't think they had a choice. "There's no way Mr. Abernathy can follow us both. You go that way"—he pointed toward the cellar stairs—"and I'll go back into the hall. If there's another way out of this house, I'm sure one of us will find it."

Ivy nodded. "You're right," she said. "But what's going to happen to the other one of us?"

"Toby?" called Mr. Abernathy from the hall. "Ivy? Where have you gone?"

Both of them took off running. Ivy flew toward the cellar stairs, and Toby skidded back into the hall. There, to his left, was Mr. Abernathy, striding across the black-and-white marble in his moss-green shoes. When he saw Toby, he smiled and raised his pistol.

Toby turned hard to the right. In half a second, he'd plunged from the well-lit hallway into a warren of darkened hallways and even darker rooms. Mr. Abernathy had transformed his house into a kind of museum, with each room displaying a different bizarre exhibit. One was filled with dozens of animals' heads mounted on plaques—Toby was very glad Percival wasn't there to see them—while another held glass cases of rocks and gemstones, and a third contained a miniature model of the city of Colebridge, complete with a clockwork train and church bells that chimed the hour. Toby scraped his shin on one of the tiny High Street shops, but he didn't even think of stopping. He didn't want to hear footsteps behind him or see the shine of Mr. Abernathy's pistol. He thought of trying to escape through a window, but all the windows on the first floor were barred from the outside; there was nowhere to go but forward.

From the dollhouse room, Toby passed into a pitch-black space with thick curtains over the windows and a chemical smell that stung his nose, and then into a room filled from floor to ceiling with insect specimens: beetles and moths and things with too many legs. Toby wasn't entirely sure that all of them were dead. Finally, he stumbled up a narrow flight of stairs and stepped out into the light, blinking at the brightness all around him.

He was back in the chessboard hallway, on the second floor, but this was a part of the house he hadn't seen yet. The first door he tried opened onto a riot of green: piney wallpaper, rugs that grew like grass from the floor, and an open wardrobe full of identical green pants and vests and shoes. This room had obviously belonged to Mr. Peartree. Toby ran to the window, but although it wasn't barred, the only thing below it was a smooth white wall dropping down to the grass below. It was much too far to jump.

Toby left Mr. Peartree's room and tried the door on the opposite side of the hallway. This one said *WEAPONS*, and it was tightly locked. The door to the next room was open, though, and Toby wished Ivy had been there to see it.

The *DISGUISES* room reminded Toby a little of the laundry at his uncle Francis's hotel, with long metal racks of clothes, towers of hats, and traveling cases overflowing with everything from wigs to waterproof boots. Dressmakers' dummies showed off a few outfits Toby recognized: a merchant seaman's togs, an opera-ready tuxedo, and what looked to Toby like Mr. Abernathy's everyday clothes. There was even a harmonica tucked into the shirt pocket. Had anyone known the real Mr. Abernathy, or had his life as the world's greatest detective been another one of his disguises? Toby wasn't sure he'd ever find out, and at that particular moment, he didn't really care: just outside the window, he could see the sturdy branches of a tree reaching toward the house. Toby had never climbed trees—they tended to leave your clothes torn up and your hands covered in sap—but if this tree could help him escape, he didn't care how messy he might get. He rolled up his shirtsleeves and ran to the window.

"I'm very sorry, Toby," said Mr. Abernathy behind him. Something in his pistol went *click*. "I'm going to have to ask you to stay."

Toby had spent years watching the trouble flit across walls and slip under doorways, but it usually stayed just at the edge of his sight. Now that Mr. Abernathy's pistol was pointed at him, though, the trouble was everywhere: oozing over his arms and legs, crawling through his hair, flooding every inch of the house, and pouring out through the cracks into the rest of Detectives' Row. How hadn't he noticed it before? Had he really believed he could beat Hugh Abernathy at a game the detective had been playing for years? What had he been thinking? He wasn't a real detective; he had no idea what had happened to Ivy; Uncle Gabriel was missing; and if he somehow managed to avoid being shot in the next few minutes, he'd be sent to the orphanage tomorrow. All around him, the trouble snickered.

"You can't kill me, you know," Toby told Mr. Abernathy,

trying to sound braver than he felt. "Ivy's probably gotten out of the house by now. She'll get the police, and they'll be here any minute."

"Maybe," said Mr. Abernathy. "Everything *is* possible. I think it's much more probable, though, that Miss Webster is stuck in the wine cellar. After all, I locked the cellar door behind her. If she does manage to escape, I'm sure she'll tell everyone exactly what's happened—but who do you think will believe her? Admit it, Toby: it's an unlikely story, and children like Ivy have very active imaginations." He sighed and sat down on a trunk full of costume jewelry, still pointing the pistol at Toby. "Anyway, I'm glad it's just the two of us now. Ivy certainly enjoys the spotlight, but between you and me, I've always thought you were the more gifted detective. Now I'd like to know for sure. Why don't you tell me how I killed Mr. Peartree?"

"Excuse me, sir?" Toby couldn't help thinking of Mrs. Arthur-Abbot, swatting at the mouse in her peach silk dress, and the thought was almost enough to make him laugh. "I don't think you need me to tell you that."

"Oh, *I* know how I did it, of course. I'm just curious to see if *you* do. Have you really outwitted every other detective on the Row, or have you just made a lucky guess?" He tapped the barrel of his pistol. "If you do well enough, I might not have to fire this."

"All right." He didn't know exactly how Mr. Abernathy

330

had murdered his assistant, and he didn't know why, but he certainly wasn't going to admit that. If there was one thing Ivy had taught him, it was how to lie with confidence. "I know you came to Coleford Manor on Friday dressed as yourself," he said, "and so did Mr. Peartree. It was the real Mr. Peartree who welcomed me to the house. You were still yourself at the badminton game that afternoon—I don't think a fake Mr. Abernathy could have gotten Julia Hartshorn quite so mad."

Mr. Abernathy nodded. "Surely not."

"You told me then that you wanted me to come see you before dinner," Toby said. "I wondered about that. I thought you were going to give me news about my parents' case, but you never planned to do that at all. You didn't even have their case file with you. I think you just wanted to make sure that someone would find the body—someone you thought you could fool easily enough."

"Harsh," said Mr. Abernathy, "but accurate. Please continue."

Toby hesitated. What *had* happened that day after the badminton game? All he could do was guess. "You and Mr. Peartree went back inside the manor," he said. "That's when you switched clothes. I bet you told Mr. Peartree that it was part of the contest—that you wanted to see if the detectives would notice you'd traded places. You dyed your hair using that leaky bottle of hair tonic you'd hidden in the broom cupboard, where no one was likely to notice it. Mr. Peartree shaved his mustache, but I don't think he could have dyed his hair, too. It's a lot harder to turn dark hair golden."

"As golden as a sheaf of wheat," Mr. Abernathy said. "You're right. He wore a wig."

"Then you switched bedrooms. You went into the Fern Room, and Mr. Peartree went into the Orchid Room. I'm guessing you'd already poisoned your own bottle of Bertram's digestive tonic by that time. Did you remind him to drink it? Did you tell him the detectives would notice if he didn't act exactly the way you would? Either way, Mr. Peartree drank the Bertram's—it was so bitter that he didn't notice the taste of Brandelburg acid—and you locked the door to the Orchid Room. By the time I came to see Mr. Abernathy, you were ready to help me discover the body. You probably splashed water in your eyes to make it look like you regretted the whole thing."

Mr. Abernathy leaned back against the wall. "Not bad work," he said. "Of course, Gabriel was impressive, too, when he was your age. Underestimating the Montrose family is one of my worst tendencies. You did miss a few details, but they're small ones. For example, did you know that being poisoned with Brandelburg acid can cause a person to cry out in pain? It's not a pleasant noise, so I put on one of my opera records to mask the sound. As for my tears, they were genuine. I was never very kind to Mr. Peartree, but he was the closest thing I had to a friend. It's a shame, really—he spent his life writing wonderful stories about me, but no one will ever know the story of why he had to die. It would have made an excellent piece in the *Sphinx*."

Mr. Abernathy was tossing his pistol from one hand to the other now, and Toby wished he'd stop. On the other hand, if he stopped, he might shoot. "You could tell me the story," Toby said. "I'd like to hear it."

There was Mr. Abernathy's spring drizzle of laughter again. Even as Mr. Peartree, he hadn't quite been able to disguise it. "You're buying time," he said. "I'm not a fool, Toby. But I *will* tell you what happened, and not only because I enjoy the sound of my own voice." He pushed up the sleeves of his meadow-colored coat and removed his verdant felt hat. "For many years, Mr. Peartree and I worked wonderfully together. I was the world's greatest detective, and he was the world's greatest assistant. I counted on Mr. Peartree to polish my cuff links and my image, and that's exactly what he did. I paid him well, and in return, he put up with me. At least, that was our agreement."

Toby remembered how Mr. Peartree had sighed as his pocket watch had flown from Hugh Abernathy's hands and shattered on the floor. What else had Mr. Peartree been asked to put up with? "Did he know you were blackmailing your clients?" Toby asked.

"He knew enough not to gripe about it. After all, as I told him more than once, why shouldn't criminals pay for their crimes? It's not strictly *legal*, of course—but neither is purchasing a stolen artifact, say, or giving out government secrets, as my friend Lord Entwhistle was doing."

The trouble was crawling up Toby's shirt collar now, and he tried to brush it away. "That doesn't make it all right to steal people's money."

Hugh Abernathy cast his eyes to the heavens. "You sound just like your uncle. Fortunately, Mr. Peartree kept whatever thoughts he might have had to himself. Last winter, though, completely out of the blue, he came to me and handed in his resignation. He was tired of being nothing more than an assistant, he said; he had the bizarre impression that his talents were being wasted, and he planned to open a detective's practice of his own. I'm sure you can imagine the pickle that put me in: if Mr. Peartree left my employment, he'd take all my secrets with him, and I couldn't allow that. The man wasn't a very good detective, but he knew enough about me to be dangerous. Unlike your uncle and those nosy neighbors of his, Mr. Peartree had real proof of my private business, and I knew he'd be willing to share it with the world for a price. What else could I do? I asked Mr. Peartree to stay on my staff for six more months, out of kindness to me, and I began to plan the greatest case of my career: the Murder at Coleford Manor."

"The third *M*," Toby said quietly. Fear had been Mr. Abernathy's motive for getting rid of his assistant, then—but that hardly answered all of Toby's questions. "It would have been easy for you to poison Mr. Peartree's breakfast," he said, "or to make sure he died in an awful accident. No one would have known it was murder. Why did you do it in public? And why invite all the detectives in the city to the scene of the crime?"

"Two excellent questions!" Mr. Abernathy clapped one hand against the pistol, making Toby jump. "You're using that brain of yours, aren't you? Now try to use it just a little more. Tell me, how's business on Detectives' Row these days?"

Toby squirmed. "Not good, sir."

"Exactly. I still have a handful of loyal clients, but even the Abernathy name isn't what it used to be. Everyone's a detective these days! Armchair sleuths think that if they read a few of my stories, they'll learn enough to be able to solve their own cases! That's alarming enough on its own, but to make matters worse, I noticed that some other detectives on the Row—Miss Hartshorn, Miss March and Miss Price, Mr. Rackham, even your uncle—were still bringing in some clients here and there. Why weren't those clients coming directly to me?

"You see, Toby, I had to do something extraordinary! Something that would put my name back on the front page of every newspaper, make my competitors look like fools, and remind everyone that only Hugh Abernathy is truly the world's greatest detective. If that same extraordinary plan could help me clean up my mess with Mr. Peartree, too, so much the better."

"So you faked your own death?"

"It worked!" cried Mr. Abernathy. "Did you see that picture of me in the *Morning Bugle*? Did you read the articles? Did you see the crowds of fans and admirers? You can't find a person in Colebridge who won't tell you I was the finest investigator in the city. Even better, my competitors' reputations are in shambles. I'd hoped those files I'd left behind about their suspicious backgrounds would be leaked to the press, but even if that never happens, they're still famous for being incompetent at best and dangerous at worst. They couldn't even solve my murder. They'll all be out of business within the month."

"So will you!" said Toby. "Everyone thinks you're dead!"

"That *is* inconvenient," Mr. Abernathy agreed. "I can't say I'm thrilled about losing all that money to charity, either, or about giving my belongings to that dust trap of a museum. But just think of how stunning it will be when, in a year or two, I make my miraculous return from the grave. I can imagine the headlines already: 'The Detective Who Outwitted Death Itself!' I'll earn back all the money I've lost, and more besides. I'll be a legend, Toby. What do you think of that?"

Toby's throat felt dry. "I think that's awful," he said. "I think you've hurt a lot of people, and you don't even care."

Mr. Abernathy sighed. "I was hoping you'd be more impressed. I've gone to a lot of trouble to keep you alive, you know. When I first realized that you and Ivy might actually be intelligent enough to solve the crime, I *could* have squashed you as flat as a pancake, but I decided to give you a good scare instead: the griffin, the ransacking, et cetera. I wanted you off the case, but I didn't want you gone altogether. I could shoot you now"—he gave his pistol a twirl—"but I'd really prefer not to. Do you remember when I said I'd give you a chance to repay me?"

Toby nodded. "Yes, sir." Ivy had been right; he *was* too polite.

"Then I'll be frank. Your parents are dead, Toby. They didn't survive that accident at the seashore. And I'm sorry to say it, but it sounds as though your uncle is also gone for good. What's next for you? The orphanage?" Mr. Abernathy peered at Toby through the rising swarm of trouble; soon it would be past Toby's neck, and over his eyes, and then it would swallow him whole. He couldn't move. He could barely think. "A boy like you shouldn't be in an orphanage,"

Mr. Abernathy said. "I meant what I told you back at the manor: I think you'll go on to do remarkable things, and I'd like you to do them with me. With Mr. Peartree gone, I happen to be in need of an assistant. If you're willing, we'll leave for Gallis next week. There's plenty for you to do: correspondence to send, clothes to iron, stories to write for the *Sphinx*. But if you're not willing . . ." He raised his pistol. "Well, you know how I feel about my secrets. I can't allow them to get away."

The trouble was clouding Toby's vision now; he could hardly see through the shadows. He could feel it pressing against him, as cold and as frightening as the steel of Mr. Abernathy's pistol, and he could hear it taunting him. Even if he went with Mr. Abernathy—and did he really have a choice?—the trouble would follow. After all, he knew the truth for sure now: his parents weren't coming home. Whether he went all the way to Gallis or stayed at the Colebridge Children's Home, there would always be someone else to please, someone else to be afraid of, more messes to clean up, and more things to apologize for, and right now, in the middle of the most disastrous moment of the eleven years of his life, Toby was sick of it.

"Go away!" he said to the trouble. "Stop following me around, stop laughing at me, and get out of here. I don't care where you go, as long as you never come back!"

Mr. Abernathy looked confused. "Are you talking to me?"

But Toby hardly heard him. It was as though he'd pulled the plug out of a bathtub drain. All around him, the trouble was receding, swirling lower and lower as he watched. First his eyes were clear, then his throat, then his waist and his ankles. It was the funniest thing: in all the years the trouble had spent chasing after him, he'd tried to hide from it, fix it, and ignore it, but he'd never once thought of telling it to leave. Now that he'd done it, though, the trouble wasn't wasting any time. With a last reluctant gurgle, it disappeared entirely, and Toby could finally see what he hadn't noticed just a moment before: three long shadows in the hallway just beyond where Mr. Abernathy sat, and the tip of a tail that might have belonged to a small brown dog.

"I do have something to say to you, actually," Toby told Mr. Abernathy. For once, it felt wonderful not to be polite. "My uncle was right about you. You really are a puffed-up, self-serving old ostrich."

"Well said, Tobias!"

Gabriel Montrose stormed into the room like a one-man hurricane, grabbing hold of Mr. Abernathy's arms and twisting them backward, trying to wrestle the pistol away. Percival went after Mr. Abernathy, too, howling loudly enough to rattle the window glass. And then there was Ivy. "Get down, Detective!" she shouted as she crashed into Toby and knocked him to the floor. At least he was used to it by now. As he fell, he thought he could see the smart leather shine of a police sergeant's boots. Then his face hit the floorboards, and the pistol went off.

CHAPTER 28

A FULL HOUSE

No one could manage to keep Uncle Gabriel in bed. Toby tried, at least for the first few days, and so did Mrs. Satterthwaite, who came to Detectives' Row full-time for a while to help. More often than not, however, the two of them would find him puttering around in the kitchen or balancing on a ladder, taking a hammer to whichever part of the house had most recently come loose. "All with a bullet in his hip!" Mrs. Satterthwaite remarked to Toby each time they'd dragged Uncle Gabriel back to his bedroom. "And to think I was ever worried about that man. He's simply impossible."

Toby agreed. He was starting to really enjoy impossible people.

On the rare occasions when Uncle Gabriel was actually lying down, he told Toby all about what had happened in Gallis. "The greatest case of my career," he said happily, "and the one that finally gave that ostrich his comeuppance. Do you know how long I spent trying to pin down solid evidence of Hugh Abernathy's blackmailing scheme?"

"Twenty years?" Toby guessed.

"Eighteen, actually," said Uncle Gabriel, "although it felt more like a hundred. His victims were too frightened to turn him in, or too crooked to admit to their own crimes, and I knew it was useless to go to the police with only my word against his. At last I got wind of a Gallian cat burglar who'd received dozens of threatening letters from Mr. Abernathy and saved each one. The rumors said she was on her deathbed, and I hoped I could persuade her to hand over the letters to the authorities. Unfortunately, she was only half as close to dying as I'd been told, and ten times wickeder. I got those letters in the end, though, and only just in time." Uncle Gabriel patted the bandage on his hip and flinched a little. "If Ivy hadn't run into me coming down the Row that morning, Tobias, I shudder to think where this bullet might have ended up."

Toby shuddered, too. Owing his life to Ivy had quickly become annoying—she'd already reminded him several times of how skillfully Mitzi, the world-famous trapeze artist and spy, had shimmied up the walls of Mr. Abernathy's wine cellar, smashed open a high window with the help of a few expensive bottles from the racks, and walked straight into Uncle Gabriel, who'd mistaken the red wine she'd been drenched in for blood. Still, listening to Ivy brag was much nicer than the alternative.

"You didn't have to take *quite* so long to find a police officer, though," he'd told her. "And you could have warned me before you knocked me over."

But Ivy had brushed him off. "Oh, Detective Montrose," she'd said. "You still have so much to learn about the element of surprise."

Ivy visited the Row as often as she could slip away from Coleford Manor, and there had been other visitors, too. Mr. Rackham brought over a basket of eggs from his hens every morning, Julia Hartshorn stopped by with a bottle of medicine for Uncle Gabriel's hip, and one evening, Miss March and Miss Price showed up, laden with a questionable meat pie, a copy of the newspaper, and several bucketfuls of gossip.

"Did you hear they found poor Mr. Peartree, dear?" Miss Price said to Toby as they ate dinner by Uncle Gabriel's bedside. "Do you remember Doctor Piper, who came to take the body away? Well, she'd had it all along. I'm afraid she was one of Mr. Abernathy's blackmail targets. He'd found out she'd been selling cadavers to anatomists at the university—*not* a very nice practice, dear—and he threatened to expose her unless she helped him with his plan."

Toby thought, suddenly, of Egbert. He nearly choked on his forkful of pie.

"After a few minutes of prodding, any good medical examiner would have discovered that the body wasn't Mr. Abernathy's at all," Miss March added. "The wig on its head, for example, would have been a very useful clue. It's no wonder Mr. Abernathy had to hide the evidence. In any case, this is good news: Mr. Peartree will have a proper send-off, and Doctor Piper has agreed to testify at the trial. With her evidence and yours, and with those letters your uncle found, I don't think Mr. Abernathy is likely to see the outside of Chokevine Prison anytime soon."

Toby frowned. "Aren't people always escaping from Chokevine?"

"Hmm," said Miss March. "I hadn't thought of that. Well, I suppose if Hugh Abernathy ever does escape, he'll make an attempt to be the world's greatest criminal, and all of us on the Row will see a lot more business."

Miss March and Miss Price had plenty of news to pass along about all the people they and Uncle Gabriel knew, but most of it wasn't very interesting to Toby. "I was wondering," he said when they'd finally paused for breath. "Did you know all along that Mr. Abernathy was still alive? You seemed to know everything else about everyone."

"Gracious, no!" Miss Price clasped her hands to her

heart. "As far as we knew, he was dead as a dodo, and we were supremely grateful to whoever had done the deed."

"Actually," Miss March said in a low voice, "we thought it was Julia Hartshorn."

Toby had wanted to ask about Julia for days. "Is she really the Colebridge Cutthroat?"

"Good heavens!" Miss March looked horrified. "Where in the world did you get that idea?"

"I saw her tattoo," Toby admitted, "and I know she escaped from Chokevine."

"I see," said Miss March. "Well, it's true she'd been in prison, but she wasn't a cutthroat. She caused a horrible accident years ago. A chemistry experiment she'd done at school went badly wrong, and I'm afraid the school's headmistress died in the explosion. Julia went to great lengths to start a new life here on the Row after she slipped out of prison, but Mr. Abernathy discovered her secret, and he didn't hesitate to let her know it."

"So you *were* protecting her!" Toby couldn't wait to tell Ivy that his hunch had been right. "I knew you were lying to that awful constable."

"We like Julia," said Miss Price. "We do *not* like Constable Trout."

"Trout?" Uncle Gabriel called from his bed. "Is that what's in this pie, Flossie? It tastes ghastly."

"It's good to see fame hasn't gone to your head, Gabriel,"

Miss March said crisply. She tossed her newspaper at him. "Your picture may be on the front page of this morning's *Bugle*, but you haven't changed one bit."

Slowly, that summer, life on Detectives' Row did begin to change. The grand white house at the corner of the High Street was taken over by the Colebridge City Museum, which strung velvet ropes across the inner doorways and began offering guided tours of the home that had once belonged to the city's most notorious new criminal. For only a nickel, you could stand in the very place where Mr. Abernathy had sat as he waved his pistol at a brave young detective who'd uncovered his secrets. The wine cellar had been turned into a gift shop, and every morning at dawn, hired gardeners stepped out onto the balconies to trim the topiary. The tourists streamed in.

Some of those tourists had other business to conduct, too. Reluctantly at first, and more eagerly after that, they brought their stories of stolen gems and picked pockets to the Row's remaining detectives. Mr. Rackham had retired after the Coleford Manor case, but Toby still saw him out and about each morning, feeding his chickens. Those clients who preferred a scientific approach to their problems lined up outside Julia Hartshorn's house, while those looking for news about their friends and enemies hurried to see Miss March and Miss Price. And everyone wanted advice from the detectives who lived in the tall, narrow house in the middle of the Row, the one with walls that tilted ever so slightly to the east. Those detectives, after all, had bested Hugh Abernathy. The money didn't pour into their pockets, but at least it did more than trickle. Toby had even started to save up for a new silk dress for Mrs. Arthur-Abbot. And he was getting very good at answering the door.

One morning in September, when Uncle Gabriel had shut himself in the kitchen and mysteriously refused to let anyone in, Toby answered the front door of one-fifteen Detectives' Row and found Ivy on the other side of it. This wasn't unusual anymore. The Websters had sold Coleford Manor to a wealthy murder enthusiast and moved to a small house in the city, where Ivy's parents could walk to the museum, Ivy could walk to Detectives' Row, and Lillie, to everyone's regret, could walk to the *Morning Bugle* offices to exchange romantic gazes with Peter Jacobson. "I have to share a room with her!" Ivy had howled at Toby. "Do you have any idea what it's like to be surrounded by all that *neatness*?" After that, Ivy and Percival showed up on the Montroses' doorstep most mornings with crates of stuff from the Investigatorium, which they were in the process of relocating to Toby's bedroom.

Today, however, Ivy was holding a small white envelope. "Look at this!" she said, pushing it into Toby's hands.

"The police sent it to me, but it's really for both of us; you'll see."

Toby reached inside the envelope and pulled out a long, narrow strip of paper with writing on one side of it. "It's a check!" said Ivy, almost bouncing out of her shoes. "Made out to Webster and Montrose! Our very first payment. It's only a hundred dollars—not ten thousand, I know—but if the police want to thank us for helping them catch Mr. Abernathy, I'm certainly not going to complain about it."

The check didn't feel entirely real to Toby. He held on to it tightly, in case it blew away or crumbled or dissolved. "What should we do with it?" he asked. "Go to Doyle's Detection Goods? Or Secondhand Sleuthery? Buy a bone for Percival?"

Ivy shook her head. "It's for you," she said, "and your uncle. I know he could use it."

"Really?" Toby looked down at the check again to make sure it was still there. "Can we give it to him right now?"

Together, they ran through the kitchen door and straight into an enormous cloud of flour. Somewhere in the cloud, Uncle Gabriel sneezed. "Tobias?" he called out. "I told you not to come in! I am extremely busy."

"Are you making pancakes again?" Toby asked. He hoped not. "I'm sorry to bother you, but we've got something for you." As the flour cleared, Toby held out the check to Uncle Gabriel. "It's a hundred dollars."

"So you don't ever have to send Toby away," Ivy explained. "And maybe so you can buy breakfast."

Uncle Gabriel rubbed the flour from his eyes. He wrinkled his forehead and examined the check. Then, with an egg-splattered hand, he handed the check back to Toby. "I think we need to set two things straight," he said. "First of all, I have absolutely no intention of sending Toby anywhere."

"But what if the clients stop coming?" Toby asked. "What if we run out of money?"

"They might," said Uncle Gabriel, "and we might, but we'll survive somehow, and we'll do it together." He wiped his hands on the front of his apron. "My god, Tobias, have you spent all this time thinking I've been fifty cents away from casting you out?"

Toby could feel his cheeks flush. "You had all those unpaid bills," he said. "Aunt Janet said you couldn't afford to keep me for long, and I wasn't sure you even wanted me to stay. After all, you're the Last Relative."

"Egads." Uncle Gabriel sat down heavily on a kitchen chair. "I wish you'd been sent to me first. I was devastated when your parents died, and I wanted to meet you right then and there, but Janet warned me to keep my distance. She said a person who rubs shoulders with the criminal element isn't a suitable guardian for a young boy, and I have to admit I agreed with her. When I found out you'd be coming to live here, I worried that you'd be miserable. You're not miserable, are you, Tobias?"

"No!" said Toby. "I want to stay here forever. Only . . ." He looked sideways at Ivy. "I was wondering, Uncle Gabriel, if I could do more than answer the door and organize your files. I'm almost done with Ivy's correspondence course now, and I don't think I'm really cut out to be a detective's assistant." He took a deep breath and coughed a little from the flour. "I think I'm better at being a detective."

Uncle Gabriel shook his head. "Of course you are!" he boomed. "Even those fools on the western end of the Row can see that! You solved the crime of the decade, for goodness' sake! I thought you *liked* organizing files." He picked the check up from the floor and handed it back to Toby. "I want you to use this to get the Webster and Montrose Investigative Offices up and running, and I won't hear a word of protest. Make sure Tobias follows my instructions, Ivy."

"I will," Ivy said solemnly. "I'd also like to know the second thing you need to set Toby straight on. It's about how much he scrubs his fingernails, isn't it?"

"No," said Uncle Gabriel, "although that is a discussion we should have. I'm not making pancakes, Tobias; I'm making a cake. I wanted it to be a surprise, but as you can probably see, I could use some help." He waved his arms at the mess in the kitchen, nearly knocking over a mixing bowl in the process. "My powers of deduction have informed me that you have a birthday coming up, and I thought we should celebrate it. You do like cake, don't you?"

Toby grinned. "I love it."

"I suspected as much," said Uncle Gabriel. "Ivy, assuming we can whack this dessert together before midnight, why don't you join us? Bring that dog of yours, too. I could even invite Tobias's aunt Janet."

"*Not* Aunt Janet," said Toby and Ivy together.

Uncle Gabriel had just taken a whisk to a bowlful of eggs when there was a knock at the front door. He looked out into the hallway, down at the eggs, and then pleadingly at Toby. "I know we just discussed this," he said, "but do you think . . ."

"Don't worry," Toby told him. "I'll get it."

He dusted himself off, shook the flour from his hair, crossed the front hall, and pulled the door partway open. A woman stood there on the steps. She wasn't any older than his mother would have been, and Toby could tell from the way she clutched her sweater around her that she was in trouble, one way or another.

"Excuse me, sir," she said to Toby. "I'm sorry to bother you. I'm looking for the world's greatest detective."

Toby opened the door wide. "Then you've come to the right place."

ACKNOWLEDGMENTS

Although the city of Colebridge, its case of "detective fever," and its resident sleuths and criminals are fictional, they are loosely based on information from several nonfiction sources, particularly *The Suspicions of Mr. Whicher: A Shocking Murder and the Undoing of a Great Victorian Detective* by Kate Summerscale, *The Invention of Murder: How the Victorians Revelled in Death and Detection and Created Modern Crime* by Judith Flanders, and *The Poisoner's Handbook: Murder and the Birth of Forensic Medicine in Jazz Age New York* by Deborah Blum.

Thanks are due, as always, to Toni Markiet for her editorial wisdom, faith, and patience, and to the irreplaceable Abbe Goldberg. Thanks also to everyone at HarperCollins Children's Books who helped bring this story into the world, including Kathryn Silsand, Kimberly Stella, Amy Ryan, Tessa Meischeid, and Janet Rosenberg.

Huge thanks to Sarah Davies at the Greenhouse for her unyielding support, and to the wonderful team at Rights People.

Kristen Kittscher and Amy Rose Capetta read early drafts and gave invaluable mystery-writing advice; Cori McCarthy helped the story find its structure. More friends and family members than I can count lent their love and encouragement during the year I spent drafting this book, and for that, I won't ever be able to thank them enough. Zach, I'm sorry I couldn't tell you whodunit. Nora, I hope you'll love a good mystery.

Finally, thanks to Agatha Christie, Ellen Raskin, and Sir Arthur Conan Doyle, with much admiration and many apologies.

DON'T MISS CAROLINE'S NEXT BOOK

The Door at the End of the World

 **1**

There's no signpost to mark the end of the world, so you need to know what you're looking for: a gatehouse, a garden, and a tall brick wall overgrown with flowering vines. The gatehouse bell is broken, but if you've managed to travel all the way to the end of the world, you're obviously persistent enough to knock on the door. You'll have to wait awhile, too, since the Gatekeeper likes to take her time. Traveling from one world to the next isn't something a person should do on a whim, and she wants to make sure you mean it.

While you're waiting, after you've checked your watch twice and wondered about the note taped to the door that says BEWARE OF BEES, you might happen to look through the window into the front room, where a girl sits behind a desk piled high with papers. That's me. My name is Lucy. I'm the one you don't quite notice as I stamp your passport, collect your travel papers, and wish you the best of luck on your trip. I'm not allowed to take you to the tall brick wall or push aside the vines or unlock the door hidden behind them—only the Gatekeeper can do that—but I like my job. At the end of the world, it's important to be organized.

This close to the door, things tend to go missing. They're odds and ends, usually: gloves, keys, spare change, the occasional pencil stub, anything that might slip or squeeze or roll into the space between the worlds. "You'll get used to it," the Gatekeeper told me when I moved in. For the most part, she was right. I'd learned to stash extra gloves in my pockets and tie my pencils to the desk with bits of string; I'd started expecting to lose things. But I can't say I ever expected to lose the Gatekeeper herself.

It happened on an unremarkable Thursday. I'd cleaned the breakfast dishes and was sorting travel papers into stacks on my desk—pink customs declarations to the left, green returnee reports to the right, and blue applications for otherworld travel straight ahead—when the Gatekeeper stomped into the room. This was still unremarkable: the Gatekeeper always stomps. She has wild white hair that frizzes around her face when she's upset, or when it looks like rain, and she walks with a cane that she thwacks and thumps when she wants to make a point. She's not a witch, but some people think she might be, and she doesn't try to persuade them otherwise.

On this particular Thursday, the sky was blue and cloudless, but the Gatekeeper's hair was already starting to frizz at the ends. As soon as I saw the basket she was carrying, I knew why. It was full of rags and rolls of fabric, sewing needles and thread, wood polish and soap, and a screwdriver with a bright orange handle. "Happy Maintenance Day!" I said.

The Gatekeeper glowered. "*Happy* isn't the word I'd choose. I'd rather have my ears nibbled off by a thistle-backed thrunt than have to spend the day with Bernard." She set down her basket. "Well, maybe just one ear."

Bernard was the gatekeeper who guarded the other side of the door, keeping an eye on the travelers who passed from his world into ours and making sure no one smuggled out illegal otherworld goods, slipped past without their Interworld Travel papers in order, or stumbled through accidentally. He and the Gatekeeper had never been friendly—but then again, the Gatekeeper didn't like anyone from the next world over. According to her, Easterners were ignorant and impolite, and besides that, they smelled. Still, twice a year, the Gatekeeper went over to East for the morning to clean and polish the door between the worlds, tighten anything that had come loose, knot the stray threads in the fabric of time and space, and argue with Bernard over which of them got to hold the screwdriver. In the afternoon, both of them came back to Southeast and repeated the whole process on this side of the door. It was fiddly, tedious work, and at the end of the day six months earlier, the Gatekeeper had vowed to retire before Maintenance Day rolled around again, but both of us had known she didn't really mean it. I couldn't imagine what the end of the world would be like without her.

"Is Bernard really that bad?" I asked. I still hadn't met him. You might think that a girl living at the end of the world would have lots of thrilling adventures, but it wasn't quite like that for me. Even the Gatekeeper hardly ever went to other worlds, and in the year I'd been working as her deputy, I'd never actually been through the door myself.

"Bernard," the Gatekeeper said, "is always worrying about *irregularities*. Last Maintenance Day he swore there was something funny about the door hinges, and the time before that he was convinced the air near the worldgate smelled of lemon pie. He always wants to know if I've noticed any irregularities on my side, and of course I never have." She shrugged. "Have you noticed anything irregular, Lucy?"

I thought about it. "The bees seemed upset a few weeks ago," I said. "They found Henry Tallard wandering near the door without any travel papers. They told me they stung him twenty-three times before he finally ran away."

"Good for them!" The Gatekeeper cackled. "I don't care how famous an explorer you are; you can't go poking around my worldgate without my permission. Henry Tallard has been inconsiderate and nosy as long as I've known him, though. That doesn't sound so irregular to me."

I couldn't think of anything else unusual that had happened lately. A whirlwind had sprung up in a corner of the garden, right beside the zinnias, but that happened at least once a month. So did the lightning strikes that zigzagged down the side of the gatehouse; at the end of the world, the weather is always temperamental and usually dramatic. Three otherworld tourists had arrived the day before, passing through Southeast on their way to see the Great Molten Lagoon over in South, and two Interworld Travel employees from headquarters had hurried through the door on business just that morning, but none of them had been remotely interesting. They had all gazed over the top of my head as I took their travel papers, and people who find a vase on a fireplace mantel more fascinating than the human sitting in front of them can't be all that fascinating themselves. "If anything strange has happened here recently," I told the Gatekeeper, "it hasn't happened to me."

"That's exactly what I like about you, Lucy," the Gatekeeper said. "Nothing happens to you. At the end of the world, that's saying something." She stomped to the coat closet and threw on her cloak. "Unless Bernard finds some more irregularities to complain about, I'll be back by lunchtime. You know the rules by now, I assume."

I nodded. The Gatekeeper's rules were sensible, just the way I liked rules to be. "Don't open the worldgate, and don't let anyone through. Make travelers wait here until the maintenance is finished. Don't leave the end of the world for any reason, and eat my vegetables."

"And if there's an emergency?"

"Shout. Scream. Make a general ruckus." I frowned. "Are you sure you'll be able to hear all that through the door?"

"I've got two perfectly good ears, and you've got two strong lungs, which I trust you know how to use." The Gatekeeper

5

smiled at me, which wasn't exactly a habit of hers. "Goodbye, Lucy." She thumped her cane three times, picked up her basket of cleaning supplies, and stomped outside.

I watched from the window as she went down the garden path, her hair throwing a tantrum around her face and her cloak swishing witchily around her ankles. When she reached the wall covered with vines, she drew a key out of her pocket, unlocked the door between the worlds, and squeezed through it. The door closed behind her, and I went back to work.

The Gatekeeper didn't come back by lunchtime. She wasn't back for dinner, either. By the time I washed the day's ink stains from my hands, combed the tangles out of my hair, and crawled underneath the quilt I'd brought from home when I came to live at the end of the world, she still hadn't returned, and I was starting to worry. It shouldn't have taken her and Bernard more than a few hours to work on the Eastern side of the door, and even if they'd found some extra snags to mend or bolts to polish, I couldn't imagine why the Gatekeeper wouldn't have stuck her head through the worldgate to tell me about it. In my nook at the back of the gatehouse, I lay awake listening for the squeak of door hinges or the thump of the Gatekeeper's cane.

By sunrise, I was prickling with panic. The Gatekeeper wasn't snoring in her bedroom or yanking weeds in the garden or calling out from the kitchen to ask whether we had any more milk for porridge. The gatehouse was eerily quiet, and there wasn't anyone else in sight. In my nightgown and bare feet, I ran down the path to the wall and pushed aside the vines, even though I knew the bees wouldn't be happy about it. Then I tugged on the door at the end of the world.

It was locked, as usual. At least *that* was as it should be. "Gatekeeper!" I shouted, using my two strong lungs as well as I could. "Bernard! Can you hear me? Are you all right?" I pounded on the door with both fists as hard as I could. Then I picked up a handful of stones from the garden and started throwing the stones one by one against the wall. "I'm making a general ruckus," I explained to the bees as they buzzed all around me, investigating the situation. "The Gatekeeper's been over in East for almost a whole day, and you know how much she hates it there. If that's not an emergency, I'm not sure what is."

I kept my ruckus up for a good long while, but if anyone could hear it from the next world over, they must not have been impressed: the door stayed shut. Maybe Bernard had been right after all, and there *was* something wrong with it. "This," I said to the bees, "is definitely an irregularity."

The bees huddled together over my head, humming to each other. After a minute or so, they spread out again to form foot-high letters against the backdrop of the sky.

SPARE KEY?

I'd thought of this, too. The Gatekeeper had taken her key with her, of course, but she always kept a copy tucked in a hat-box in the darkest corner of the coat closet. "In a place like this, where things tend to go missing," she'd explained to me when

I'd first arrived, "having only one gatekey would be extremely foolish. But you're never to touch the spare one, Lucy, or I'll make sure you won't find a respectable job again—in this world or any other. Just ask my last deputy what happened to him." The Gatekeeper had smiled at me as she'd said this, but I was sure she hadn't been joking.

"Do you really think that's a good idea?" I asked the bees now. "I'm not supposed to go anywhere near that key, and I'm definitely not supposed to open the door."

EMERGENCY, spelled the bees.

"I know, I know." The thought of breaking one of the Gatekeeper's rules made me uncomfortably itchy, but if she was really in trouble on the other side of that door, I wasn't sure what else to do. "Just out of curiosity," I said to the bees, "do you know what happened to the Gatekeeper's last deputy?"

The bees hesitated. They looked a little nervous.

I sighed. "Never mind. I'll go and get the key."

The Gatekeeper, I discovered, owned a lot of hats. By the time I found the right dusty hatbox, the one that held a small saw-toothed key instead of a bonnet or a bowler, the sun had risen above the treetops. This gave me something else to worry about. I'd been lucky so far, but eventually some explorer or trader or half-witted adventurer was going to arrive at the gatehouse, waving their papers at me and demanding to go to the next world over. How would I explain what had happened to the Gatekeeper, or when she'd be back? How would I keep an increasingly large and grumpy pack of travelers safely inside? There wasn't that much space around the dining room table.

I crawled out of the coat closet and dusted myself off. "Stop worrying," I told myself, holding the spare key tighter. "The Gatekeeper will be home by then." It would be simple enough to unlock the door and let her through, I thought as I went back down the path toward the wall. I'd never opened a worldgate before, but it looked just like any other door; how complicated could it be?

FINALLY, said the bees.

"I'd like to see *you* search through forty-three hatboxes," I told them. They hovered around me as I pushed aside the vines and slipped the gatekey into the lock.

"I'm sorry, Gatekeeper," I whispered. I turned the key until something clicked. "Please don't fire me."

Then I pulled open the door at the end of the world.

2

Not many people get an opportunity to stand with their feet in one world and their eyes gazing into the next—and I didn't, either. As the door swung toward me, someone tumbled through it.

"Oh dear!" he said as he fell.

I didn't have time to think. I let go of the doorknob and leaped aside to avoid being squashed, and the door in the wall slammed shut.

It took a few moments for me to realize what had happened. A boy was lying on his back on the ground, and his eyes were wide. He looked older than me—I'd turned thirteen last summer—but not nearly as old as my brother, Thomas, who was twenty-three and extremely grown-up. "Bernard?" I asked, frowning down at him. The bees, who had zipped away in the confusion, flew back to get a better look at the boy. This made his eyes open even wider.

"Who are you?" he asked me. "Where am I? Bees!"

He sounded a little worried, but that was understandable. I was worried, too. "I'm Lucy Eberslee," I said, "the Gatekeeper's deputy. You're at the end of the world, of course. And you're not Bernard, are you?"

The boy shook his head. "I'm Arthur," he said, squinting up at me through wire-rimmed glasses. "Did you say the end of the world?" He blinked. "Does the world end in bees?"

Now I was sure something was wrong. The Gatekeeper would have been angry enough if I'd broken just one of her rules, but to open the door *and* to let an ignorant Easterner crash through it? Her hair would be frizzing around her face for at least the next ten years—not that I'd be working at the gatehouse to see it. "I don't suppose you have your travel papers?" I asked, feeling desperate. "Your passport? Your customs form? Your visitation fee?" I looked over my shoulder at the gatehouse. "Anything I could file?"

Arthur was still shaking his head. "I think," he said, "they're going to sting me."

He wasn't wrong. The bees were circling him faster now, and their hum had changed from curious to threatening. "It's their job not to let anyone come through the door without permission," I said. "If you don't have any papers, how in the worlds did Bernard let you come here?" The Gatekeeper had always said Bernard was useless at his job, but even for him, this was an unthinkable mistake. Traveling to another world without documentation was dangerous, not to mention extremely illegal.

"Why do you keep asking about Bernard?" Arthur winced as he picked himself up off the ground. "I've never met a Bernard. My tutor is named Joseph."

"Your tutor?"

Arthur nodded. "I was supposed to meet him in the library. But I hadn't read the awful old book he'd assigned me, and I thought maybe I'd hide from him instead. I ran to the back of the library and leaned against a door to catch my breath, and right after that I was falling backward into this garden, which you say is the end of the world, even though it seems like a very nice garden to me, and I think I've sprained my ankle." He winced again. "If you don't mind my asking, why is it springtime on this side of the door and autumn on that one?"

The bees must have decided Arthur wasn't an immediate threat, because they stopped circling him and settled for hovering a few feet over his head. I wasn't quite as convinced. "Let me be sure I've got this right," I said. "You stopped to lean against a door, which just happened to be the door at the end of the world, and no one stopped you? Not someone named Bernard? Not a witchy sort of woman with frizzy hair and a cane?"

"I didn't see anyone like that," said Arthur. "I didn't see anyone at all, except for you!" He looked around the garden and adjusted his glasses. "I don't think Joseph will ever find me here. Would it be all right with you if I stayed for a while? Just for an hour or—"

"No," I said. "No way. You've got to get back on your side of the door, and I need you to do it right now." I was more worried than ever about the Gatekeeper, and I couldn't spend any more time taking care of an otherworld traveler, especially not an illegal one I'd accidentally brought through the worldgate. If anyone found out about *that* particular disaster, I'd be in at least ten different kinds of trouble, and not just with the Gatekeeper. The Interworld Travel Commission would be downright furious. What if they put me on trial in the House of Governors? What if they found me guilty? I tried not to think about all that as I walked past Arthur and went to open the door in the wall.

It wouldn't budge.

I jostled, jiggled, cajoled, and tugged. The key swiveled in the lock, and the knob turned on its spindle, but the door wouldn't open no matter how hard I pulled. "It's stuck," I said to the bees, trying to keep my voice low enough that Arthur couldn't overhear me. As a rule, it's not a good idea to give travelers any reason to panic.

"Stuck?" said Arthur. (I groaned.) "May I try?" Before I could explain any of the reasons why he shouldn't, Arthur strode past me, grabbed the gatekey, and twisted it hard. Then there was a sharp snap, and he stepped back from the door, holding the key in his hand. Or, rather, half the key.

"Hmm," said Arthur. "That's too bad. I think I might have broken it."

I stared at him in horror. "You *think* you *might* have?"

"I can fix it, though!" Arthur said quickly. "I'm sure I can!" He

13

went back to the door, fiddled with the lock, peered at it, took his glasses off, put them back on again, wiggled the doorknob up and down, said "Ah!" a few times, and turned back to me.

"It doesn't look fixed," I pointed out.

Arthur looked uncomfortable. "I can't quite see the problem," he admitted, "but I don't think you'll be getting this door open again anytime soon."

I could see the problem, and he was standing right in front of me. "You don't understand," I said. "I *have* to get the door open. It can't be stuck for good."

"Don't worry." Arthur smiled and handed me the useless half of the spare gatekey. "I'll just take the long way around."

I'd like you to know that I always try to be professional, even in a crisis. A few months earlier, the Gatekeeper had caught a woman trying to smuggle bags full of Eastern spices through the worldgate, and I was the one who typed out the whole incident report for Interworld Travel while the Gatekeeper shouted and waved her cane in all sorts of directions I'd never known about before. This time, though, I couldn't stay calm. "It's not as simple as that!" I snapped. "You've traveled into another world, and now you're stuck in it, and the Gatekeeper's stuck over in your world somewhere, and worst of all, *I'm* stuck here with *you*. Do you know what the punishment is for breaking the door between the worlds?"

"Um," said Arthur. He wasn't smiling any longer. "No?"

"That's because no one has done it before! It's not possible! But you've managed to figure it out somehow, and we'll probably both be arrested before the day is out, and I'll never find the Gatekeeper, and it's all thanks to you!"

Arthur stared at me. Without blinking, he leaned against the wall and slid down it until he was sitting on the grass. "That's a lot to take in, Miss Eberslee," he said at last. "May I call you Lucy?"

I glared at him.

"All right. Miss Eberslee." Arthur plucked a handful of clover from the ground and held the little plants up to his face, one at a time. "Four leaves," he said quietly. "They've all got four leaves."

"Of course they do." I knew I shouldn't have shouted; I'd managed to make Arthur even more useless than he'd already been. "All clovers have four leaves."

"Not in my world." Arthur let the stems fall back to the ground. I could see his hands weren't entirely steady. "You're serious, aren't you? If this isn't my world, what is it?"

The Gatekeeper had told me that most ordinary Easterners didn't know much about the worlds beyond their own, but I hadn't realized exactly how serious the situation was until now. I sighed and sat down next to Arthur. We were going to have to start at the very beginning. "You're in the world next door to yours," I said. "This world is called Southeast. Your world is called East."

"It is?" Arthur frowned. "And East is just on the other side of that wall?"

"Sort of. Not really. It's complicated." If I started trying to

15

explain the fabric of time and space to an Easterner, we'd both be sitting there until we were ninety. "If you climbed over the wall, you wouldn't see anything but fields. The only opening between our two worlds is right behind the door. At least, that's where it *was*. Now there aren't any openings at all."

"Because I broke the door?"

"Well, yes."

Arthur looked so alarmed at this that I actually felt a little sorry for him. "To be fair, though," I added, "you wouldn't have broken the door if I hadn't opened it. And I shouldn't have shouted at you. I apologize for that." I stood up and brushed the dirt off my hands. "Anyway, I'm sure you have lots of questions, but they're going to have to wait. We're both in trouble up to our ears right now. You're not allowed to be here, I wasn't allowed to open that door in the first place, and the Gatekeeper, who *is* allowed to open it, is lost somewhere on the other side of it. If you didn't see her in your world, I have no idea where she might be, and now I've got no way to find out, and for all I know she's stuck over there permanently." I took a long breath. "Honestly, I'm not sure what to do next. What would you do if you were over in East and a person went missing?"

"I suppose," said Arthur, getting to his feet, "I'd call the authorities."

I shook my head. "That's no good. I *am* the authorities!"

Arthur squinted at me. "But you're a child."

"I'm thirteen," I corrected him. "I finished school last year, and I'm in charge here when the Gatekeeper's away."

"Well, I'm sixteen," said Arthur, "or I will be in a few months, and in my world, neither of us would be old enough to be in charge of anything. You're the Gatekeeper's deputy, and the Gatekeeper is missing?"

I nodded.

"Who's in charge of the Gatekeeper, then?"

I tried to imagine someone telling the Gatekeeper what to do. The idea of it was so preposterous that I almost laughed. "She'd probably tell you no one is," I said, "but we both work for the Southeastern Interworld Travel Commission. That's a government agency," I added when Arthur stared at me blankly. "Anyway, Interworld Travel can't find out what we've done. Their rules are the ones we've broken! Remember what I told you about getting arrested?"

"Right," said Arthur, but he sounded distracted. He scratched his mouse-brown hair and gazed past me. "Who's Florence?"

I blinked. "Excuse me?"

"Or where is Florence? I suppose it could be a place instead of a person. In my world, it's a place in Italy. Do you have Italy here?"

I had no idea what he was talking about. "Florence," I said, "is a person. An awfully important person, as a matter of fact. Why do you ask?"

Arthur pointed out into the garden beyond us. "The bees," he said. "They seem to have something to say about her." He lowered his voice to a whisper. "Did you know your bees can spell?"

Arthur was right. I'd been too distracted to notice, but at that very moment, the bees were spelling out FLORENCE and

17

getting more and more agitated about it; they didn't like being ignored. "You don't need to whisper," I told Arthur. "They know they're talented." Truthfully, they could be a little conceited about it sometimes. "They were a gift to the Gatekeeper from the next world over."

"Are you sure about that?" he said. "We don't have spelling bees in my world." He paused, frowning. "I mean, actually, we *do* have spelling bees, but . . . they're very different."

"Oh, the bees aren't from your world." I kept forgetting how much Arthur had to learn. Even his tutor hadn't managed to teach him a simple otherworld geography lesson. "Southeast has two ends. The near end, where we are now, is connected to East. And the far end is connected to the next world over on the other side."

Arthur looked dubious. "A world with magical bees?"

"Exactly," I said. "That world's called South. They've got lots of other magical things in South, too, but when they want to send a diplomatic gift of goodwill, it's usually bees. I'm not exactly sure why." I glanced back at our own colony. A few more bees had flown over to lend their assistance, and now they said, FLORENCE!!!!! After what had happened with the spare key, I wasn't exactly keen to take their advice again, but they were right: we needed help from an expert.

"Is there a door leading into South, too?" Arthur wanted to know. "A door like the one that's here?"

"Of course," I said. "And that door has a gatekeeper." I raised an eyebrow at him. "Her name is Florence."